HALF
PAST

ALSO BY
VICTORIA HELEN STONE

Evelyn, After

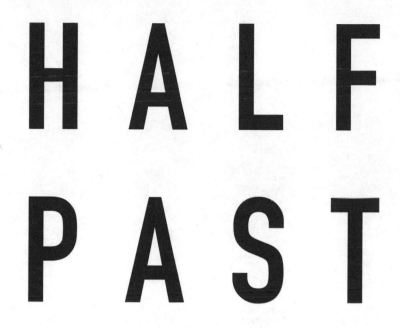

HALF PAST

A Novel

Victoria Helen Stone

Published by Lake Union Publishing, Seattle

www.apub.com

Amazon, the Amazon logo, and Lake Union Publishing are trademarks of Amazon.com, Inc., or its affiliates.

ISBN-13: 9781477819791
ISBN-10: 1477819797

Cover design by Damon Freeman

Printed in the United States of America

This book is for my mother, who's always been there.
I love you, Mom.

IOWA

CHAPTER 1

"You're not my daughter."

Hannah Smith had heard the same thing at least a dozen times in the past month. Often enough that she'd grown impatient with the conversation, but not so often that it didn't still shock.

She drew a deep breath and held it for a moment. "Mom . . ."

"I want Rachel."

Hannah forced all the hurt and impatience from her throat before she spoke again. She swallowed the emotions to store them with the rest of the feelings she'd been stuffing down for months. "Mom, I already told you. Rachel moved to Blue Lake. I'm taking care of you now. I'm Hannah. Remember?"

"I want Rachel!"

"I know. She'll be here on Saturday." Her mother's blue eyes swam with confusion. Hannah patted her arm. "That's three days away."

Her mom recoiled. The hand that had changed Hannah's diapers, combed her hair, fed her, hugged her, tended her wounds . . . it curled in on itself in horror that Hannah had touched her.

"Where's Becky?" she asked in a querulous voice that none of them had ever heard before the dementia. It was a child's voice. A helpless, demanding whine from a woman who'd never whined about anything. *Nose to the grindstone* had been her favorite saying. *No time for complaining if a body keeps busy.* But Dorothy's body wasn't busy anymore.

Hannah bit back a sigh. She had no right to her weariness. Her sisters had been dealing with this for years while Hannah had lived in a Chicago high-rise six hours away. She'd been back home for less than a month. She hadn't put in enough time to be impatient yet. She'd only just started paying her dues.

Surely this would get easier.

She smiled. "Becky's at home with her family. She's coming on Saturday too." Hoping she could wrap it all up into something her mom could understand, she added a cheerful footnote. "All three of your daughters to yourself for a whole afternoon! Rachel, Becky, and Hannah! Won't that be nice?"

Judging by the scowl her mom aimed in her direction, it wouldn't be nice at all. Or maybe she was still sharp enough not to buy the upbeat helpfulness Hannah was trying to sell her. Rachel and Becky had always provided enough sunshine for the whole family. On her best days, Hannah was more of a crisp, bracing breeze. On bad days . . . well, her dad had sometimes described her as a handful. Generous of him, but he had always been the generous sort. They were a good Midwestern family. Respectful. Hardworking. God-fearing.

Then there was Hannah.

Maybe it was her differentness that made it so hard for their mother to remember her. After all, Rachel and Becky looked like their mom. She could recognize her older two daughters if only because she'd spent a lifetime seeing them in the mirror. Blond hair, blue eyes, plump cheeks. They were corn-fed wholesomeness incarnate.

Hannah was darker. Black hair, tan skin, eyes a mysterious midnight brown. She looked exactly like her father, which had been consolation for a girl who'd otherwise felt as if fairies might have left her on the Smith doorstep. A changeling to replace their true child.

Maybe Dorothy Smith's dementia had taken even the memory of her husband's face, and that was why Hannah so often looked unfamiliar.

Whatever it was, she tried not to take it personally. Tried and failed.

Settling back into the recliner with her book, she ignored her mother's suspicious glances until they finally faded into placidness. A few minutes later, Dorothy perked up again, her fear of Hannah seemingly forgotten as she leaned close in conspiracy.

"Someone has stolen my things," she whispered. Her right hand had begun to shake, jittering rhythmically along the cheap fabric of the chair they'd brought from home. Dorothy's favorite chair, despite that it stained easily and the places where her hands trembled were getting worn and bare.

Hannah didn't reach to comfort her this time. "No one has stolen your things."

"They have. I can't find my husband's ring anywhere."

"It's at home, Mom. I'm taking care of everything."

"Home?" her mother asked.

"At home. This is Sunrise Village, remember? You're staying here for a time so the nurses can help you at night." She was staying here for a good long while, actually. Until she died. Hannah forced another smile, the muscles of her face stretching so tight she thought they'd break. "Your friend Sylvie is here too. You have dinner with her every night."

"Sylvie," she said as if it were a reassurance, but Hannah could tell that the name felt unfamiliar on her tongue. "Sylvie."

"That's right. Dad's ring is at home, safe and sound. And I'm back in my old room, watching over the house."

"He died last month," she murmured. He'd died six years ago, but what was the point of telling her that? In Dorothy's mind, she'd only just lost her husband, and nothing was going to change that.

"I'm sorry, Mom. You must miss him so much."

Her mother's shaky right hand went to her wedding band and twisted it around. Hannah glanced down at her own ring finger before she remembered it was bare.

She was jobless, living in her childhood bedroom, in the middle of a divorce, and taking care of a mother who didn't seem to even have a daughter named Hannah. Damn, she was really kicking ass and taking names. Living the dream. Killing the blues. Being her best self.

"Someone," Hannah murmured, "has stolen my things." Repeating her mother's words felt surprisingly good. Someone else must be at fault if she couldn't figure out what had happened to her own life.

But it wasn't any truer for Hannah than it was for her mom. No one had taken anything from her. Hannah was here, in this place at this moment, because she'd chosen to be. She *was* being her best self, damn it. She was taking care of a mother who'd spent her life taking care of the rest of them. There was no shame in that. Nothing stolen or lost.

Hannah returned to her novel, realized she had no idea what was going on with the plot, and backed up a few pages. A few minutes later, she backed up again before finally giving up and closing the book with a hard snap.

Some days her mother enjoyed the various activities organized by the center, and some days she was afraid to leave the room. She'd had two of those days in a row, and Hannah felt a little stir-crazy. When the afternoon aide knocked and opened the door of Dorothy's room, Hannah nearly gasped with relief. "Cory! How are you?"

The young woman smiled with a genuine warmth that made Hannah feel less guilty about leaving every day at five. "Wonderful. How is Ms. Dorothy today?"

"Great," Hannah lied.

"Are you ready for your bath, Ms. Dorothy?"

Her mother's face screwed up as if she might protest, but after a moment she nodded.

Hannah stood so quickly that her book dropped to the floor. "All right! You have a lovely bath and a nice dinner, Mom. I'll be back tomorrow." As she leaned to pick up the book, she pressed a quick kiss to her mother's head. Dementia had taken her scent away too. Now, instead of Suave conditioner and Doublemint gum, her mom smelled of Johnson's baby shampoo and hospital sanitizer.

"We'll see you tomorrow!" Cory called as Hannah made her escape. Her mother said nothing. Probably for the best. Some days weren't so bad. Some days she recognized Hannah, even if she did seem confused about how her youngest daughter had gotten so freakishly old.

But surely forty-five wasn't that old. She likely had more than half her life still in front of her. Hell, she had time to turn her two failed marriages into six or seven if she tried hard enough.

She didn't bother to hide the bitterness of her smile as she pushed through the front doors of the care center and stepped back into the real world. She existed out here, at least. She was a person, harmless, if still unknown. No one pulled away in horror as she passed.

Sucking a deep breath of clean, disinfectant-free air into her lungs, she fled to her car. The feeling was terrible on every level. She shouldn't want to run from her mother. The woman was sick. Dying. And losing everything bit by bit as she did it. That was true suffering. Hannah's frustration didn't even qualify as a hangnail in the face of her mom's slow, steady decline.

The worst part of callously wanting to escape was that she had nothing to escape *to*. Where would she go? Back to her old bedroom in her parents' home? Back to the months-long divorce negotiations with her husband? Back to sorting through the remains of her mom's passing life?

She slammed the door of her car and huddled in the surprising heat for a moment. A breeze had cooled the May afternoon, but the sun was bright enough that the interior temperature was probably close to ninety. Her body drank in the heat as if she'd been slowly freezing all day. Maybe she'd fall into bed as soon as she got home. Twelve hours of sleep might recharge her enough to face tomorrow bravely.

As soon as she started the car, Hannah's phone rang. She cringed, imagining a call from the care center with a last-minute emergency. She'd have to get out of the car. Return to the memory unit of the center. Calm her mother down. Stay another hour or two.

Or maybe it was one of her sisters checking to be sure Hannah hadn't run away screaming yet. Running was kind of her thing. Screaming was too, sometimes.

The car display finally caught up with the call and flashed *Jasmine*. Hannah squeaked in surprise at the sight of her former coworker's name; then she shut off the car and answered the phone. "Jasmine! Hello!"

"Hey, girl. How's life in Iowa?"

Hannah groaned, but it quickly broke into laughter. "It's life in Iowa."

"When are you moving back?"

She didn't even bother groaning this time. It was understood. "I'm not. I've told you that a hundred times."

"Yeah, you keep saying it, but we both know it's not true. You won't last a year in that town."

"I have to," she answered.

Jasmine's voice dropped. "How's your mom?"

"The same."

"And how's Jeff?"

Hannah waited a few heartbeats for her stomach to settle. She didn't exactly miss her soon-to-be ex-husband. But she was so used to having him in her life that it felt strange to live without him. "We haven't spoken. Have you . . . have you seen him?"

"Just in passing. We don't run in the same circles now that you're gone. But I saw him coming out of Wiley's. He said there's still no good barbecue in your old neighborhood."

"Oh. So he looked okay?"

"He looked fine."

That was good. Hannah didn't want him suffering. She just wanted him to let go of his grip on their relationship. Leave her and her severance package alone.

"Why don't you come back and visit? You can stay at my place. You won't run into Jeff up here, if that's why you're staying away."

"I just . . ." She wanted to go. Wanted to start the engine and point her car toward Chicago right now. But she couldn't. "It'll be a while. Maybe I can make it in for a quick weekend sometime." She missed her friends. Missed the restaurants and people and *life* of Chicago. She missed everything. But if she went back now, she might stay, and she couldn't do that to her mom and sisters.

"Well, we all hate you for leaving. The new management is . . . oh, hell, it's fine, I guess."

"Yeah?"

"No."

"I'm sorry," she said sincerely.

"Oh, no one blames you for getting out while the getting was good. If I'd been offered a package, I would have taken it in a hot second, believe me. I'm just jealous. Okay, I'm not jealous of Iowa, but I'm jealous of the severance." A phone trilled in the background, and Jasmine's chair squeaked. "Crap. I've got to take this. Call me this weekend?"

"Absolutely. I'll—" But Jasmine had already hung up.

Hannah realized that her heart was beating hard, just that brush with her old job leaving her breathless. Most people thought there was nothing exciting about accounting, but she hadn't been the addition-and-subtraction kind of accountant. She'd been more of a . . . how-to-legally-shield-your-billions-from-taxation kind of accountant. Money and flash and legal loopholes. She'd been good at that. Great at it. And she hadn't even been the front man for the team, so she'd rarely had to deal with rich assholes.

But as exciting as the work had been, it had eaten away at her soul. She'd stopped taking pride in making more money for people who had too much already. The severance package had been a relief. One year's salary and a payout of all her stock options. She'd even gotten paid for the four weeks of vacation she'd never bothered taking.

At her age, with no rent and very few ways of spending money in Coswell, Iowa, it was more like an early retirement than a termination. When she'd walked away, she'd felt triumphant. But the triumph had worn off quickly. Now she felt like a bump on a log, to use another of her mother's favorite expressions.

Don't just sit there like a bump on a log. But here she was turning into wood.

Her hairline began to prickle with sweat, so Hannah restarted the car and headed for home. The care center was two towns over, but it was still only a twenty-minute drive.

The towns around here were tiny and scattered, but they all shared one overriding need: health care for their rapidly aging populations. The young people who could leave had been leaving for decades. The ones who couldn't get out stayed home and worked at hospitals and hospices and care centers. Senior care was the new Midwestern crop.

Surely even that industry would dry up soon. Or maybe it wouldn't. Maybe the caregivers would be aging by then and the cycle would start over. They'd move into the rooms where they'd once tended patients, and someone young would show up to care for them.

Still sweating, whether from the heat or anxiety, Hannah rolled down the windows and enjoyed the bright evening drive past acres and acres of turned soil that would soon sprout corn. In late summer, the rustling crops could sound almost like the lapping waves of Lake Michigan on a windy day, but today the breeze moved nothing. It just picked up the dark scent of rich dirt and spring grass. The wind smelled like her childhood.

Despite her jokes about Iowa, she'd never hated it. It was a beautiful place. A good place. But she'd always felt like a visitor. As if she were observing the people and taking notes on their behavior. She wasn't blond and bubbly. She wasn't interested in basketball or wrestling championships. She didn't want babies. She didn't even believe in God. Growing up, she'd had no place here, no comfort, but this time she'd returned hoping to find at least a peaceful resting spot for a year or two.

She waved lazily at a man in a passing pickup because that was what people did here. Coswell had only about two thousand residents now, but it had been closer to three when she'd been in high school. In a town that size, you knew everyone, and almost everyone in the surrounding county too. Certainly you knew someone's cousins or one of the family's kids. Everybody was intertwined. A net of people that reached out and out to the curves of the horizon. And Hannah had been a puzzle to all of them.

Not an outcast, really. Not hated. Just . . . nothing like the rest of the Smiths.

Rachel and Becky had been more like twins than simple siblings. They'd both been homecoming queens. Valentine's Dance sweethearts. Cheerleaders. Not even mean-girl cheerleaders, but the upstanding kind who cared about their community and classmates. They'd been members of 4-H, raising rabbits to show at the state fair. Hell, they'd even been successive vice presidents of Future Homemakers of America. A legacy family!

Hannah snorted at the very idea of FHA, wondering whether that club was legal anymore. Surely not. Or if it was, the name had been changed to Rising Household Engineers or something.

Hannah had skipped homemaking classes and 4-H. Her biggest interest had been music, and not the country kind everyone else in town had loved. She'd been into punk and alt-rock. Though she'd never gone for a full punk look, she'd had four piercings in her right ear and she'd chopped her hair into a pixie cut when big hair had been the fashion.

Instead of saving her money for Jordache jeans and stylish jackets, she'd saved it for bus trips to see the Ramones play in Minneapolis. Or L7. Or Sonic Youth. Sometimes she'd had to skip school to do it. Once she'd even disappeared for two days, only to be grounded for two months afterward.

Not that she'd been all "buck the system." She'd gotten As and Bs in high school and had chosen accounting pretty quickly in college. She'd never been a bad kid, really; she'd just been full of an energy that had vibrated at a different frequency from the rest of her family.

She'd embraced feminism and women's studies while her sisters had announced engagements. She'd concentrated on her career while her parents had been absorbed with their new grandchildren. Her family had loved her. Always. But they'd loved her cautiously because they'd never understood her.

Which was fine. She didn't quite get them either.

Regardless of their differences, she was back now. Putting in the time. Here to relieve her sisters of their caregiving duties for a little while. Hannah would never contribute to the Smith gene pool, but she could contribute her time and love to this family, damn it.

It might even feel natural after a few more weeks.

She passed the old grain elevator at the outskirts of town, then the new grocery store. She should go in. Stock up. Maybe cook a good meal tonight.

She drove on by and headed into town.

Forty years ago there'd been a four-way stoplight where the highway bisected Main Street, but now it was just a flashing red. She slowed and looked both ways before rolling through.

She approached the older, smaller market. She'd viewed it as a fantasyland of possibilities when she'd been small. There had been five-cent gumballs that she could count on most of the time and twenty-five-cent cupcakes she could only talk her mom into once a month or so. Her dad, though . . . he'd been a reliable source of quarters.

But she didn't stop there either. She was a terrible cook, she was hungry, and she was craving sushi. Good sushi. Not that there was a possibility of even bad sushi in this town. Resigned, she pulled into the off-brand fast-food joint some enterprising family had opened in the old Dairy Queen and walked in to order a fish fillet sandwich. "It's almost sushi," she assured herself as the door jingled shut behind her. The heavy grease on the air belied her words, but it also made her stomach clench with hunger.

Since returning home, she'd lived in fear of running into people she'd known in her youth, but she was trying to get over it. If the boy she'd lost her virginity to was now deep-frying fish for her, she'd just smile distantly and tell him he looked great. Luckily, the place seemed to be staffed by teenagers. She breathed a sigh of relief.

The sigh stuck in her throat when the customer in front of her moved away and she saw a familiar name on the flyer taped to the register.

Jensen. Common enough around here. But this Jensen was a five-year-old girl who was battling leukemia, and her parents needed help covering medical costs and travel to the Twin Cities. Olivia Jensen. Her parents' names weren't listed, likely because everyone else knew who they were.

"Ready to order?" the girl behind the register asked. Hannah nodded, but the words that formed on her tongue were *Who are her parents?* The words stayed there and dissolved. She was afraid to ask. She didn't want to know if the bald, smiling girl in the picture was related to one of Hannah's old friends. Jesus, she could be the daughter of her junior-high boyfriend, Alex. Shit, the girl could be his *grand*daughter.

"I'll have the fish fillet," she forced out. "And tater tots."

"Anything to drink?"

Despite her dry mouth, she shook her head.

She paid for the food, then stared at the flyer. When the girl turned around to work on the order, Hannah hurriedly dug back into her wallet and withdrew a fifty. She stuffed it into the donation can, watching to be sure the girl didn't see. After a few seconds, she took an additional forty dollars from her wallet and stuffed that in too. Palms sweating, she closed her purse and cleared her throat.

The girl wasn't Alex's, she assured herself. She wasn't anyone Hannah might know. Probably.

There were just too many unsought connections in a town this size. No matter where you went, someone saw you, knew you, wanted something from you. Someone remembered the lowest point in your life and you remembered theirs. It was like dragging an open book around with you all day long, with the details of your family and your setbacks and all the ways you'd fallen.

Some people felt lost in a big city, but Hannah had felt free. Her emotions were hers to feel when she wanted, not surprises to be dredged up in every encounter.

Arms crossed, she waited impatiently for her food, then beat a hasty retreat to her car as soon as the bag was in her hand.

A few minutes later, she was home. The driveway was all hers now, and it felt so strange. No competing with her sisters' cars and her dad's truck. Their mother's old Buick was still in the one-car garage. She needed to take it out soon. Drive it around to be sure the battery held a charge. This winter she'd move the old car outside and buy a cover for it so that Hannah could keep her own car snow-free.

Not that her mother would ever need her car again, but selling it felt wrong.

She shook her head as she hauled her purse and dinner to the kitchen door.

Lewy body dementia. That was the thing eating her mother's mind away. *Lewy body.* A scourge she'd never heard of until her sister had spoken the words. They'd thought it was Parkinson's disease when the first symptoms had started five years before. A frightening enough diagnosis on its own, but then the mood swings had started. Then the hallucinations.

That had been the clincher for the diagnosis, apparently. Most seniors with dementia didn't see imaginary people. But Dorothy did. Not always, but often enough.

It must have been terrifying for Rachel, who'd been the one coming to their mom's house every day at that point. It was still scary to Hannah, and she was surrounded by nurses and aides who were there to help at the drop of a hat.

She sighed as she set her dinner on the kitchen table and kicked off her shoes. It had been terrifying for her mother too, especially at the start, when she'd still realized how much she was losing. She'd tried to hide it. Tried to compensate. Just the trembling of her hands had been an embarrassment for her, a woman who'd always been so steady and never wanted a fuss.

Another wave of exhaustion hit Hannah, rolling through her skull and the taut muscles of her neck, then all the way down until even her legs felt weak. She washed her hands, grabbed the bag of food and a cold beer, and made it to the couch before collapsing.

Why the heck was this so exhausting? All she did was sit there and talk with her mother, help her with lunch and the bathroom, keep her supplied with music and television shows. It was barely work at all, but Hannah felt weak as a baby.

She should go out for a run. Keep herself healthy. But one sip of the beer and she groaned and sank deeper into the overstuffed couch. This was heaven. She wasn't going anywhere. Except to bed if she could make it.

She propped her feet up on the pile of divorce papers scattered over the coffee table and flicked on the television to lose herself in the latest iteration of her favorite crime show.

"CSI: Criminal Laziness," she muttered.

Raising her beer in a toast to the TV, she vowed she'd do better tomorrow. Better at caring and committing and settling down like a good, decent Midwesterner.

"I'll bake brownies," she said. Her mom's favorite treat. "I'll clean the kitchen." That felt all right too. "And I'll . . . I'll smile at everyone." That one felt like utter bullshit, but she nodded solemnly. Time to finally learn how to be an Iowan. Really. She had to stop fighting it and fit in. How hard could it be if she applied herself? She'd lived here half her life.

CHAPTER 2

Hannah paid the sleepy-eyed cashier for the brownies and hurried to her car to transfer them to a plastic container she'd brought from home. Okay, they weren't homemade, but did her mom even remember what homemade tasted like? And brownies were brownies. Hannah had never had a *bad* one, really.

After she pushed the empty supermarket container under the seat, she felt better. Small towns were breweries for paranoia. In any other place, it would be insane to think someone would see her buying brownies and mention it to her mother, but these things happened in Coswell, Iowa. *Dorothy, you didn't tell me Hannah was back in town! I saw her at the SuperValu, buying brownies, and I couldn't believe it.*

Of course, Hannah had the perfect immunization against gossip nowadays. Her mom would be just as likely to ask, *Hannah who?* as she would to realize Hannah had told a little white lie. In all likelihood, she wouldn't remember that anyone had brought her brownies at all.

That wasn't quite fair. Dorothy had good days when everything seemed almost normal. But those good days were becoming rarer. There had only been one in the past month.

Hannah had meant to make the brownies. She honestly had. In fact, she'd awoken at six thirty feeling more energetic than she had in weeks. Ten solid hours of sleep had done her good, and she'd grabbed a cup of coffee and started digging in to a pile of her parents' documents, hoping to get through one stack before breakfast. There were so many stacks.

Her father's death from stomach cancer had taken two years, and there'd been dozens of hospitalizations. Back then her mother had been sharp as a tack, and she'd demanded copies of every medical record he had.

After he'd died, and before anyone had realized Dorothy was getting sick, she'd also started saving every bit of mail that arrived. In the past month, Hannah must have thrown away five hundred credit card offers. But she was finally starting to make a dent.

Not that the house was in bad shape. The piles of paper were all confined to the den. Rachel and Becky were far too meticulous to have allowed their mother to slide into sloppiness.

So she'd meant to spend an hour going through papers before she made brownies and cleaned the kitchen. But at the end of that hour, she'd found something that had pissed her off. A thin file that contained her mother's medical records.

Nothing too important. An X-ray report for the wrist she'd broken slipping on ice ten years before. An unfilled prescription for calcium supplements. Receipts for her Medicare payments. And a blood workup from a physical.

Hannah had glanced through everything to be sure they weren't records the current doctors might need. But there must have been another, separate file with more important papers delivered to the care home at some point. Hannah had been about to tuck everything back into the folder when she'd noticed the blood type listed on the one-page report. AB positive.

"Jesus Christ," she'd muttered. "Are they trying to kill her?"

Now, pulling out of the parking lot of the supermarket, she glanced down at the report in disgust. It was seven years old, so hopefully it wasn't something that had been given to the current doctors, but what if they had it on file? What if they'd just entered the incorrect information without even checking it?

Hannah's blood type was O negative, a fact she couldn't forget if she wanted to. She was a universal donor, and the Red Cross sent her a postcard every six months reminding her to come in and donate. Her blood was the holy grail of emergency medicine, transferable to any accident victim who needed blood so badly they couldn't wait for their type to be tested.

Anyone who remembered junior-high science knew that an O-negative offspring couldn't have an AB-positive parent. It didn't work that way. Someone at the lab had screwed up, and if her mom got the wrong blood, it could kill her.

So instead of baking brownies, Hannah had torn through a few more piles of paper, looking for more of her mother's medical documents. When she hadn't found any, she'd showered and headed out. She would present her mother with the brownies and the nurse on duty with the report.

Twenty minutes later, she breezed through the doors of the care center with a big smile. Irritated as she was by the mistake, she was also well rested and determined to stay positive today.

Thursday was movie day, after all. The activity director always chose upbeat movies. Hannah and the residents could lose themselves in hope and happiness for a couple of hours. *Fake* hope and happiness, but she'd take it.

She waved at the attendant behind the door of the care center's memory wing and tried to ignore the fact that the lock sounded like a prison gate latching behind her once she was in.

When she drew close enough to the central desk to read the nurse's name tag, she offered a greeting. "Hi, Tonya!"

"Good morning, Hannah!"

The nurse didn't need a name tag to remember Hannah's name, and she felt a quick jolt of familiar shame. She was selfish. She didn't pay enough attention to people. She wasn't part of the community.

Hannah smiled to hide her guilt. "Could you do me a favor? I ran across an old medical report of Mom's that has an incorrect blood type. I'm hoping you can find out what you have on file here."

"Absolutely." She took the report Hannah offered. "I'll check into it as soon as morning rounds are done. What should it be?"

"I'm not sure, but definitely not AB positive."

"Got it. I'll let you know what I find."

First duty done, Hannah headed for her mother's room, the bowl of lies clenched in her grip.

"Hi, Mom! I brought you brownies. Frosted. Your favorite. And don't worry; I cleaned up my mess."

Her mom smiled vaguely. "Hello, dear!"

Hannah tried not to let her smile waver. "Hello, dear" was the greeting Dorothy gave to people she didn't remember. It had been silly for Hannah to count on something more just because she was feeling good today. At least her mom was upbeat this morning. Hannah would take that over sullen and frightened any day.

"Did you have a good breakfast?" she asked.

Her mom's smile widened. "French toast. My favorite."

Dorothy remembered the meal she'd had an hour ago, and she remembered which breakfast was her favorite, but couldn't remember her youngest daughter.

Stop it, she commanded herself. *Just smile and make her day a little better.*

Why was this so damn hard to pull off? Why was it so easy for her to reassure obnoxious strangers about their millions of dollars and so hard to play along with her own parent?

"It's movie day today," she said with forced cheer as she retrieved a paper towel from the bathroom and presented her mother with a slightly squished brownie. "Have you heard what they're playing?"

"I don't think so . . ."

Right. Hannah wasn't supposed to challenge her that way. "Let's see, then." She found the sheet of daily activities presented to the residents as if they were on a fun cruise instead of waiting to fade away. "Oh, it's *Grumpy Old Men*. I haven't seen that in years. I think you'll love it. The movie isn't until ten, but there's a sing-along at nine."

"Oh, I love singing!"

"I know! Should we pick out something to wear? Maybe throw on some lipstick?"

Despite her cheeriness, Dorothy's hands were shaking badly today, so Hannah helped her eat the brownie first, then set about finding something bright for her to wear to match her mood. She supposed she should help her brush her teeth after the chocolate, but tooth decay wasn't high on Hannah's list of concerns at this point. She laid out the clothes, then scooted close to her mom to help her with a tiny bit of powder and blush, as if they were going to dinner and a show instead of to the rec room.

"You're such a pretty girl," her mother said.

"Thank you."

"Do you have any children?"

God, she was disappointingly infertile even as a stranger. "No. No kids."

"I'm so sorry." Her mother reached out to pat her hand, and Hannah had to resist the urge to hold tight and curl in close for a hug.

She missed being held. Her mother sighed. "Sometimes it's just not meant to be."

Well, it hadn't been meant to be because of the birth control Hannah had been diligently using for nearly thirty years, but she didn't mention that. Her mom had never understood Hannah's desire to remain childless. Dementia wasn't going to make the idea any easier to grasp.

"You must be married, though."

"I used to be," Hannah answered.

Her mother leaned close to whisper. "Not . . . not a *divorce?*"

"I'm afraid so."

"Oh, no! You poor thing."

Was she a poor thing? She felt pretty okay about it all. The truth was that she should never had said yes to Jeff's proposal. She'd warned him that she wasn't good at love and was even worse at forever.

But he'd convinced her with his awful patience and love and under-standing. He'd tricked her into thinking she was like other people. She wasn't. She'd known damn well she wasn't, but she'd married him any-way out of pure hope. And as soon as the ring was on her finger, she'd started to hate him.

It was her fault. All of it. But that didn't mean she was giving him half of her settlement. He'd been earning his own money as a history professor the whole time they'd been married. He'd have a damn *pension* by the time he left teaching.

She smiled and slapped her hands to her knees as she stood. "Clothes before lipstick. I don't want to get red all over your pretty yel-low blouse. I'll call a nurse to help, all right?" When she was this shaky, Dorothy normally couldn't stand for even a few minutes at a time, and Hannah couldn't support her alone. Becky probably could. Rachel definitely could. But not Hannah.

She rang for a nurse.

The sing-along would be fun. When she thought about it impersonally, Hannah found herself fascinated by the way the brain retreated for those affected by dementia or Alzheimer's, brightening old memories even as it stole new ones. Her mother's memory seemed to function on a sliding scale these days, thick and sturdy at the farthest end, and frayed to nothing at the nearest. Sometimes her recall rolled close, touching briefly on the present, but it usually settled somewhere in the middle. On the worst days, it hovered near the start.

Once Dorothy was dressed and colored, Hannah wheeled her slowly toward the rec room, pausing so her mom could talk to other patients on the way. Hannah recognized some of the last names, but most of the faces had hidden their familiarity behind deep wrinkles and watery eyes.

The halls here were cheery and bright, but there was no way to fully mask the smell of urine in the air. She hoped her mom was inured to it. Hannah hoped she got used to it soon too.

A few minutes after they were settled near the piano, Hannah felt her mother's shaking hand tug at her sleeve, and when she looked toward her, Hannah jumped in surprise. Suddenly, just like that, her mother's blue eyes were full again. Not confused. Not vague. She was in there and shining through.

Dorothy winked. "Don't let the nurse know about those brownies or they might not give me a cookie with lunch."

"Sure, Mom."

"They're nice girls, but they're like prison guards sometimes, I swear. And don't tell them I said that either."

"I won't."

"Hide the brownies in my nightstand before you go. You've never been a blue-ribbon baker, Hannah, but those are delicious."

"Thanks, Mom." She took her mother's hand and held it tight, pressing a kiss to the thin skin of her knuckles. The best goddamn brownies she'd ever baked, and they'd been mass-produced in a store by people who couldn't care less. She deserved the stab of hurt that closed her throat.

It was the nicest day they'd had since Hannah had taken up vigil at her mother's side. Before moving back home, she would have pictured the senior citizens singing songs like "Over There" and "Chattanooga Choo Choo," but life wasn't a nostalgic old movie, and most of the people in the home hadn't fought in World War II. They sang a lot of Beatles songs. Some Elvis. Peter, Paul and Mary. Even a little Willie Nelson.

Grumpy Old Men was hilarious, if only for the raucous laughter it inspired in the audience. And though Dorothy's moment of clarity passed quickly, she later complained that she'd smiled so much her cheeks hurt.

Claiming those fake brownies had been well worth the guilt. Not that they'd created magic, but every little bit of joy helped.

When the nurse came in after lunch and said they needed a quick draw of Dorothy's blood to confirm those records, Hannah simply nodded and went back to her book. Mistakes happened. She wasn't going to read these people the riot act. If there'd been an error in the file, it would be resolved with no harm done, and Hannah could be sure she'd made a small difference in her mother's outcome.

By four, her mother was tired enough that she was nodding off in her chair, and Hannah helped her into bed for a quick nap before dinner. Ironic, of course. This was the first day Hannah wasn't eager to leave early.

Ten minutes later she was softly closing the door of her mother's room behind her when the nurse approached. This time she was accompanied by the doctor.

"Everything all right?" Hannah asked.

"Ms. Smith, I'm Dr. Kapur. If we could take a moment of your time in one of our consultation rooms."

Hannah laughed. "Honestly, it's no big deal. Just get the records corrected."

"It's . . . not that."

Hannah looked from the doctor to Nurse Karen, whose eyes dropped. "Is something wrong?"

"Not wrong, per se," the doctor said, as if that clarified anything. "Are you sure about your blood type, Ms. Smith?"

"As sure as a girl can be. I get phone calls from the Red Cross if I skip a donation. Why?"

He cleared his throat and tipped his head toward the small room to their right. Hannah gave in with a roll of her eyes and walked toward it. "If you could just spit it out?"

"Yes, well." He followed her in and closed the door behind them. Karen hovered near the door while Dr. Kapur waved a hand toward one of the chairs. Impatient now, Hannah sat, trying to hide her irritation. She knew most of it was fear for her mother. But surely a simple blood typing couldn't reveal anything dangerous. She was worried over nothing.

"We retested your mother's blood," the doctor said as he perched on the edge of the chair. "We sent it over to the hospital. It is AB positive."

Hannah rolled her eyes again. "Then test it one more time. Come on."

"You don't understand. Her blood type was tested when she was admitted to the hospital two years ago. Then again today. Plus there is the report you brought in. Your mother's type is AB positive. No question."

"So what does that mean?"

He cleared his throat again and glanced at the nurse before clasping his hands carefully together. "Ms. Smith, every person has two markers, one from each parent. If the parent is an A type, the child could get an A, or in some cases an O. If the type is AB, the child could get an A or a B."

"Yeah, I get that."

"So you understand what I'm saying." He slumped back a little, his body language screaming relief.

Hannah wasn't feeling anything like relief. She was feeling a surge of white-hot anger. "No, I definitely *don't* get what you're saying."

He glanced at the nurse again, as if begging for help.

"Hannah," the nurse said softly, "an AB parent can only give an A or a B marker to a child. Not an O. An O is an absence of either—"

"I know that!" she snapped. "I just don't get what you're saying!"

"Ms. Smith," the doctor tried again, "I'm sorry you have to learn this way, but you must have been adopted."

You're not my daughter.

She looked from the doctor to the nurse. "What?" she whispered.

"Closed adoptions were common in the '70s. The rule, really. Open adoptions were very rare at that time."

Who are you? Where's Rachel?

Hannah clutched the arms of the chair, digging her nails into the rough fabric, wondering how many other devastated children had done the same in this room. "No. That's not possible."

"If you were adopted at birth, all the records would have been sealed, and—"

"No. My father is . . ." What did she mean to tell them? *My father is my father. I look just like him. I can't be adopted.* As if they would care. "Excuse me. I need to speak with my mother."

"Hannah, wait," Nurse Karen said, but Hannah was already past her and opening the door. "If you'd like to have your blood re-typed to be sure—"

But she didn't need another test. The Red Cross hadn't been wrong for twenty-five years. But Hannah had been wrong. All wrong from the start.

"Mom," she said as she shoved open her mother's door. "Mom!" The word rang through her head, discordant. Too sharp. And not accurate.

Dorothy didn't stir, so Hannah rushed over to touch her. "Mom, they're saying I'm not your daughter." She shook her awake. "Mom, they're—"

"Help!" her mother croaked, the word splintering before she drew a breath and tried again. "Help! Help! Please!"

"Ms. Smith!" She heard a rush of voices behind her, felt hands on her shoulders, but she clung hard to her mother's arm.

"Mom, who am I? They're saying I'm adopted. Who am I?"

But her mother only gave a wordless, terrified cry and closed her eyes, covering her face with her hands as if Hannah were about to hit her.

"Mom!" she screamed as the hands finally pulled her away. *"Please."*

But her mother was sobbing, her clawed fingers shaking against her cheeks as she wept.

"Hannah," the nurse said, "this isn't helping anything. You're only scaring her."

Hannah shook her head. This couldn't be happening. Not now. Not like this.

"You need to leave," the woman said, most of the sympathy gone from her voice.

"No, I need her to tell me the truth."

"Even if that were possible at this point, we can't have you terrifying her. And she obviously can't tell you anything right now."

Hannah took a deep breath, squeezing her hands into fists as she closed her eyes.

"Help," she heard her mother whimpering over and over. "Help."

Hannah wanted to scream "Help!" right back at her. *Help, Mommy! Help me!* But she backed away instead.

She found people gathered in the hallway, watching as she rushed from her mother's room. Hannah brushed past the group of attendants and patients and hurried toward the locked doors. She was buzzed out and free within seconds.

She couldn't be adopted. She was her father's daughter. She even had his strange little fingers that flared out at the last joint. The lab work had to be wrong. All of it. Every time.

But when she finally reached the exit of the care center and raced toward her car, the truth chased after her. She couldn't escape it. Three separate tests couldn't have been wrong.

She drove too quickly toward home, speeding past houses and fields she'd passed a hundred times. A thousand. The world blurred around her. Her pulse muted every sound but her heart. No, not her heart, but her fear and horror. That was the thump, thump, thump that drummed through her body.

You're not my daughter. You're not my daughter.

This wasn't fair. Hannah was already lost. Already floating in an uncertain place between her past and future. She didn't need this right now. It wasn't fair.

Help. Please help.

She was home in fifteen minutes instead of twenty. The house was stifling and still when she burst in. It would storm later, but right now, the air was heavy and humid. Still, she didn't stop to open windows. She marched to her bedroom closet and tore down the piles of boxes she'd lined against the wall.

Almost all her possessions were in storage, but she'd brought her most important documents and keepsakes with her. She opened box after box until she found what she was looking for; then she sat down hard on her ass and stared at it.

She'd looked at her birth certificate a dozen times before, so she would have noticed if someone other than Dorothy were listed as her mother, but somehow she'd hoped to find a straightforward answer there. As if she'd open the folder and see "Jane Doe" listed on the mother's name line and she'd smack her forehead for never registering it before.

But no, it said the mother's maiden name was Dorothy Baylor just as it always had. And Peter Smith was listed as her father. Her birthday was the one she'd always celebrated: February 5, 1972.

The information under place of birth and witness was strange, but it had always been strange. It was an address on Highway 1 in Big Sur, California. Not a hospital, but a house. And the attending witness to the birth hadn't been a doctor. It had been a woman named Maria Diaz, no MD following her name. A home birth.

She'd been astounded the first time she'd seen it. Horrified, even. But the explanation from her mother had been simple. They'd had no money, so they'd done it the old-fashioned way. Lots of people did back then. The end.

But Hannah didn't know of any old-fashioned way of giving birth that would result in the wrong baby.

She read the birth certificate again. Everything was the same as it had always been, but this time she noticed something odd. She'd been born on February 5, but the birth hadn't been recorded by the county until March 27. Was that normal with home births?

She needed to know more about her sisters' births, but she couldn't quite bring herself to call them yet. At this point, no one else knew aside from a couple of medical professionals. Telling her sisters would make it real. Permanent. She couldn't face it right now.

But maybe she didn't have to. One of the many files she'd sorted through last week had contained copies of all their birth certificates. She'd noticed it because she'd thought maybe someday she'd work on their genealogy. Their parents never spoke about family. They hadn't seemed secretive about it, just close-mouthed in the way that Midwesterners were.

Her father had lost his parents by age eighteen, and her mother had spent her teen years in an orphanage. Tough times, but they'd survived. Today they would have blogged endlessly about overcoming hardship, but back then people had straightened their spines and kept moving, and any hard feelings were kept to themselves.

Nose to the grindstone. Simple folk living simple lives.

Or not. They might have been utter frauds this whole time. What could she trust when she couldn't trust her own *life*?

"Calm down, girl," she muttered to herself. This wasn't a made-for-TV movie. There was an answer somewhere. Something straightforward and not at all awful.

She carried the birth certificate to the den and opened the file box she'd nearly filled since moving in. Right at the start of it was a file she'd neatly labeled "Birth Certificates" in bold, sure letters. What an innocent conceit.

She laid her siblings' papers on the cracked leather ottoman and set hers between them. All the documents looked the same. She dragged her fingertips over the raised seal on hers. It was missing on the photocopies of her sisters' certificates, but she could see the gray shadow of it on both, hovering like a ghost.

The address of birth was the same on all three: 47105 Highway 1. The attendant was the same too: the mysterious Maria Diaz.

Her sisters' births were a year apart, in 1968 and '69. Hannah had come a little later in '72. Three years was time enough for a remarriage or a change in relationship status, but that hadn't happened. Her parents had been married since 1966. They'd still been married when her father had died forty-five years later.

So what was different?

She checked the signatures and the name of the clerk, and then she looked at the filing dates and frowned.

Her sisters' certificates had both been filed within a week of their births. Only Hannah's had been delayed by more than a month.

It must mean something.

Whether she was ready or not, she had to call Rachel. They weren't the closest of sisters, but Rachel might be the only one who could help her figure this out.

Keenly aware that she was about to ruin a lot of her sister's child-hood memories, Hannah slipped her phone from her pocket and dialed.

"Hannah!" Rachel answered happily. "How are you holding up?"

She lied automatically. "I'm good."

"Is Mom okay?"

"Sure," she said, deciding not to say, *Of course not, she's lost her mind!* "What's up?"

Hannah cleared her throat. "Are you busy?"

"I'm setting up for a wedding reception in the church basement, but it's no big deal."

"Oh, you're not at home?"

"Not yet. Why?"

What the hell was she supposed to say? How was she supposed to introduce this? But maybe Rachel knew already. She was the oldest. She could be part of the secret.

Her head went light and her scalp tingled. Hannah rubbed her brow. "What do you remember about me as a baby?"

"As a baby? I was only four when you were born. I don't really remember anything except that time Mom spanked me for giving you a haircut, and you were almost a year old by then. She must have just about died when she pictured me wielding a pair of scissors an inch above your eyes. Can you even imagine?"

Rachel laughed, but all Hannah could do was frown in confusion over what she was about to say. "So you don't remember anything about me being born?"

"No."

"Not even, like, Mom being pregnant?"

"Not at all. What's going on?" Rachel paused for a beat and then sucked in a quick breath. "Oh my God, Hannah, are you pregnant?"

She nearly squealed the word *pregnant*. It didn't matter that Hannah was in the middle of a divorce. A baby was a baby, and babies only brought joy as far as Rachel was concerned. That was why she'd had five of them.

Five. Even in her current preoccupied state, Hannah cringed. "No, I am not pregnant."

"Are you sure?"

"If I were, I'd be a good eight months along, so yeah. I'm sure." She heard the muted sounds of other people talking in the room with Rachel, and she realized what a bad idea this was. "Listen. You're busy. I'll call back later."

"I'm not busy. We're wrapping up. Tell me what's going on."

"Rachel . . ." Her stomach twisted itself into a knot. How the hell was she supposed to say this? Maybe there was some good way to put it, but she couldn't think of anything but the obvious. "Rachel, I'm not related to Mom."

"You're not relating to her?"

"I'm not *related* to her. Biologically. She's not my mother."

"Hannah," Rachel huffed, her voice edging up with exasperation. "What are you talking about?"

"Our blood types aren't compatible."

A moment of silence indicated she'd finally realized what Hannah was saying. "That's obviously wrong. Was it a test? Have them redo it."

"There have been three tests. It's not wrong."

"Hannah . . ."

"She's not my mom. I know I'm just springing this on you and it's hard to believe, but she's not. The doctor kept saying I must have been adopted, but . . ."

"You look just like Dad." Rachel wasn't finishing Hannah's thought. The words snapped out of her. An accusation. A cry.

"I know."

"If you're Dad's daughter, then she has to be your mom. The end."

"No. No, she doesn't have to be."

"Hannah," she said again, harder this time. Horror and disgust sharpened the edges of Rachel's voice and asked that age-old question: *Hannah, why do you always cause so much trouble?*

Because she'd been born trouble, apparently. "What do you want me to say, Rachel? She's not my mother. It's not scientifically possible. And Dad is obviously my dad! So what the hell happened?"

"How should I know?"

"You were there!"

"I can't even believe what you're saying!" Rachel cried. "How could Mom . . . ? That doesn't make any sense. She and Dad were married for forty-five years!"

"You must remember something. Arguments, drama, upheaval?"

"No."

"Do you remember moving to Iowa?"

"No."

"Do you remember anything about California?"

"I don't . . ." Rachel blew out a breath. "I don't know. I remember chickens, I think. Holding the eggs. And playing in a river, maybe? That's it. I was four."

"Rachel, what am I supposed to—?"

"There has to be some explanation for this," Rachel cut in. "Some rare exception. This is absurd."

"Absurd? It's fucking *horrifying!*" Her shout echoed into silence. When she registered the pain in her scalp, she unclenched her fist and shook away the hairs she'd accidently torn free at the roots. "This is my life," she whispered.

"Listen," Rachel said in her soothing oldest-sister voice. "This has to be a mistake. Don't tell anyone else. Don't freak out. Becky and I will be there the day after tomorrow. We'll figure it out, okay?"

"Should I call her?"

"No. Not yet. Becky was even younger than I am. She can't help if I can't."

Hannah shook her head. "What am I supposed to do?"

"We'll figure this out. We *will*. I promise."

If she'd said it about anything else, Hannah would have believed her. Rachel kept her promises. And she was *so good* at taking care of people. Gifted, really.

But there was no neat answer here. No innocent explanation. Her dad had fathered a child with someone else. Her mother had helped cover it up. And there might not be enough of Mom's memory left in this world to ever find the truth.

CHAPTER 3

Hannah waited patiently for the morning aide to finish his duties. She sat placidly in the armchair with her book, telling herself that the man, Miguel, wasn't shooting her careful looks. He'd probably always watched her with a bit of caution in his eyes. It was difficult to perform professional work in front of an audience, after all. This had nothing to do with yesterday's outburst.

But everyone must have heard that she'd caused trouble. Maybe she'd even been accused of attacking her own mother, because the doctor couldn't reveal private patient information to explain her behavior. She must seem unstable and cruel and awful.

Or maybe they knew all of it. Even medical professionals gossiped, privacy rights be damned. She hoped they did. Hoped they didn't just think she'd lost her temper and yelled at her disabled mother for no reason.

She shouldn't have frightened her mom. Of course she shouldn't have. But anyone might have behaved irrationally after getting that kind of news.

She met the aide's eyes and smiled reassuringly as he helped Dorothy shuffle from the bed to her chair. "Thank you so much, Miguel," Hannah said, the words nearly edging into a Southern drawl in her attempt to ooze polite calm. "I'll help her pick out something to wear in a little while."

He seemed relieved at the normalness of the conversation and smiled back. "Have a good morning, ma'am," he called to Dorothy as he left.

Dorothy didn't respond. Her eyes weren't clear today. She looked away from Hannah's gaze.

The impatience inside Hannah was a living, hungry thing, but she couldn't do anything that might frighten her mother. Even on a good day, she could easily be sent into a state of confused terror. This was not a good day.

So no accusations. No anger. No direct questions. And definitely no grabbing.

Chastising herself for even entertaining the impulse, Hannah steadied her breath. The truth was, she did want to grab her mother. She wanted to grab her and shake her and scream with rage for this betrayal.

Another deep breath. And another. She calmed down a little. Made herself patient.

Her mother's state today could be a good thing. She might want to deny everything to Hannah, but maybe she'd talk to someone she thought was a stranger. Maybe she'd forget that she'd meant to keep this all secret.

"Hi, Dorothy."

Her mother's eyes darted away, but she offered a flash of a polite smile. She might have lost most of her mind, but she still knew her manners.

"Could you tell me about your husband?"

"They've stolen his ring," she responded immediately.

Steeling herself against her own mercenary plan, Hannah smiled. "But I have it right here." She withdrew her father's gold band from her pocket and held it out.

"Oh!" her mother cried. "I couldn't find it!"

"I found it," she said in the same soothing murmur a TV villain might use. "You can trust me."

Hannah had no idea how the vagaries of memory loss worked. How could her mother focus on the ring being missing, yet rarely ask where her husband was? Perhaps her husband's death had been such a blow it was stamped on her brain and couldn't be blurred by even this disease.

It didn't matter, she supposed, not if the ring could get Dorothy talking.

She pressed it into the palm of her mother's shaking hand, and Dorothy tucked her fingers against her heart. "Thank you. Thank you so much."

"You're welcome."

"Are you sure it's his?"

"Your initials are engraved right inside. You two used to live in California, didn't you?"

Dorothy's expression flashed from happy to sour in a split second. She pressed her hand tighter to her chest.

"In Big Sur," Hannah suggested.

"We left."

"Sure, but you lived there for years, right?"

Dorothy raised her chin and looked away. "No."

"You had your daughters there. It was your home."

She turned sullen. "We don't talk about California."

Hannah's heart leapt into a frantic beat. "What? Why don't you talk about California?"

"Because," she snapped, "we don't."

"But you had a farm there, didn't you?"

Dorothy curled tighter around her hand, as if she were trying to protect it. "We had a lot of things."

"Like what?"

"Things, things, things."

"So you had a lot of money?"

"No! We had God. We had God there. He was with us. Always with us."

God? What did that mean? "Miss Dorothy." She leaned closer. "I'd like to know about your family. Peter and Rachel and Becky. And Hannah. She was born in California, wasn't she?"

"We don't talk about Hannah."

Hannah's hands clenched at the rush of fear. Her nails dug into her palms, a bite of physical pain to match her emotions. "Why?" She didn't get an answer. She wasn't even expecting one at this point. "Mom, please. *Please*. I need to know."

No answer. Dorothy's body was frozen, guarding that wedding band, shutting Hannah out.

"Who is she?" Hannah pressed. "Who is Hannah? Who's her mother?"

Dorothy looked up, and for one heartbeat, Hannah thought her mom had heard and would answer. But her watery gaze focused somewhere past Hannah's shoulder. "He's here!"

"Who's here?" She looked back automatically even though she knew the room was empty behind her.

"He's here to take me to the puzzle room!"

"No one's here, Mom."

"He's here. He brought a puzzle."

Hannah closed her eyes and felt tears well behind them. Once a hallucination started, it could go on for hours. "Is it Dad?" she asked in the vain hope she could get her mom back on the subject of their family.

"I need to go to the puzzle room."

Jesus. There was no puzzle room just like there was no man there to collect her. Hannah rubbed a hand over her burning eyes. "Just tell me who my mother is."

"He's here. I'm late. I need to get dressed."

"Jesus Christ, Mom, there's no one there!"

"Don't be rude. He gets mad when you're rude. I need to get to the puzzle room."

Hannah glanced over her shoulder one more time, then gave an exaggerated nod. "Yes. But first he says he wants to know about Big Sur."

Dorothy blanched. "Why?"

"He says it's a puzzle of Big Sur and you have to tell him the right thing to get it."

"He didn't say that!"

"I talked to him before I came in the room. He says you need to do the right thing and then you can have the puzzle."

"W-what?" She looked confused now, her eyes darting from Hannah to that imaginary man behind her.

This was a terrible trick to play. Hannah was a terrible daughter. Oh, hell, she wasn't a daughter at all.

"What's the right thing?" Dorothy whispered.

"The right thing is to tell him what happened in Big Sur."

Dorothy's gaze slid to the side, and her eyes narrowed. "We left the garden."

"Which garden?"

"I had to do it, so we left the garden."

"Mom, do what? What did you do?"

She wouldn't look at Hannah now, not even for a moment. Her gaze bounced restlessly from object to object. The table, the floor, the window. "I need to go to the puzzle room now. I'm late."

"Who is Hannah's mother?"

"I've always loved puzzles."

"I know, Mom, but—"

"I need to go now!" she shouted, lurching forward until she teetered on the edge of her chair. "He's getting angry!"

Hannah's rage tried to push out, but she held it down, stuffing it deep into her gut, pressing until it felt tight and hard and nearly secure. "All right," Hannah ground out. "Let's pick out some clothes."

"I don't want your clothes! I don't know you!"

"Mom—"

"You're not my daughter!"

This time the arrow struck. This time it found a soft place and sank deep and true. The thunk of it reverberated through her body. She wasn't Dorothy's daughter, which was why Dorothy only recognized Rachel and Becky now.

"I'll get someone to help you," Hannah whispered before grabbing her purse and pushing out the door. Halfway down the hall, she spotted Miguel carrying a tray from another room. "She'd like to get dressed, please," she said past numb lips.

A rumbling filled her head, a quiet roll of vibration that chased her through the security door. It was her world breaking down. And her sanity. And all her love and softness. It was crumbling inside her, and she was a monster now. The selfish, heartless bitch her family had always feared she'd grow into.

The rumbling swelled and swelled until it gave way with a sudden crack.

It wasn't until Hannah slammed through the front doors of the care center that she realized the sound was only a storm. The gray sky lit up with another bolt of lightning just before rain began to fall in fast, hard drops that hit the ground like bullets. Thunder rolled again, shaking her guts and her brain.

She didn't bother racing for the car; she just stepped right out into the rain. It was ice-cold and numbing, a counter to the hot anger coiled inside her. The rain plastered her hair to her head and sneaked in rivulets down her shirt. Even after she got into her car, the tiny streams of water kept flowing as she sat there shivering.

She wanted to be back in Chicago. Back in her apartment. In her bed. In her marriage. She wanted to wake up, dry and warm, and realize the past six months had been a bad dream. A nightmare that didn't make any sense in the morning. Why had she come back to Iowa? And how could Jeff possibly hate her so much? It was nonsense. Jeff didn't hate anyone. And what utter foolishness to think her sweet, steady mother wasn't her mother at all.

It was one of those dreams you couldn't even explain to another person because it made so little sense. *It was me, but I wasn't myself. I lived in my old room in my parents' home, but my mom wasn't my mom and I didn't know who I was.*

She sat there, trembling and waiting to wake up. A flash of lightning cracked with such fierce nearness that she jumped and hit her temple on the car window. A smaller, duller crack, but one that would have woken her if she'd been dreaming.

So. This was all real, and she couldn't wake up from reality no matter how hard she tried.

The chill had settled into her bones, so she started her car and cranked the heat up. Now she was a creepy, wet lady trembling in her car in the rain. Her breath fogged the windows. She was breathing too hard. Nearly hyperventilating.

She turned on her seat heater and tried to get control.

It was only 10:00 a.m. The whole day stretched out in front of her, awful and endless. She couldn't go back into the center or she'd lose it and scream and yell and be reported for elder abuse. She couldn't go home and be productive. Just the idea of shifting through meaningless piles of papers nearly broke her.

But maybe they weren't all meaningless. Maybe there was a secret stash somewhere. A box that held adoption papers or a diary with a scrawled confession of . . . whatever had happened. Her father's affair. Faking the birth certificate. Or something about "leaving the garden," whatever the hell that meant.

She could try to do some research. Figure out who lived at that address now and whether they knew anything.

Or she could just do some determined day drinking.

"Yeah," she murmured into the foggy blank of her windshield. "Day drinking. That feels right."

She grabbed tissues from her purse and wiped off her side of the windshield. The automatic windshield wipers were already working furiously to try to cut through the steady wash of rain. Another bolt of lightning cracked the sky in two, but Hannah didn't jump this time. She just pulled out of the parking space and headed for the liquor store for a bottle of her favorite expensive vodka. She needed orange juice too. And maybe a terrible frozen pizza and a pint of good ice cream.

By the time she got home with her vodka and groceries, the impulse to start drinking had passed. Not the desire, certainly. She desperately wanted to *not* be sober right now. But she could wait until after noon. She might even be able to wait until happy hour.

She set her bag on the salmon-pink Formica of her parents' kitchen and looked down at the worn spot in the countertop where her dad had set his keys every night. Every single night. Never a change in habit. Never even an overnight trip with his fishing buddies.

"God, Dad," she sighed. "What the hell did you do?"

Touching the spot with two fingers, she could almost smell her father. A hint of grain and sorghum from the feed store, underlaid by the smell of Old Spice and Dial soap.

No, she definitely wouldn't make it until happy hour. But she could get a little sleuthing done before she retired to the couch with a bottle.

After putting the drinks in the fridge, she maneuvered the frozen pizza box until it fit in the freezer and set the ice cream on top of it. She'd gained five pounds since the move but couldn't bother caring much about it. She'd stayed slim her whole life, kept her clothing hip but age appropriate, and updated her hairstyle and highlights to match current trends. She'd stayed relevant. Listened to new music. Read the latest books. Maintained a busy social life.

And what did any of that matter? She was no longer a successful businesswoman with a confident style. She was just an aging failure. No marriage, no kids, no home, no job.

No parents.

She had to get something back. Had to pull something from this rubble.

She'd seen shows about people searching for a birth parent. Reunions between strangers who somehow felt a spark of recognition at first sight. Was that what had always been missing from her life? The certainty of belonging? Some animal sense of rightness?

Maybe her birth mother was just like her. Dark haired and dark eyed and dark souled. Maybe she pushed too hard at boundaries and couldn't settle down and always caused too much trouble.

That made sense, didn't it? That's what had happened. Her real mother had slept with a married man. Seduced him, maybe. And when she'd realized she was in trouble, she'd stuck around just long enough to have Hannah. Then she'd rolled out of town again, back to her restless life of wandering. That had been Hannah's birthright from the beginning.

The story felt like a deep breath filling Hannah's lungs. A cool rush of relief. The relief lasted only a moment, though, because her father didn't fit very neatly into that scene.

Peter Smith had been just as steady and sweet as his wife. A bit harder, yes, as men of his generation were. He hadn't been given to deep conversation or emotional declarations, but he'd taken his girls out for ice cream on summer weekends, kissed their foreheads goodnight, and always been the voice of calm during Hannah's temperamental teen years. She couldn't imagine him engaged in a wild affair, even in his youth.

He'd gotten up at 6:00 a.m. seven days a week. He'd never once called in sick to his job as manager of the feed store. He'd saved his earnings every year so he could take ownership of the store in 1989 when his old boss retired. He went to church early on Sunday mornings and led Bible study for the men on Sunday afternoons. He'd listened to baseball on the radio, but football and hockey had been too violent for him. His only hobby had been fishing, and not the kind that involved throwing one line into the water and drinking beer all day long.

He wasn't the kind of man to hook up with a wild traveling woman for a few weeks of passion. Or maybe he'd done it once and learned his lesson? Gotten it out of his system?

Hannah realized she'd been standing in front of the open freezer for a long time. The old motor whirred. Her breath fogged. She shut the door and went to the kitchen table to open her laptop.

She tried a half dozen searches first. "Peter Smith" and "California." "Peter Smith" and "Big Sur." Then "Dorothy Smith." Then "Dorothy Baylor." But every travelogue and blog post in the world seemed to pop up with those searches. Smith, especially, was far too common a name to track down online.

And that was the first time it occurred to her—that their names might not even be Smith. Smith was the kind of name people chose when they were running from something. Smith was a name for hiding.

We don't talk about California.

"No," she murmured. She was losing her grip. The most likely explanation for her existence was an affair, and the illegitimate child of an affair was reason enough for a couple to never speak of the past. Whatever the truth was, they'd done a good job of leaving it behind. They'd tried hard and they'd built a good life for their bastard child.

Giving up her search for some elusive off-the-grid Smith family from the '70s, Hannah instead pulled up a satellite map and typed in the address of her birthplace. She expected an aerial shot of a small town to appear on the screen, but all she saw were trees. Acres of them.

Frowning, she zoomed in until a tiny group of buildings came into view. Well, *view* was a strong word. There were glimpses of black roofs through the green canopy of trees and a few small clearings that looked like parking areas.

She zoomed out again until she could see the pale line of a highway snaking through the landscape. A few icons popped up. A gas station. A motel. A roadhouse. And right next to the little circle of her search address, an icon read "Riverfall Inn." She clicked on it, and there was her address: 47105 Highway 1.

Shit. She'd been born in a motel?

But no, of course not. Her parents hadn't lived in a motel room for years. She clicked to the Riverfall Inn website and immediately saw that the inn was an old house that had been converted to a B and B. The history it offered was brief.

The Riverfall Inn has been operating as a Big Sur Bed and Breakfast since 1993. Now we are excited to announce the opening of the riverside cabins that were originally built on our property in 1968! Each cabin was lovingly restored using eco-friendly designs and local materials. You'll find all the comforts of home right here in the redwoods. Please see our accommodations page for more information about our inn rooms and our riverside cabins. We'll see you in Big Sur soon!

Cabins built in 1968. Was that what her parents had been doing there? Building tourist cabins?

From what she could see on the accommodations page, the cabins were tiny squares outfitted with modern amenities. No useful information there.

She clicked through to the pictures of the inn, which looked like an old farmhouse that had been restored. Surely the inn house was a more likely find. She could imagine a midwife there, helping a woman through labor. A young, long-haired woman who looked like Hannah.

Had it been a private home until 1993? She tried finding an article about the opening of the Riverfall Inn, but thousands of reviews and traveler photos popped up. She couldn't sift through them fast enough to find any other information. Admitting defeat, she opened an email window and sent a simple query to the inn. Could you please tell me a little about the history of the property? Thank you.

At a loss about how to proceed from there, Hannah turned on the oven to preheat it. It was almost eleven. She'd dig through a few more piles of papers, and then she'd drown her sorrows in cheap pizza and screwdrivers while she waited to hear back from Big Sur.

CHAPTER 4

"Hannah?"

She opened her eyes and saw a dark shape moving through her bedroom moments before she was assaulted by the bright explosion of a flash bomb. She grunted out a cry of horror and threw her hands over her face.

"Are you okay?" her sister asked. Hannah wasn't sure which one it was. They both had the same sweet warble.

"What time is it?" Hannah groaned.

"Eight. In the morning. Are you *drunk*?"

"Not anymore, unfortunately." It had to be Rachel. Becky rarely used that judgmental tone.

"Hannah," her sister scolded.

"Oh, for God's sake. Don't you think I deserved a good, solid night of drinking?" Or a good, solid day. She'd managed to hold off until three after all. She'd lost count of the screwdrivers after that, though. All she remembered was that she'd woken up at four in the morning, thrown up, then dosed herself with water and ibuprofen before stumbling from the couch to her bed.

"Could you close those damn curtains?" she growled.

Rachel sniffed but she tugged the curtains closed.

Thank God for the Advil and water. And probably the vomiting. Aside from the sunlight allergy and a dry mouth, she didn't feel that bad. She managed to sit up and swing her legs over the side of the bed without even a hint of nausea.

"I need coffee," she muttered.

"Becky's making it right now."

Hannah grunted and pushed up from the bed to shuffle toward the kitchen. All the curtains and blinds were open, of course, but she squinted against the assault and headed toward the smell of drip coffee.

Becky stood at the sink, wearing honest-to-God rubber gloves as she washed the dishes that had been piling up over the past few days. Hannah tried to ignore the guilty anger that burned her gut. She would have cleaned the kitchen last night if her life hadn't been falling apart.

Becky tugged off the gloves and turned to watch as Hannah grabbed a coffee cup from the cupboard. She almost put it back when she realized the mug was printed with "Have a Blessed Day!" above a smiling sun, but she didn't have the energy to fight the small battles today.

"Are you all right?" Becky asked.

"I'm sure I look like death warmed over, but I'm fine."

"I meant . . . the other thing."

Hannah had only filled the mug halfway, but she set the pot and mug down and spun to glare at Rachel. "You *told* her?"

"I . . . um." Rachel shrugged.

"You asked *me* not to tell her!"

"I know, but we were driving all the way here and . . . I didn't want her walking in blind."

"Did it occur to you that maybe I should be the one to tell her I'm not really her sister?"

"Hannah!" Becky gasped. "Of course you're my sister! Don't say things like that."

"Half sister at most, apparently."

"As if that matters to me."

"It matters to me!" Hannah countered.

But her nasty, snapping words didn't make Becky angry. Instead, her mouth tipped down into sadness and she opened her arms and rushed over to give Hannah a hug. "I'm so sorry, baby. Are you sure this is even true? I can't believe it."

"At this point all I'm sure of is Mom isn't my mom. It's not scientifically possible." She gave Becky a brief squeeze, then waited to be released. The other women in her family always hung on too long.

Becky finally let her go. "But Dad has to be your dad. You're a smaller version of him."

"Slightly smaller," Hannah conceded. "But you know what that means. If I'm his daughter, Dad cheated."

Becky pressed her lips together and shook her head.

Hannah sympathized with the impulse, but she wasn't going to deny the obvious. "I know it's hard to accept, but an affair is the only explanation."

"Shh!" Becky shook her head again. "The kids will hear!"

"What kids?" When Becky glanced into the living room, Hannah turned to see two blond heads bent close together over an iPad. Becky's youngest two kids. Probably. They were both gangly tweens now. Or teens.

Rachel slammed a cupboard door, but she kept her voice low. "Maybe you're a scientific wonder. There's no way Dad had an affair."

"How would we know? He was young. It was a different time. And they were sure as hell running from something when they left California."

"They just wanted a simpler life," Rachel insisted.

"You know what Mom said to me yesterday? She said, 'We don't talk about California.' Does that sound simple to you?"

Rachel's brow furrowed in anger. "Don't tell me you've been asking Mom about this?"

"Don't look at me like I'm crazy! Who else am I supposed to ask?"

"Not a helpless old woman, for heaven's sake!"

Hannah's huff of laughter was anything but amused. "Rachel, are you kidding me? I just found out I've been lied to my whole life. Mom is the only one who can tell me anything, and you want me to . . . What? Just drop it? Just let it go?"

"She can't even remember why she's in that care center, and you expect her to answer questions about something that happened forty-five years ago?"

"Yes, I do."

"I can't believe you even brought it up. She must have been so upset."

"She was," Hannah said.

"Hannah!" Rachel used the same shocked tone she'd been using since Hannah could walk.

"Yes, she was upset. She got scared and freaked out and yelled that I wasn't her daughter. Funny, I didn't realize she'd been telling me the truth this whole time."

Becky laid a hand on her shoulder. "That's just the dementia talking."

"No, I really don't think it is. I think it's the dementia destroying her filters. She stopped remembering to lie. Does she ever tell you you're not her daughter?"

Becky didn't answer. Neither did Rachel. Hannah fought the urge to give them both the finger. Sure, she'd tried to rationalize some of this to herself, but she didn't want to hear it from them.

"I'll make you breakfast," Becky offered. "You'll feel better after you've had something to eat."

Ah, the constant refrain of Midwestern life. Illness? Offer food. Funeral? Bring food. New baby? Drop off food. Suddenly discover you're some sort of illegitimate secret orphan? Food, food, food.

But she was hungry, so she didn't object.

Becky quickly whipped up some corn fritter batter, and the smell of the pancakes frying made Hannah feel ten years old again. As a teenager, she'd grown scornful of the constant pushing of corn as a vital vegetable. It was a grain, she'd insisted, and not even a healthy one. But her scorn hadn't stopped the pushing. Corn fritters for breakfast, corn on the cob for lunch, creamed corn for dinner. It was everywhere, boiled and cut off the cob during the summer, packed into boxes and stacked in the deep freeze in the cellar so they wouldn't run out for the rest of the year. God forbid they ever run out.

She hadn't eaten corn in years. She'd refused. But as soon as Becky set the plate in front of her, Hannah slathered the fritters with butter and syrup and dug in. Food was comfort after all, and damned if it didn't work. She felt nearly high with pleasure as she swallowed.

When the memory popped up that she wasn't truly a Midwesterner and neither were her parents, Hannah chewed that too. She washed it down with a gulp of coffee. By the time Rachel and Becky and the two kids—Ruby and Ethan—sat at the table with their own plates, Hannah was halfway through hers.

It was a subdued breakfast, with none of the normal, pleasant conversations that her sisters had perfected over countless potlucks and fish fries. Hannah was surprised to realize she missed their chatter. The kids' eyes focused on whatever they were watching on their phones. "How's it going, guys?" she asked.

"Great," they both said without looking up.

Hannah nodded. "School's out in three weeks?"

"Yes." Another joint reply.

Becky perked up. "Can you believe my baby is graduating high school?"

"Well, he is almost six feet tall now."

"I know. But he'll always be my baby. My first baby! Right, Rachel?"

"Heck, Tom is thirty, and he's still my baby."

Silence fell into the place where Hannah should have spoken about her own children. Rachel cleared her throat. "I have news, actually."

"Jesus," Hannah said. "You're not pregnant, are you?"

She'd failed to keep the abject horror out of her voice, and they both frowned briefly at her before Rachel shook her head. "No . . . but Mindy is!"

Hannah's jaw dropped. Mindy was Tom's wife. That meant Rachel was—

"You're going to be a grandma!" Becky squealed.

"Oh my God," Hannah breathed. Her sister was a grandmother. No. Hannah couldn't possibly be that old.

But of course she was. Hannah could've been a grandma already too if she'd started as young as her sisters.

Rachel and Becky were hugging, their blond hair mingling until Hannah couldn't tell whose head started where.

Becky's hair was shoulder length and bouncy. Rachel's was shorter, but the same shade of burnished gold. The practical bob made her look like a younger version of their mother. *Their* mother.

"She's only two and a half months along, so they're not telling everyone yet, but I had to tell someone!"

That someone was obviously Becky. Hannah just happened to be sitting there too.

This discovery that she was only a half sister wasn't truly a revelation; it was only confirmation. Her sisters' worlds revolved around children and home and family, just as Dorothy's always had.

Hannah, on the other hand . . . Well. She remembered the first two nephews' birthdates. Usually. The rest were just a jumble of ages she couldn't guess, their birthdays running together into one long series of screaming romper rooms. She'd given up on attending birthday parties years ago, and she'd given up on sending presents not long after that. She did give them each fifty dollars at Christmas, though.

Now there would be more. More babies and cooing and sighs about how children made life worth living. Followed by the awkward silence when they noticed Hannah sitting there, nursing a glass of wine and counting the minutes until she could escape the chaos.

Maybe the discovery that she didn't belong to this family wasn't horrifying or hurtful. Maybe it was validation.

"Let me jump in the shower," she said. "I'll be ready in fifteen minutes."

When she returned with her dark hair gathered into a damp bun, her sisters were still discussing babies, though they were both wiping down countertops as they talked. She'd expected nothing less. "Ready?"

She was getting into Rachel's huge Suburban when she realized what a mistake that was after the way she'd left the center yesterday. And the day before. There was a good chance she'd need an escape hatch. It was her preferred mode of travel.

"Actually," she said as she stepped back out to the curb, "I'll take my car and meet you two there."

Rachel frowned.

"I need to get groceries on the way home."

"I put a casserole in the fridge for you."

Of course she had. "I'm out of cereal," she lied.

Shrugging, Rachel started her car, and Hannah breathed a sigh of relief as she retreated to her own. She'd just bought herself twenty minutes of not feeling like the circus freak sitting with the preacher's kids.

Yesterday's storm had blown out all the clouds and humidity, and the day was fresh and bright. She slipped on her sunglasses and rolled down the windows as she followed the Suburban through town. When she turned on the radio, the song made her smile. "Three Times a Lady" by the Commodores. The music brought such a rush of memory of the radio playing during summer drives that she could practically feel her sisters pressed up against her legs.

Being the youngest, she'd always been relegated to the middle seat, while her sisters had hung their arms out the windows and waved at everyone they'd passed. But whenever her dad had glanced into the rearview mirror and smiled at her, Hannah had felt special. Her sisters were too busy looking out the windows to notice his secret winks.

God, she missed him.

She'd missed him for years, but now she *needed* him. Whatever he'd done, she'd forgive it, if only he could tell her.

After today's visit, she'd spend every free hour going through his papers. Surely there was a sealed envelope somewhere. Maybe there was a hint she'd missed in his will. He must have left her an answer. She couldn't just be adrift.

It wasn't until she was halfway to the care center that she remembered the query she'd sent to the inn. She dug her phone from her purse and opened her email, darting her eyes from the screen to the road and back again, watching for runaway cows or tractors broken down on the shoulder. Her email application chimed, and Tucker@

RiverfallInn.com appeared at the top of her inbox. Hannah's heart tripped.

She opened the email, but when she saw the paragraph, she knew she couldn't safely read the whole thing while driving.

Under normal circumstances, she would've pulled over to read it, but one of her sisters would notice and freak out, and they'd turn around and demand to know what was wrong. Snarling, she put the phone facedown on the passenger seat and made herself drive on.

"Come on, come on," she urged her sister's car. At least Rachel wasn't such a goody two-shoes that she drove the speed limit. On country roads the speed limit was more of a suggestion, really, especially if you were friendly with the local officers. And the Smith family had always been good citizens. Once they'd arrived in Iowa, at least.

By the time they pulled into the care center lot, her palms were slick with sweat against the steering wheel, but she managed to put the car in park before she grabbed her phone. She opened the email and had only gotten past the "Thank you so much for your interest!" opening when Becky tapped on her window.

She rolled it down and nodded reassuringly. "I'll be inside in a second. I need to answer this email."

"Sure." Becky, her arms piled with Tupperware containers holding genuine homemade treats, started toward the entrance, then turned back around. "We'll meet back at the house this afternoon and talk about all this, okay?"

"Yeah. Thanks."

"We'll get it figured out."

"Right." Her fingers twitched as she fought the urge to shoo her sister away. "Just give me a minute. I'll meet you in Mom's room."

Not giving her sister a chance to engage again, Hannah raised her phone.

Thank you so much for your interest! Our property has been operating as a B and B since 1993. Before that, it was private property. If you've visited before, please keep in mind that though the house was updated in 1993, I did a complete renovation and restoration in 2010 when I purchased the inn and surrounding acreage. I think you'll find the rooms much improved in comfort and design. I'm also very excited to let you know that we recently restored the riverside cabins that were built in the 1960s and had fallen into disrepair. You can see pictures of all our accommodations on the website. We'll see you in Big Sur soon!

—Tucker Neff

Hannah's lip curled. The email hadn't told her one damn thing. Maybe she could call and explain to Tucker Neff what information she needed and why. See if he could help.

Her face burned at the thought. She wasn't going to lay her secrets at a stranger's feet so he could back away in horror. He didn't sound like he knew much, anyway. All he cared about was the business. Confessing the truth wouldn't be worth the shame.

Surely in this digital age she could send away for property records and start her search quietly. No one else needed to know. Even with Becky, Hannah had felt a shock of horror that Rachel had revealed her secret. It was bad enough that Hannah herself knew. If one or two more people found out, the entire town would get the news.

And Rachel must have told her husband. Becky would tell hers. Maybe even the older kids.

No. Her sisters wouldn't want their children to know anything sordid about their grandparents. And they wouldn't want the neighbors to know. This wouldn't spread further. She was safe.

But safe from what, exactly? Not pain or betrayal or confusion. Not the knowledge that she was truly, utterly alone in this.

Clutching the steering wheel, she stared at the front doors of the care center and considered driving away. She could just pull out, grab a cup of coffee, and keep driving. All the way back to Chicago. Or even farther than that. Maybe all the way to the East Coast. Find a job in a small office, rent a studio with an ocean view, start a new life, and never look back.

Sure.

With a wistful sigh, she got out of the car and headed inside.

Her sisters weren't in their mother's room. They were at the nurses' station, passing around Tupperware containers full of delicious treats and catching up on the caregivers' lives. The kids were visiting too, the earbuds dangling free as they smiled and laughed.

Hannah had spent her days here for a full month, and she'd had no idea that Nurse Quinn's brother played for a minor-league baseball team in Kansas or that Nurse Brenda had a daughter with cerebral palsy. The caregivers beamed with happiness at this little reunion.

"She must be eight by now?" Rachel asked Brenda. "Third grade in the fall?"

Hell, even matching ages to grades was a mystery to Hannah, aside from placing five-year-olds in kindergarten and teenagers in high school.

But her sisters settled into their places in this group as if they'd always belonged there and always would. Hannah walked past them and slipped into her mother's room.

Her mom was seated at the small desk, a puzzle piece clutched in her hand. She looked up, her face a pale moon of polite confusion. "Hello," she ventured carefully.

"Good morning!" Hannah offered, going for cheerful neutrality today. She pulled a chair close to her mom and took a seat. "I see you finally got a puzzle."

"Yes. It's a painting."

It wasn't a painting, but the vivid photo of flowers was so bright it looked almost surreal even to Hannah's clearer eyes. The pieces were oversized and easy for shaky hands to fit together. "It's beautiful. I know how much you love gardening."

"I do!" Dorothy said. "Flowers are pretty, of course, but vegetables are so much more satisfying. Don't you think?" Always so practical. She slowly angled her trembling hand into place and pressed the piece in.

Hannah glanced over her shoulder. She couldn't see her sisters in the hallway, but she could still hear the laughter and conversation. She'd meant to at least start this day with a nice reunion. She'd planned to pretend for an hour or two. But once her family came in, Hannah wouldn't be able to ask any significant questions. Rachel would interfere. The kids would listen.

She cleared her throat. "Your vegetable garden was always the envy of our block. Remember when Lorraine Davenport said you should be banned from competing in the county fair because your winter squash won every year?"

This time her mother's smile wasn't vague at all. It shone bright and wide. "I didn't want to cause a fuss, so I bowed out that year. And she still didn't win."

Hannah laughed. "That's right. She didn't say much about your squash after that."

"No, she did not."

"Are you sure you didn't mean to cause a fuss?"

Her mother laughed. "I really didn't."

And Hannah believed her. She leaned a little closer and lowered her voice. "My favorite part of your garden was the zucchini, because you'd make zucchini bread. Loaves and loaves of it until the deep freeze was piled high. God, I can still remember the smell of it, and the pats of butter melting on a warm slice."

"That was always Hannah's favorite," she said.

Hannah froze and tried to think how to proceed without scaring Dorothy out of this good mood. "Yes. Hannah loved it. How did you get so good at gardening?"

"Oh, you know, when I was a girl, we didn't have any choice. If we didn't garden, we had nothing to eat. And at the orphanage . . ." She trailed off, frowning a little as she picked up a puzzle piece of pink and red petals.

"And in Big Sur?" Hannah tried gently. "Did you grow vegetables there?"

"My, yes. We had almost two acres of garden. It was a lot of work, but the kids helped too."

"Rachel and Rebecca?"

"Yes. They loved helping. We all helped each other."

"Who did?"

"The whole community."

"Even Hannah's mother?"

Dorothy's hand stopped its restless wandering in the air above the puzzle. The piece wobbled in her clawed hand.

"Did she help in the garden? Hannah's mother?"

She set the piece against the edge of the puzzle and pushed. The lines weren't right. The pink and red petals mashed up against a yellow daisy.

"Dorothy," Hannah pressed. "What was her name? Did you know her?"

The tips of her mom's fingers turned white as she pressed harder at the piece, trying to mash it into the wrong spot.

"Please. Please, Mom, just tell me who she was."

"We left her there," her mother whispered.

"What?"

"We left her there."

"In Big Sur?"

"Yes," she rasped. "We left her there."

"Who was she? I need to know her name! I need to—"

"We don't talk about that!" Dorothy cried. Then her palm came down hard on the table, a terrible boom of sound. *"We don't talk about that!"*

Her shout stopped the laughter in the hall, and sudden footsteps brought her sisters to the doorway. They paused for a moment, taking in the scene; then Rachel rushed forward. "Hannah, what are you doing?"

"I'm just asking questions."

"I told you not to do that!"

Hannah glared. "And I told you I needed to ask."

Her mom's hand hit the table again, the slap echoing through the room. "We don't talk about that! We don't talk about that!"

"I know, Mom," Rachel said soothingly as she knelt down and took her mom's hand in both of hers. Her eyes stabbed through Hannah, as if trying to burn her with shame and scorn. "Shh. Don't talk. It's okay."

"It's not okay," Hannah snapped.

"Yes," Rachel ground out, "it is. It's fine, Mom. I see you're working on a puzzle."

Hannah glared at her sister and refused to back down. "It's *not* okay. She just told me they left her there."

"Who?"

"My *mother*. She just said they left her in Big Sur."

"We don't talk about that!" Dorothy cried again.

"Christ," Rachel cursed. "Becky, would you get her out of here?"

Hannah jumped to her feet. "I don't need to be handled, Rachel."

"Apparently you do."

What the hell was Hannah supposed to say to that? Yes, her mother was upset. Yes, she was crying, but Hannah had a right to know her own truth. "She could still be there, don't you get that? She could still be in Big Sur. I could still find out who I am."

"You're Hannah Smith." Rachel drew her mother's trembling hand to her mouth and kissed it. "*This* woman is your mother, right here in front of you, and you're being cruel to her. She raised you. She loved you. We're your family and we're here with you, so what could it possibly matter who they left behind in Big Sur?"

She drew a deep breath, pulling in enough air to tell Rachel exactly what she thought of such a shitty dismissal of her feelings. But Becky's arm curled over her shoulders and pulled her into an embrace. "Come on. Let's go outside and talk."

Hannah held her breath. If she walked away, Rachel would go on thinking she was right, and she wasn't.

But did it matter what Hannah might say? Rachel wouldn't be swayed. She was the oldest sister, and she had utter confidence in the rights and wrongs of the world. Of course it was wrong to upset an old woman with dementia. Of course it was wrong to dig into your family's closet of dried and dusty skeletons. Hannah was being selfish again. She was always being selfish.

When Becky tugged her carefully around, Hannah let herself be guided to the door, then down the hall toward the little walled yard that let the memory care patients wander safely outside.

"I've been thinking," Becky said as she led them to a bench shaded by a maple tree. "Maybe it isn't what you suspect. Maybe you're a niece or something like that. If Dad had a sister who got into trouble, Mom and Dad might have raised you as their own. That would explain why you look like him."

Hannah frowned, considering the possibility for a few heart-beats. Long enough that her pulse sped with hope. Hope that there was a more innocent explanation. Maybe even a generous one. And yet . . . "I could understand raising me as their own, but why would he have covered up having siblings at all? Why run to Iowa and lie about their past?"

"Maybe she was troubled."

"Mom isn't reacting as if it's something innocent, is she?"

"These days Mom isn't reacting to anything the way she should."

Hannah nibbled on her thumbnail. "She said they left her there."

"I know, but—"

"I think I need to go."

"Go where?"

"To Big Sur. I can't just sit around here every day wondering about this. If my mother is still in California, I need to know. And I can't . . . I can't stay here with all these secrets."

A foot scuffed the cement behind them. "Of course you can't," Rachel said. She circled the bench to face them, arms crossed over her chest, face set in anger. "Of course you can't stay. I should've known."

"What's that supposed to mean?" Hannah demanded.

"*One month*. You finally come back to help take care of Mom and you only manage one month before you decide to leave."

"That's not fair!"

"Isn't it?"

"No! I moved here for the long haul. I've been here every day and I had no intentions of leaving. But even you have to admit this changes everything."

"How? You're going to run off to California and somehow find a woman who's been missing for forty-five years? And then what? Mom is still the one who raised you, and she's the one who needs you now."

"She doesn't need me! She doesn't even know who I am! Oh, she recognizes the two of you. Great. I'm happy for you both. It must be nice. But for some mysterious reason, she tells me I'm not her daughter."

"But you are," Rachel snapped.

Hannah surged to her feet. "I wouldn't expect you to understand. You've always belonged. You've always been just like her. I'm the one who never felt right."

"That's ridiculous."

"What the hell would you know about it, Ms. Homecoming Queen?"

"Oh, come on. So we had different interests in high school. Do you think I always felt like I fit in?"

"Yes," Hannah answered. "Yes, I think you always fit in perfectly. With this place, with this family. I don't think you ever lay in your bed at night and wondered why you were so damn different from everybody in your whole world."

Rachel rolled her eyes. "So you're going to run off and abandon your sick mother because of some ancient teenage angst? You're forty-five years old, for God's sake. It's time for you to stick with *something*."

"Ha." She hadn't meant to make the sound. It sprang from her mouth like a cough. A harsh, blank, one-syllable laugh.

Ha. She'd always known that was what her family thought of her. She'd seen it in their eyes and felt it in the deepest pits of her own guilt. At least someone was finally saying it.

"Rachel," Becky said, the word drowning in caution.

"No," Rachel bit back. "I'm tired of always putting up with her artsy, angsty bullshit. Always smarter than the rest of us, always too sophisticated for this town and our little worries. Well, it's easy to keep up with music and fashion and politics when you only have to look out for yourself, isn't it, Hannah?

"You never have to worry about what to make for dinner or how to pay for new athletic uniforms for five kids or whether or not Medicare is going to cover Mom's new prescription. You never have to worry how the town will float new books for the high school or if the church can keep paying out pensions to three retired secretaries. You don't even have to worry about your husband anymore, do you? All that matters is what *Hannah* feels. What *Hannah* wants."

Hannah sneered, though she suspected the tears pooling in her eyes gave away her hurt. "You're a self-righteous bitch."

"Stop!" Becky said, moving to stand between her sisters. "Stop it right now. Rachel, go back inside."

"Sure," Rachel snapped. "I'll go take care of Mom. Hannah, go ahead and run away like you always do. Don't worry about us. We'll be fine. Just do whatever you want. That's your specialty." She marched across the garden and flung the door open.

Hannah stared at the door closing slowly behind her sister until it latched with a cold, hard click.

Becky put a hand on her arm. "Hannah—"

"Don't apologize for her. She said exactly what she meant."

"She's upset. We're all upset. This is all . . . This is *crazy*, Hannah! The idea that Dad might have . . . God, I can't even say it."

"Well, try to imagine how I feel." She barely got the words out before her throat swelled with choking tears. They spilled over her eyes, and she couldn't stop the sobs from escaping. "I didn't bring this on!" she pushed out past the pain. "This isn't my fault!"

"I know." Becky, despite being five inches shorter, wrapped her arms tight around Hannah and tried to hold her. "I'm sorry. I'm so sorry."

"It's not fair!"

"I know. It's not fair at all. But you're so upset right now. There's no need to decide anything today. We'll see what we can find out from here."

"I already looked into Big Sur. There are only a thousand full-time residents. If my real mom is there, she'll be easy to find."

"And if she's not?"

"Then it should be easy to find someone who remembers her. During the winter the place is even smaller than Coswell. Easier for me to go ask a few questions than write a thousand letters."

"Hannah." Becky's voice was broken, pleading. "If she's been there for forty-five years, she'll be there for another month. Please take a few days to let it sink in."

"I can't, Becks. It's making me crazy. I can't sit with Mom every day and not ask questions. And Rachel is going to have me arrested for elder abuse if I don't stop."

"She will not."

"Maybe she'll just tell me I'm a worthless, selfish piece of shit again."

"That's not what she said."

Hannah drew up, pulling out of Becky's arms. She swiped her sleeve over her face and sniffed hard. "That's exactly what she said. But it doesn't matter. She's right. I am running away. I always do."

"You don't—"

"It doesn't matter! I don't care. If my mother is still there, I need to know."

"*Why?*" Becky pressed, and it wasn't sarcasm or disdain or disagreement. She honestly didn't understand. Hannah could see the desperation in her pleading eyes.

"Because, Becky . . . what if I'm just like her?"

"What do you mean?"

"I mean, maybe there's nothing *wrong* with me. Maybe I just got my mother's personality."

"Hannah, stop! There's nothing wrong with you!"

But that wasn't true. Oh, she'd been pleased with herself and her life for quite a few years, but the divorce meant she had to face all her doubts again. Why couldn't she just stay in place and settle?

Rachel had been right about that, at least. Hannah walked away from things. She ran away. She turned her back and moved on. It was what she'd always done.

She may as well try it one more time. She wasn't doing any good here anyway. She never had.

CALIFORNIA

CHAPTER 5

California had always unsettled her. Los Angeles, especially, but even the Bay Area. The faint, fuzzy haze that blurred the air disturbed her. She wasn't sure why.

It was there even on clear days, adding a sheen to every view. Every landscape or city skyline or beach day was coated in it.

She knew it was just moisture and cold from the Pacific mixing with the heat of the land, but it felt eerie to her. She was a Midwestern girl, despite her birth certificate. In Iowa, a strangeness in the air meant danger. A sign of an impending storm, and a bad one at that. Years and years of tornado warnings and trips to huddle in the basement had scarred her.

Strange air was never good. And she couldn't seem to reassure her brain with logic. That wall of fog that hung off the coast every morning looked like alien mist from a Stephen King novel. Anything could be lurking there. Soviet submarines, UFOs, monsters.

Most likely monsters.

No, thanks. She'd take a Chicago beach any day. She should never have left that city.

If she'd stayed, she wouldn't have found her mother's medical documents and felt her life cleave in two, the opening filling swiftly with this gnawing doubt. And she wouldn't be driving through California haze and traffic, squinting against a sun that somehow pounded down even as it hid behind that weird nimbus.

The cities were the worst, of course, the haze shimmering off acres of cement. But as she drove south out of San Francisco, Hannah only found more of the same crowding. Yes, it was hillier here. More natural. A bit more spread out. But there was no true openness.

The canyons here were the same as the canyons surrounding LA: logjams of houses that had caught on any flat surface, as if they'd tumbled in on a flash flood. Some were propped on logs and pilings to keep them upright. They sat perched on cliffs, jammed into slots, stacked one above another. So many people. So many souls. Their homes jostled for position just as their cars did on the freeway, one giant traffic jam of humanity.

But after what felt like an endless drive, something changed. Past the freeways of San Jose, the road construction of Santa Cruz, and the glitz and money of Monterey and Carmel . . . the landscape shifted. She crossed a boundary. The two-lane highway narrowed even further. The haze faded into clouds and moisture, and just like that, she was somewhere wild.

She drove more slowly, expecting at any moment to pass through another town of pseudo-quaint clapboard houses and manicured lawns, yet she found nothing but angry water and treacherous roads. The coast here was dangerous. Untamed. Uninhabited.

Not that she was alone. There were other cars filled with tourists and maybe a few pilgrims like herself. But no one just passing through. No one trying to get anywhere. These roads were too slow and steep for speed.

Clouds drifted in and out. The sea glowed gray blue below the cliffs. Tourists pulled onto gravel turnouts to take pictures, but Hannah drove on, tugged forward by the GPS directions on her phone.

It wasn't far now. The blinking blue dot told her that, but she imagined she could feel it in her gut too. Some sort of homing organ.

Thirty minutes later, she drove right past the sign she'd been watching so carefully for. A soft "Oh" pushed from her lips as if she'd been jabbed in the stomach.

The Riverfall Inn. Just a sign sticking out from the trees, too subtle to catch her attention in time. The trees were redwoods, she realized then. Her first redwoods and she hadn't noticed them either.

After making a careful turn on a steep dirt road, she edged back onto the highway, driving more slowly lest she miss the turn again. She spotted the sign just in time, and then the paved narrow lane that slipped into the trees past it.

At first she tried to ease up the rising hill, tentative in this unfamiliar car, but that didn't work. She had to gun the engine to hop up over the steep rise. After that, the road leveled out and curled through the trees.

The paved road turned to dirt. Now she was driving through a false dusk. Tunneling into a strange forest. A hidden house appeared next to her before she even realized she'd reached her destination. Hannah slammed on the brakes, and the car slid to a dusty stop.

Heart racing, she turned off the engine and stared at the inn. It looked just like the pictures. A two-story blue farmhouse with white railings around the front porch. Lovely round lanterns flickered on either side of the redwood door. The Riverfall Inn. Beautiful and expensive. This was where she'd been born, but the high-end finishes made it feel like a movie set instead of a truth.

As she stepped out of the car, she looked around for the cabins and saw only trees and ferns. Water rushed somewhere in the distance, but she couldn't see even a hint of it from here.

The house before her was so covered in vines and brush that she couldn't tell how old it was, though surely these plants had been growing for decades. Hannah walked up the steps and carefully opened the door. Her arms felt too light, as if she were a visiting ghost.

The girl behind the counter glanced up over her glasses without lifting her head. "Welcome to the Riverfall Inn."

The insincerity of her words matched her dreary clothes and dark makeup. Hannah glanced around the tiny front room and found it was all wood and natural colors, the sleek lines polishing away any hint of the farmhouse it had once been.

"Hi," Hannah ventured.

The girl—Jolene if her name tag was correct—sat straighter and stared.

"Um. I rented a cabin?" Hannah couldn't recall the last time she'd sounded so uncertain about anything. This place didn't give her any feelings at all, and there were no cabins around. If it were the right place, wouldn't she have a sense of coming home? A reaction in her bones?

"Your name?"

"Smith," she answered, unsure of even that. "Hannah Smith."

"Have you stayed with us before?"

Yes. Maybe. "No."

Jolene whipped out a map. "You're in cabin three. We're here." She pointed at a large rectangle on the map labeled CHECK-IN, then slid her finger across the paper. "You're going to take the right fork in the road and park right here." She made an X and then circled one of the six little squares that were laid out in a semicircle. "Maid service includes new kindling each evening, and there's breakfast here in the dining room from eight to ten every morning. You're here for four nights?"

"Yes."

"With four nights, you get a complimentary bottle of wine."

"Oh. All right." She stared, unable to wipe her confusion off her face while too many questions pushed against the back of her teeth.

72

"It's already in your room," the girl prompted.

"Sure. Thank you."

Jolene's forehead crumpled into an irritated frown for a bare second. "Here's your key," she offered, placing an old-fashioned motel key on top of the map. "Will you be exploring the area?"

Hannah blinked several times, worried she was acting suspicious enough to prompt questions. Then she realized it was a canned phrase. *Exploring the area.* As if Jolene gave a damn what anyone did around here. She was someone's teenage daughter, eager to escape this place as soon as she could. She probably wanted to get out of the fog of the coast and into the haze of LA.

"Yes," Hannah finally answered, "I'll be looking around. Big Sur, I mean."

Jolene produced another sheet of paper. "Hiking map." This one had smaller squares and rectangles. "Here's your cabin. Here's the river. The river trail is great." If it was as great as the tone implied, the trail was likely packed with dog shit and trash.

Hannah gathered up the papers and the key and stuffed it all into her purse. "Thanks." She was three steps toward the door when her tongue finally shoved out a question. "Do you know what this place was before?"

The girl had already slumped into her chair, but she straightened when Hannah turned back to face her. "Before?"

"Yes. Before it was an inn."

"It was another bed and breakfast."

"I mean before that. The history of the property."

Jolene shrugged, just as Hannah had known she would. It was a dumb question to ask a disaffected teenager.

"Is the owner around? I'd like to speak with him."

"He's out surfing. He'll be here in the morning, though. Or you could try coming by later. The cell reception sucks, so don't count on your phone."

Hannah nodded and let herself out. As she took a deep breath of woody air, she realized she was thankful it had been Jolene checking her in instead of the owner. She hadn't gotten her bearings yet. Didn't know what she wanted to ask, much less what answers she was hoping for. She should know. She'd spent hours on the plane and in the car thinking it out, but she felt muffled and disoriented now that she was actually here.

She hopped in her car and drove deeper into the woods.

The shocking beauty of the coast had let her forget why she was traveling, if only for a few heartbeats at a time. But the urgency was back now. The reason. The weight of it was an odd, pressing knowledge that wasn't knowledge at all. It was *question*. Doubt. Erasure. Fear. As deep and primal as these woods.

The car bounced into a pothole, shaking her as she rounded a curve, and then the cabins were in front of her.

She pulled into the space marked **#3**, turned off the car, and sat there, too scared to get out.

The engine ticked to silence. She waited for that feeling again. A sense of belonging or coming home. The cabins were just small brown squares that blended into the trees. She'd meant to stay in the inn itself, but it had been sold out, so she was here without even knowing if the cabins were the right place. Shouldn't she feel *something*?

But she never felt the right things, did she? She'd never felt pulled toward community, never appreciated the love and security that everyone else craved. Her mother and sisters had always been so close, so content. And everyone in her family was still on a first marriage, while Hannah was relieved to be leaving her second. She was wrong. Always wrong. Why had she expected to conjure up the right emotions here?

The sun began to set, and true dusk settled in, shrouding the woods and Hannah's fear.

She got out of the car and walked toward whatever answers waited.

CHAPTER 6

There were no answers here.

As soon as she walked into the cabin, she knew she would've been better off just calling the owner to ask as many questions as she could. Even if these cabins had been here in '72, everything but the foundations had been stripped out and rebuilt years ago.

The floors were smooth, heated wood, the walls were glossy layers of warm plaster, and the interior doors were frosted glass. And the bathroom . . . well, Hannah heartily doubted anyone had installed river-stone shower floors in the 1970s.

She dropped her bags on the self-warming floor and collapsed into a deep armchair. Tears burned her eyes. She let her head fall back so the tears could run into her hair and disappear as if they'd never existed.

"Not fair," she growled. "Not fair, not fair."

She might have screwed up important things in her life, but this was one thing she hadn't deserved. This, at least, was something simple that every child was promised. Here is your father. Here is your mother. Here are their names, even if you're adopted and have never met them. Here is a legal document to tell you who you are.

She'd always found it strange that so many adopted kids became obsessed with that question: *Who am I?* She'd felt sorry for them. Didn't they know who they were already? Did they need someone else to tell them? You were who you were, no matter who'd given birth to you.

But now she saw the flip side of it. There'd been one tiny correction to her path, and she suddenly needed to know the truth. She needed to see it. See herself carved into someone else's face. A mirror of her features. The original sketch of her genetics.

But why? What could it possibly matter? She was who she was, regardless. There were no answers here. There was no genetic sketch. And the only mirror was a backlit oval perched over a ridiculously shallow ceramic sink.

Hannah wiped the wet trails from her temples and pulled out her phone. Without even thinking about it, she pulled up Jeff's name and hit "Call."

It was only as she waited for the ringing to start that she wondered what the hell she was doing. He wasn't her husband anymore. He wasn't even her friend. They were adversaries now, fighting over the money she'd earned with her own hard work.

"Bastard," she said automatically, even as she crossed her fingers that he'd pick up.

He didn't. Maybe he finally hated her enough that he'd blocked her number. Or maybe he was on a date and he'd silenced the phone as soon as he saw who was calling. But she didn't hear his voicemail. She didn't hear anything at all.

Hannah pulled her phone back and looked at the screen. The one tiny bar of signal changed to a blank.

"Shit."

She needed him and she couldn't have him. Even if that was what she'd chosen when she'd walked away, it didn't make it hurt less. In fact, it hurt more, because she couldn't blame anyone but herself.

Well, she could if she tried. She was mad at him for quite a few things. For the settlement fight. For the million arguments about her stupid dissatisfaction. For ever wanting to marry her in the first place, damn it.

She'd warned him. She'd told him it wouldn't work.

The flash of familiar anger burned off some of her self-pity, and she sat forward, though the chair tried its best to pull her back into its cushions.

Had she expected there to be an interactive exhibit waiting for her in the cabin, with pictures of the farm and its previous inhabitants? Maybe she'd thought her room would feature a framed photograph of her father with his arm looped around a strange woman, a caption offering her name.

"Ha." Hannah shook her head at her impatience, another constant in her life. Impatience was good for a career. Not so good for solving a forty-five-year-old mystery. Or making a marriage.

Before she lost all the light, she opened the back door of the cabin and stepped onto the packed-dirt patio. A fire pit sat in the center, already prepped with kindling and wood. Two chairs were angled toward each other, awaiting a pair of lovers. Or Hannah and her feet.

The sound of water drew her off the patio, and she only had to take a few steps before she saw the rushing, bubbling water of the river. No waterfall in sight, but she could hear it somewhere to the east, rumbling its existence.

She followed a trail to the right, checking out each cabin as she passed. They were all the same style as hers, eco-chic or some such descriptor. When she reached a fence that said **PRIVATE PROPERTY**, she turned back and tried the other direction as the air turned twilight blue around her.

After passing all six cabins, the trail continued uphill along the river. She followed it for a few dozen yards, then decided it was a trip better saved for the morning. The redwoods—she assumed they were all redwoods—blocked the last of the pale light glowing in the west, and she needed a bit of that light to get the fire started.

It wasn't until she turned back, guided by the glowing windows of her cabin, that it struck her. Her mother must have walked here. Certainly her father had. He and Dorothy and her sisters had lived here for years. They'd tended a garden. They'd likely made that trail along the river themselves. Made the cabins. Made Hannah.

She stopped at her cabin door and turned back, looking up at the trees and the sky beyond it. And finally she felt it. A shift in her body. A recognition that opened something inside her. It felt like heartache. Or like the strange, painful hope that you weren't falling in love again when you knew damn well you were.

God, she was tired. She'd spent the past forty-eight hours tearing through the remaining stacks of documents in her parents' den, sure she'd find an answer. Any break she'd taken had only been to get back online and order birth certificates. For herself. For her sisters. For her father. For Dorothy. New copies to compare to the old in case any details had been forged. The birth certificates might be waiting when she got home. Hopefully they'd be useless to her by then, but she'd needed to do something.

She needed to do something now. But instead of building the fire, she opened the bottle of wine and sat in one of the chairs. The impossibly tall trees rustled around her and blocked out the stars. Hannah drank her wine and wondered if her heart was about to break yet again.

CHAPTER 7

She woke with a headache and cottonmouth and the sharp smell of her own sweat. Though she didn't remember any nightmares, it had obviously been a restless night. The sheets were twisted and damp around her waist.

It was already nine, but that was fine. She'd needed the sleep, and she didn't mind getting to breakfast late. Better to have the inn owner to herself than share him with ambitious sightseers.

Hannah showered and girded her loins and hiked up to the main house for answers.

When she found the dining room, she was relieved to see only one couple at the table, and by the looks of it, they were wrapping up their last cup of coffee. They both appeared to be in their early fifties when they glanced up from their guidebook and offered friendly hellos. Hannah smiled weakly back and took a seat.

When the owner appeared, he looked exactly as she would've imagined if she'd thought that far ahead. Tousled brown hair that was sun bleached at the ragged tips. Skin that had sustained a damaging shade of tan for dozens of years. If he'd been a lean surfer dude in his youth, he'd thickened up now. Too many beers and burgers, she guessed. But he still had that golden beach-child look about him.

"Welcome to Riverfall!" he called as soon as he looked up from the coffeepot he was setting carefully on a sideboard. His greeting felt a thousand times more genuine than the girl's had been last night. "Care for coffee?"

"Thank you." She suddenly had enough adrenaline to power a small town, but she'd never say no to coffee. He poured a cup and tipped his head at the pastries. "Help yourself to as many as you want. I've got quiche in the kitchen. Bacon and Swiss or fire-roasted veggie. Or one of each, if you like."

Unsure about putting something heavy into her stomach, Hannah chose the veggie option and turned down a glass of orange juice. When he disappeared to the kitchen, the couple rose and said their goodbyes to Hannah, then disappeared as well.

Once she was alone, she sipped her coffee and looked around the room with curiosity. The walls were pale gray and hung with artsy prints of cliffs and redwoods. The floor looked old though, the dark, wide planks scattered with scars. She felt dizzy looking at them, imagining her sisters playing on that surface, crawling around or huddled in the corner, serving tea to dolls.

She jumped in surprise when the owner reappeared, plate in hand. Hannah introduced herself.

"I remember! I'm Tucker. We exchanged emails. You're in cabin three, right?"

"Yes. It's beautiful. How long have the cabins been here?"

"Two years." His voice sang with pride. "I bought this place seven years ago, but the cabins are a recent addition."

"They were here, though? When you bought the place?"

He winced. "So to speak. They were basically falling down. We stripped them to the foundations and started over."

Nothing left of the originals. Nothing for her to see. "And the inn itself?"

"We preserved what we could. The floors. The exterior walls. But we needed to add private baths to each bedroom, so we lost a lot of the original layout."

"And before that? Do you know who owned this place?"

"Some guy from San Jose who wanted a piece of Big Sur. He was an awful B-and-B manager, though. Not hands-on at all. This place really went to hell."

"Well, it's beautiful now."

His chest puffed up and she saw her chance. He liked talking about his property. If she let some of her guard down, she could get all the information she wanted from him.

"I'm in the area researching some family history. I-I think my family may have lived here a really long time ago. The Smiths?"

"I don't know any Smiths around here, but I'm not native to the area. Not that many are. Were they settlers here? It feels isolated now, but it used to be nearly unreachable. Some of the state parks have some great information on the ranchers and loggers who used to live here."

"No, it wasn't that long ago. Not that I know of anyway. More like the '60s."

"The '60s?" His eyebrows flew nearly to his hairline. A laugh burst from his throat. "You're not talking about the commune?"

"The *what?*"

He waved a dismissive hand. "Just a rumor. I'm sure it had nothing to do with your family."

"Wait. Are you saying there was a *commune* here?"

He grinned with delight. "That's what I've heard."

"Here on the property or just here in Big Sur?"

"Right where we're standing. They say that's what the cabins were. Housing for hippies."

Her lips parted, but she couldn't make a sound.

Tucker, on the other hand, was warming to the topic. "Free love. Peace. Communal living. The whole shebang. They came down from San Francisco or something. That big meadow on the way to the cabins was supposedly used to farm vegetables. I'm sure it's all an exaggeration, but it's a fun story. It's pretty boring here during the winter. People like to talk and there's not much to talk about."

"I . . ." Her throat clicked when she tried to swallow. She grabbed her coffee and downed a gulp. "I don't think my family was involved in that." They couldn't have been.

He shook his head. "I'm sure they weren't. This was all late '60s, early '70s. Summer of love and all that. It didn't last long."

Early '70s. A commune. Free love. Whether he realized it or not, he was talking about the Smiths. He was talking about *Hannah*. "That's crazy," she whispered.

"I know, right? I've never checked it out. It's more fun to think it's true than to find out it was a just some guy running a campground."

A campground. It could have been a campground. Not as romantic, but definitely more likely. "Do you think that was all it was?"

He shrugged. "That would be my best guess. Cabins and a clearing for campers and tents. There weren't a lot of motels around back then. But I'm sure there were hippies passing through, staying here, and a campground isn't nearly as interesting as a commune. Gossip twists things."

Her brain was only working in fits and starts. Because he was wrong. A campground wasn't the best guess at all. Pregnant girls didn't hang around campgrounds for nine months, did they? Or had she only returned to have the baby? "Do you have property records?"

"I don't think so. I could dig out the contracts from the purchase, but I can't imagine that jackass gave me anything he didn't have to. Shouldn't be hard to find, though. The county seat is up in Salinas."

She nodded. She'd passed a sign for Salinas on her way down.

"If you find any documents, I'd love to get copies. Never thought much about it, but I guess I could really spice up the website with some background stuff."

She looked up to see his wide grin, and for a split second, Hannah hated him. Hated the way his eyes creased with delight at the idea of spicing things up. She wanted to toss her coffee in his face and then slap his burned cheek. But the flash of rage passed like heat lightning. She settled for pushing the quiche away, untouched.

"Thanks for the information."

When she emerged from the house, she looked around with new eyes. Now she pictured hippie girls with braided hair hurrying up the dirt road, long sundresses flaring around their legs. Young men with dirty shirts and dirtier beards gathered around a fire pit, playing guitar and bongo. And her father standing among them with his clean, barber-cut hair, wearing a short-sleeved dress shirt and comfortable slacks.

It was absurd. Unimaginable. And the only thing that made sense.

Somehow her steady, conservative parents had started their married life in a hippie commune. Somehow her father, a deacon in his church and a man who wore socks with his sandals, had been a practitioner of free love. And his wife, who listened to Judy Garland and had maintained until 1988 that pants "just weren't ladylike," had lived a bohemian lifestyle in the middle of the woods and let her husband have sex with other women.

And from that era of love, drugs, and communal gardening had sprung Hannah.

She walked slowly back to her cabin, so stunned it felt like a contact high, as if the walls of the inn were still leaching '60s pot smoke into the atmosphere.

The commune story made perfect sense . . . aside from the fact that she knew her parents. She couldn't picture them as part of an antiestablishment movement, but maybe that was why they'd never told a soul. People in Iowa wouldn't understand. Hannah didn't understand.

And both of them must have been lost souls back then. Both parentless. God only knew what Dorothy had experienced in an old-fashioned orphanage as a young girl. And her dad had been supporting himself from an early age. Hannah could imagine how they'd both been swept up into a counterculture for a few years.

Except she honestly couldn't.

She reached the clearing Tucker had mentioned. The dirt road curved to avoid a meadow that hadn't caught her eye on the drive in. In the evening it must have been only a darkening space, but in the late-morning sun, the long grass shone emerald green, a startling jewel in the midst of redwood shade. A few tiny trees had begun to shoot up at the edges of the grass, softening what must have once been a rectangle of cleared land.

We had almost two acres of garden.

Hannah's knees went weak.

We all helped each other.

She sank slowly into the waves of grass as her mother's own words confirmed the truth. Dorothy had been speaking of this place. Of working together, all the women and children, tending this soil, feeding a community. And then they'd left, and Hannah's mother had stayed.

A smile trembled on her lips even as her vision swam beneath tears. She couldn't picture the Smiths here. She couldn't picture that at all. But she could see her real mother in clear detail. Her tanned arms bared to the sun. Long black hair sliding across her back as she bent to tug a weed free from the stubborn ground. Flowy skirt knotted above her knees to keep it out of the way while she worked. The woman tossed her head back in laughter and joy, the sun catching the line of her cheek. But Hannah couldn't quite see her face. Not yet.

Hannah had been born in this wild place to that woman. She'd been conceived out of love or lust or a need to make a better, newer world. Her mother had been a woman who'd wanted something more than what she'd been raised for. Just as Hannah had. Maybe she'd been running from something, but she'd found a place and an idea, at least for a moment.

And now Hannah had done the same thing. If she'd been running from the boring cruelty of watching Dorothy Smith die, she'd at least found *this*.

It had been right to come here, no matter what her sisters thought.

She clutched at the grass for a moment, closed her eyes, felt the earth beneath her knees. Even if this experimental Shangri-la had failed, it felt right to know she'd come from it. So much more right than living in Coswell, Iowa, had ever made her feel. Kneeling there, Hannah felt like she'd shed the stiff, uncomfortable suit she'd been wearing her whole life, and now she was naked in her own skin for the first time.

Her hippie mother would love that, surely.

Telling herself the time to run naked through the meadow would come later, if at all, Hannah stood and walked through the grass until she reached the middle. She looked up at the sky, where the sun shone lazily between thick clouds. She dragged her shoes along the ground around her, checking to see if there were still garden furrows here. But the ground was smooth.

Smaller trees made up a far line of forest, and when Hannah noticed the even spacing of the trunks, she headed that way. Sure enough, when she got close, the toe of her shoe caught a soggy, ancient apple. Fruit trees had marked this boundary of the garden.

If the Smith family hadn't moved to Iowa, this would have been Hannah's life. Working under this sun in this garden, gathering apples for lunch, discussing social justice and inequality. Sneaking off to splash naked in the river on hot days.

Then again, she wasn't exactly an earth-mother type. Maybe Big Sur would have been just as stifling as Coswell. There weren't any numbers to crunch here, there were definitely no punk concerts, and she'd seen no evidence that an ocean view would bring out her nurturing side any more effectively than corn fritters had.

Still. There was the possibility that she would have fit in. Or at the very least had a mother who *understood* her.

Had her awkwardness in her own family been the source of all her failings in life? Was that why she had so much trouble connecting? Hannah had never felt that Dorothy didn't love her, but there must have been some hesitance there. Some resentment that Hannah had sensed even as a small child. No woman could take in her husband's bastard without at least a little resentment. Hannah had picked up on something.

She just . . . couldn't seem to lock into relationships. There was never a definitive *click* to let her know she'd finally made something solid and lasting. It always felt more like grasping something that was too hot and seeing how long she could stand to hold on.

Had her birth mother been the same? Hannah needed to find out if the woman was still here or if she'd drifted away with the tides long ago.

As she turned to walk back across the meadow, her eye caught on a shade of brown that stood out from the rest of the forest. She moved toward the northwestern corner of the meadow and narrowed her eyes, trying to make an image from the puzzle of shifting shadows and crossing branches. Beyond the fruit trees, nestled beneath the canopy of the redwoods, an angle of gray led her gaze to the remains of a wooden wall.

Hannah parted the branches of the apple trees on either side of her and hunched over to pick her way closer. It was definitely an old building. Between two parted boards, she caught the glint of something white. A sink, maybe.

"That's poison oak," a gravelly voice said from behind her.

Hannah spun around and nearly poked out an eye on a branch. Squinting protectively, she looked for the man past her eyelashes. "What?"

"You're about to step into a whole patch of poison oak." His words were weary, as if he'd explained this to stupid tourists a hundred times already this week.

She clawed her way out of the apple-tree branches and lurched into the open meadow again. The man's grizzled, worn face matched his voice. He didn't have to protect himself from branches, but his eyes were as tightly squinted as hers had been. A gray beard hid any other sign of expression.

"Sorry. And thanks. I was just trying to see what that old building was."

"Bathhouse," he explained, then added, "The toilet. You've probably seen plenty of those. Not worth getting a rash over."

"Was it from before?"

He lifted the shovel he held and poked it impatiently against the ground at his feet. "Before what?"

"Before this place was a bed and breakfast."

"Well, it's definitely from before something." He turned and started to walk away.

"Do you work here?" she called to his narrow back.

"Yep."

"Do you know anything about the commune?"

He stopped moving for a second, pausing midstep. But he didn't look back. "Nope," he finally said, the word faint on the breeze. His legs shushed through the long grass as he resumed his path.

Hannah couldn't tell if that *nope* had meant he knew nothing or everything.

She glanced toward the bathhouse, now invisible in the trees, and when she looked back toward the old man, he was nearly at the dirt road. "Sir!" she called, finally deciding he was the best hope she had for immediate information. "Have you lived around here your whole life?"

He kept walking as she tried to high-step it through the meadow toward him. She heard the crunch of his feet on gravel as he disappeared beyond the bushes at the edge of the trees. Just as Hannah reached the road herself, an engine growled to life. An ancient all-terrain vehicle roared from the side of the road and disappeared around a curve, carrying her bearded stranger away.

She forced herself not to chase after him like a lunatic. After all, the man worked here. Even if he was a close-mouthed recluse, she'd see him again.

Hannah picked a few burrs off her pant legs and headed toward her cabin to wet her suddenly dry mouth. These woods weren't going to whisper their secrets to her no matter how long she lurked, but Google would. She had a starting point now, even if it was the last thing she'd expected.

A goddamn hippie commune.

A reckless thrill shot through her at the thought of telling her sisters about this. It was pure meanness on her part, she knew that, but it was better than the bone-deep sorrow she'd been feeling.

She wouldn't call them yet, though. She needed more details or they'd just deny the possibility, tell her it was a mistake. Anyway, maybe she'd wait until she got back home so she could watch their faces go slack with shock.

"You're the worst," she muttered to herself as she unlocked her cabin and grabbed her laptop. No point sitting inside when the day was so nice. Hannah plopped down in a patio chair and logged in to the hotel's Wi-Fi. Thank God the place catered to eco-geeks and not real hippies, or she would've had to drive for miles to find a hotspot.

Her previous attempts at searching for information online had been too broad, but now she could narrow it down to hippie communes in Big Sur. Surely there hadn't been that many.

Okay. There had been a lot. Hannah's jaw dropped within two seconds of starting the search. A few clicks later, she was whispering several choice curse words to herself.

Big Sur had seemingly been some sort of wilderness retreat for hippies trying to escape the crowds in San Francisco. They'd camped out in the woods and in public parks and even bought their own land to found mini utopias. In fact, there was still a hippie commune going strong just a few miles up the highway from the Riverfall Inn.

No wonder Tucker had never bothered doing much research. Every landowner around probably had a similar story.

The place that was still operating didn't seem to be much of a commune anymore. It had drifted solidly into New Agey self-help retreat status, but she imagined it was still worth a visit. There could be people working there who'd remember the communes that had disappeared.

As for those . . . she tried several different searches, but she couldn't find anything specific. Nobody had spent time blogging back then, and the newspapers didn't seem to consider hippies to be newsworthy, except as a public nuisance. The most promising link was about a lawsuit against the town of Carmel, and that only because it referenced the "filthy hippie communes" near Big Sur.

The far-fetched theory about what had happened to the Smith family in 1972 didn't seem so far-fetched anymore. And now Hannah had a real-life hippie commune to visit. Maybe this trip wouldn't be all Sturm und Drang after all.

CHAPTER 8

Hippie communes weren't quite what they used to be.

Hannah shot a sullen glance at the driveway that dipped down toward the famous seaside commune, but she couldn't even see the buildings from here, much less the people. Instead of being welcomed with warm, patchouli-scented arms, she'd been stopped at the gate by a security guard with a crew cut and a polyester uniform shirt.

"I just want to take a look around," she repeated.

He regarded her with a bored stare that said he'd heard it a million times before. "Only residents and workshop attendees are allowed on the grounds."

"How am I supposed to know if I want to spend a week here if I've never even seen the place?"

"Ma'am, please turn your car around."

"This is ridiculous. Is the leader of a small country vacationing here or something? I just want to walk around for a few minutes. I can leave my car here if you like."

"I'm afraid that's not an option." He was less friendly than guards she'd encountered at government buildings. She didn't know what kind of peace and love they were selling inside, but it definitely wasn't the counterculture kind.

"So the only way to visit is to sign up for a workshop."

"Or you can schedule a massage."

Hannah brightened at that. "A massage! That would be great. I've been pretty damn tense. Can I go in and see if there's a therapist available?"

"You'll have to call ahead, ma'am."

"But I don't have cell service."

"There's a pay phone at the state park down the road."

"Are you kidding me?" she snapped.

His flat-mouthed glare answered the question.

"Can't you just get on your radio and ask if there are any openings?"

A Mercedes-Benz SUV pulled up behind her, and the guard stepped away. "Please move your vehicle, ma'am."

Hannah nearly growled at him, but she threw the car into gear and twisted the wheel. "You should think about taking one of those workshops on positivity," she muttered. "Learn to let a little kindness into your life. Asshole."

She made a careful three-point turn and sped back up the drive to the highway. Unbelievable. She just wanted to talk to some old hippies. Maybe she'd be better off hanging out at the nearest marijuana dispensary. Then again, she suspected people around here just grew their own.

She didn't have any change to use for a public phone, so she turned north and drove toward civilization. The view of aqua water and soaring cliffs helped calm some of her anger. How could it not?

This place must have been magical when her parents had lived here. No cell phones. No European SUVs. No high-end spas masquerading as spiritual retreats. Just people looking for a peaceful spot to hide.

Hannah rolled down her windows and let the wind whip her ponytail around her head. Even above the traffic, she could hear the waves crashing below and the seagulls screaming. She wanted to park and hike down to one of the isolated beaches she kept glimpsing below her as she turned into curves, but she wasn't here for a vacation. She'd find no answers down there.

So she drove toward Monterey and set her phone on the dash, hoping it would grab a signal better from there. She was nearly to Carmel before her phone beeped. And beeped. And beeped.

She could see the flash of text messages coming through, but she didn't dare try to read anything on this road. As soon as she spotted an overlook, she pulled onto the gravel and parked. A huge spit of land loomed up out of the sea in front of her. Far above the water, a lighthouse flashed toward the clouds that were rolling in from the Pacific.

She let herself watch it for a moment, shivering a little at the ominous beauty of the sight. The spot reminded her of Alcatraz, and she wondered how many tragedies those stone block buildings had witnessed. Not that the buildings cared. They simply watched and waited for the pounding sea to eventually grind them into sand.

"You're not here for beauty," she reminded herself. But the sad gorgeousness stayed with her as she reached for the phone.

Five messages. Most were from Becky. None were from Rachel. But there was also the one name she'd dreaded seeing: Jeff.

"Damn it, damn it, *damn it*." She'd reached out in a moment of weakness, and her stupid phone had apparently found just enough of a signal to screw her over. His text message response did not convey warmth. Did you want to talk, or are you just fucking with me?

God.

They'd spoken fairly often right after the split, but recent communication had been through lawyers only . . . at her insistence. And now she'd been caught calling him.

It had been pure weakness on her part. Jeff had been her best friend for years, and she *needed* a best friend right now. She couldn't talk to her sisters. They'd taken a side, as if this were an argument instead of the worst moment of her life.

Speaking of . . .

She clicked back to Becky's texts, and her eyes immediately filled with tears.

Please call me and let me know how you are.

Are you okay?

What's going on?

Rachel's sorry for what she said. We both love you. Please call.

Hannah rolled her eyes even as a tear spilled over and tickled its way down her right cheek. If Rachel was sorry, she could get in touch herself. The rest of the messages, Hannah believed. She knew Becky loved her. She knew she was worried. But that didn't mean Becky could begin to understand what Hannah was going through.

And Rachel? Rachel didn't even want to understand. She just wanted it all to go away. She liked to fix things. To keep them orderly. And there was no possibility of making this right.

Hannah started to write back to Becky, then changed her mind and closed the box. She opened it again before she'd even moved to another screen. It wouldn't be okay to let her sister worry. Becky's ambivalence didn't call for cruelty.

Arrived safely and am looking into some promising leads. Phone service is pretty much nonexistent, so don't worry if I don't get in touch. I love you too.

She left off the *tell our big sister to kiss my selfish ass* ending that scrolled through her mind. If her car went off a cliff, those shouldn't be the last words she sent to her sisters. Even if she did mean them.

Becky responded immediately. Are you somewhere you can call me? I'd like to know what's going on.

Hannah ignored it and clicked back to Jeff's message.

If he cared about her, he would have been nice. He would've said, *Did you want to talk?* instead of *Are you just fucking with me?* He could have even shown some concern and said, *Hey, is everything okay?*

Thank God she hadn't reached him and admitted vulnerability. Her face flushed at the thought.

At first, when she'd been fantasizing about divorce, she'd imagined it would be amicable. Mature. One of those conscious uncouplings people did these days. After all, they didn't hate each other. Hell, she still loved him. It wasn't that she'd hated being married to *him*; she just couldn't stand being married, period.

It was too much for her. The constant awareness of another person's needs. The worry that a spouse wasn't happy and fulfilled. The bone-deep knowledge that she couldn't be her true self with anyone. Not really. Her true self wasn't lovable enough.

She didn't want to take every vacation with Jeff. She didn't want to find another barbecue restaurant for him when she felt like sushi. She didn't want to check in and see if he was okay with girls' night on a Tuesday because Jasmine had been dumped by her boyfriend.

Then he'd started making wistful comments about other people's kids when he'd always denied wanting his own. His observations about children and legacy and family had made Hannah feel as if she were sinking deeper and deeper into water, the pressure pushing at her lungs and ears and eyes.

She'd read once that men were happier in marriage than women were. Funny, considering the stereotype of women always pushing for marriage. But once in it, men were happier because they were *cared for*. Looked after. But what happened when the woman wasn't great at caring for people? Nothing good. Constantly trying to be better than she was had worn her down until she'd turned into a moody, unhappy beast.

And still, she couldn't understand how it had all gotten so ugly.

Yes, she was a shitty wife, but she'd warned him about that up front. He'd said, *Let's just try.* Let's try. No pressure. Let's give it a go.

She'd tried, and it hadn't worked, and now they couldn't speak without screaming at each other.

She just wanted to get back to being friends. She just wanted to *call* him. Instead, she deleted his message and looked up the phone number for scheduling a massage.

When she asked if there were any appointments available today, she assumed the pause meant the woman was looking through the schedule. But apparently she was taking a moment to process her disbelief. "No," she finally said, "I'm afraid we're booked solid for the next nine days."

"*Nine* days?" What the hell was this place? The holy grail of seaside self-improvement? "I just . . ." She was getting the feeling that *just wanting to ask a few questions* wasn't going to garner her any love and trust in this place. "I'm really interested in getting a glimpse of this experience before I book a workshop. Funds are tight, you know? Is there any way I could just come see the spa? Or maybe you have a manicure appointment available?"

It sounded like the woman on the other end swallowed a gasp. "We don't do manicures here, ma'am. This is a holistic wellness center."

"Right. Of course. I apologize."

"If you just want to set foot here, you could come during the public hot springs hours."

"That sounds perfect! Yes, absolutely. Thank you!"

"Great. Wednesday nights from two a.m. to four a.m."

"What now?" Hannah pulled her phone from her ear to frown at it for a brief second. "Did you say two a.m.?"

"That's right. The rules are posted at the top of the trail and again at the hot springs entrance. You'll need a flashlight for the walk."

Hannah hung up before she could say anything rude to the woman. She definitely wasn't getting into this commune. Time to think of another option. She strained the muscles of her face, squeezing her eyes shut. Still, nothing ingenious popped into her mind.

Defeated again, she headed back south on the highway. Solving this mystery was going to take some old-fashioned footwork, but that was why she'd flown to California, right? This wasn't a defeat. This was the start. She was kicking ass.

"No you're not," she grumbled, then decided to ignore that BS and put her nose to the grindstone, just the way she'd been raised. "You're not a quitter," she said aloud. And then she laughed. And laughed harder. Because she definitely was a quitter; she just hadn't quit this yet.

CHAPTER 9

As soon as she got back to Riverfall, she stashed her purse in the cabin and grabbed a jacket. She kept expecting it to be pleasantly warm on the coast of California, but it wasn't. In fact, the afternoon was downright chilly, and the sun she'd glimpsed earlier had vanished.

Zipping up her jacket, she made her way to the river trail and followed it east toward the **PRIVATE PROPERTY** sign. Her hand dragged along a young redwood as she rounded a curve, and the softness of the needles surprised her. She'd expected they'd be hard like pine needles, but they were more like narrow leaves, pliant and yielding when she reached for them.

Walking among the strange trees and the ferns that grew huge in all the ambient moisture, Hannah could imagine she'd stepped back in time. Maybe she had. It felt magical here. Primeval. Perhaps that was what had attracted so many lost souls decades before.

Lost souls. Lost parents.

Had her father loved this other woman? Had it been happy and meaningful and out in the open?

Some people had lived like that then. No jealousy. No judgment. She couldn't picture her Lutheran parents living life that way, but she couldn't picture them here at all. What was one more detail added to the mix? Maybe they'd lived in this Garden of Eden and let the expectations of the outside world fall away.

Or maybe the affair had been secret. A messy, needful passion in the forest. Late nights beneath the stars, always in the dark, until Hannah had come along to expose them.

Whichever it had been, they must have created her in happiness. They'd needed each other, at least for a time. She'd inherited that restless intensity. She understood it. There was love and passion and travel in her bones, and her parents had come together to make it.

She slowed to take in this place where she'd been born, this place where the earth was far more powerful than people. The ground beneath her feet felt light and hollow, and she imagined the thousands of years of redwood needles that had fallen to create the layers of this path. Just a few inches down, there were needles her own father had stepped on. And her mother. They'd walked here. They must have.

A few minutes later, she reached the fence with the sign. The trail turned and disappeared into the shallow river, only to reappear on the other side. A few stones visible above the waterline offered a hopeful hint of passage, but she wasn't looking to continue a hike.

The fence of the adjoining property didn't quite reach the river, so she picked her way carefully over tree roots and rocks until she was past the long wall of wood and found another dirt road to step onto. A hundred yards ahead, she reached a walkway of redwood chips that led to the door of a modest ranch house. Hoping they were long-term residents who might know something about previous neighbors, she approached.

When she was ten feet from the door, she heard the high-pitched squeal of a child from inside. The good news was that someone was home. The bad news was a kid might answer her knock.

It seemed unbelievable even to her, but talking to children made Hannah feel as if she were the inexperienced one in the interaction. The kid was always the calm one, watching her with big eyes, waiting for her to say the right thing, and all she could do was babble and squirm. Why was she so inept at talking to humans with a kindergarten vocabulary? Shouldn't that be *easy*?

She knocked and practiced saying, "Hello, is your mommy home?" over and over. A rush of wheels approached from the other side of the door, and she braced herself. But the loud rumble of plastic against the floor retreated again, and the house fell quiet.

Hannah tried the doorbell, wincing at the way the chime echoed somewhere inside. This time, footsteps approached. Adult footsteps. Followed by more squealing.

The door flew inward.

"Hello!" she said thankfully at the sight of the woman, though it was the first time she'd ever felt thankful to see a woman with a baby on her hip and a toddler wobbling behind her to catch up. Another toddler peeked from around a corner. Hannah had stumbled onto a hive.

The woman smiled brightly despite the sheen of sweat on her forehead and the black hair escaping her braid and dancing madly about her head. She waved a rag she held in her right hand. "Hi! You're here about the opening?"

"Opening?" Hannah asked.

"For the baby," the woman said, clearing up nothing.

"I'm sorry, I . . ." Hannah glanced toward the farthest kid and watched him jerk back around the corner to hide. "I don't know anything about babies. I wanted to ask you something about the property next door. But you seem busy?"

Laughing, the woman waved the towel again. "Not busy at all. We just finished up snack time. Come on in."

"You've obviously got your hands full." Hannah's feet had already backed her up two steps.

"Nonsense. I'm down one baby right now. Things are quiet."

Hannah felt her face twisting in some mixture of confusion and fear.

The woman laughed. "This is a daycare. Well, it's my home too, but a daycare during the day! Three babies, three preschoolers. That's what I'm allowed. Right now I only have two of each."

"That . . . seems like a lot."

"It is. I'm only looking for one more right now, frankly. Babies take more work, but at least they can't climb things."

Hannah laughed as if she understood.

"I'm Jenny," the woman said. She swiped at the baby's cheek with the towel one more time, then let the child grab the rag so she could reach out to shake Hannah's hand.

"I'm Hannah. Hannah Smith."

"Come on in. I'm taking the kids out back."

Hannah stepped in and closed the door carefully behind her, lest any small people escape. The closest toddler stepped right up and grabbed the leg of Hannah's jeans. When Jenny led the way down a hall, Hannah found herself following in a strange shuffle, half dragging that leg so she wouldn't pull the toddler onto his face.

Even counting the discovery that her parents had been orgiastic hippies, this was the last thing she'd expected to happen in California.

Ahead of her, Jenny grabbed a baby monitor off a hallway table and opened a door to a fenced backyard, letting in a bright glow of green. The sun had emerged temporarily and it filtered through the giant trees of the yard to shine its mottled light on a little play set. The toddler attached to Hannah's leg broke for the door and raced into the yard. Thank God.

"The little one's sleeping," Jenny explained.

Hannah marveled at her calmness, the same way she'd always marveled at her sisters' calm in the face of so many children.

She'd sometimes tried to convince herself she might grow that kind of peace along with a fetus if she decided to become a mom. But she knew from her own experience that Rachel and Becky had been born with it. Jenny looked like another girl who'd started babysitting at age eleven. And had been good at it. Hannah had tried it once at twelve, and she'd spent the entire three hours terrified she was going to screw up.

"Is this one yours?" she asked, nodding toward the plump baby who'd wound its fist around Jenny's braid.

"Oh, no. Mine are both in school now. But I have these monkeys to keep me company."

"Mm. Sure." She smiled awkwardly toward the playground where both boys were trying to fit down the slide at the same time and bottling up at the top of it. The kids looked more confused than upset.

"You said you were interested in the property next door?"

"My parents lived there many years ago. I'm just knocking on doors to see if anyone remembers who owned it in the '60s."

"I'm sorry. I don't know. This house belongs to my in-laws. I can ask my husband when he gets home, but he's only thirty-seven. He might not know."

One of the boys had made it down the slide and was eyeing Hannah as if he might approach. "Oh, that would be great if you can ask. Can I leave you my email address? My phone isn't working well out here."

"They never do. Frankly, I'm thankful for that. Sometimes it's nice not to be found."

Hannah eyed the boy warily. He took a few steps away from the slide and toward her.

"My mother-in-law lives in the Bay Area now, but my husband could call her."

"Thank you! If he could, that would be amazing. I'm trying to figure out who all was living there. Track down some relatives. That kind of thing."

"Try a DNA test!" Jenny suggested.

Hannah glanced away from her tiny stalker in surprise. "What?"

"Haven't you seen those commercials? You can do a DNA test to find out your background, but they also match you up with family members who've taken one."

"Really?"

"Yep. It's pretty cool. A friend of my mom's got a kit for her birthday."

"I'll check it out. Thank you."

She left Jenny her email address and managed to escape without another mauling, though Jenny did lean in for a one-armed hug. Hannah was surprised to find herself hugging Jenny back. In fact, when the woman whispered, "I hope you find what you're looking for," Hannah's eyes welled.

Embarrassed, she turned quickly away and stepped into the dimness of the house. "Thank you so much. And I hope the baby search works out."

"Maybe we'll both have good luck."

It seemed possible. Right now Hannah *felt* lucky. A DNA test would be a long-term approach, but it seemed a promising way to find her mother's last name if her inquiries here didn't work out. She might even track down her mom. Hannah would never have thought of it without Jenny's help.

She walked up the road, hoping she might pass another house.

If only she could see a census from the area. It would list every person living on the property in 1970, and her mother might be among them. But she knew it took a long time for those to become public. Useful for finding the name of a great-grandparent, not so useful for a mother.

Come to think of it, she didn't even know any grandparents' names, and wasn't that strange? Shouldn't she know something even if they'd all died years ago? Maybe her sisters had asked those questions. That was the sort of thing people became interested in once they had kids. She'd have to ask Becky the next time they spoke. She didn't know when she'd be talking to Rachel again.

The road rose up to the highway without passing any other houses. There wasn't much of a shoulder to speak of, and Hannah's neck tightened as cars rushed by at speeds that felt way too high for the curves. Luckily, she could see the Riverfall Inn sign just ahead.

After a pack of motorcycles passed, she glanced across the highway toward the roadhouse and suddenly realized she was starving. She needed to get back and look into the DNA search, but maybe she'd be better off starting that on a full stomach.

A raindrop hit the top of her head. Then another. When the rain started to fall in earnest, that decided it for her. She tugged up her hood, looked both ways, and sprinted across the road.

The roadhouse looked as ancient on the inside as it did on the out. Ancient, but clean. The long slab of dark wood that made up the bar was polished to a shine.

She glanced toward the wood-paneled dining area. Her eyes adjusted enough to spot two couples sharing a bottle of wine, so Hannah headed for the bar instead. She usually had no problem with eating alone, but she was not going to sit at a table by herself next to people celebrating their twenty-year romances together.

The tension in her neck had risen to her head. She pulled her hair free from the ponytail and rubbed her scalp, hoping to relieve the tightness. It helped a little. A drink would help more.

When the door to the kitchen swung open, she looked up gratefully, but when she saw who walked through, she didn't exactly feel relief. Now the tightness concentrated in her gut.

She'd expected a young, seasonal worker. Someone who moved on every year with the tourists. But this man was around her age. A little older, actually. And handsome as hell.

While she was still noticing that his light-brown eyes perfectly matched the color of his skin, he smiled, and Hannah's heart jolted. This guy was a silver fox. The lines around his eyes deepened into creases with the smile. His black hair had gone white at the temples in gorgeous contrast to his skin.

"Good afternoon," he said as he slid a menu across the bar to her. "Late lunch? Early dinner?"

"Both," she answered. "And happy hour too."

"I've hit the jackpot. What can I get you to drink?"

She wasn't going to flirt with the bartender. She *never* flirted with bartenders. They were inundated with flirting every day, and she had always been determined not to add to the ridiculous pile on. But instead of ordering, she raised an eyebrow. "What do I look like I need?"

He raised a matching eyebrow. Crossed his arms. And studied her.

The nape of her neck tingled and goose bumps spread out from there. Shit.

"I was going to suggest my favorite local red."

"Not a bad idea."

"Maybe. But today . . . today you look like you need whisky."

She winced, suddenly conscious of the ridge the ponytail had left behind in her hair. "That bad, huh?" She swiped a few damp strands of hair off her cheek. "But you're right. Whisky sounds perfect."

"I make a mean old-fashioned with grapefruit bitters if you're interested."

"I am so goddamn interested," she responded. His flash of a smile rewarded her eagerness.

"Coming right up."

He moved at an easy pace, his hands sure and steady as he mixed the drink. When a younger guy appeared in the dining room to check on the table, Hannah saw the bartender glance up and watch for a moment.

"Is this your place?" she asked, recognizing the ownership in his eagle eyes.

"It is. My stepfather owned it for years, then sold it. I bought it back about five years ago."

Hannah sat a little straighter. "So you grew up here?"

"Yep. Spent a decade down in LA, but I eventually made it back home. I'm Gabriel Cabrillo." He wiped his fingers on a towel before holding out a hand.

"Hannah. Hannah Smith." She liked how his warm hand turned suddenly cold at the fingertips from where he'd held the glass. His grip felt nice. Sturdy and not watered down for a woman.

"Pleased to meet you," he said as his hand left hers with a promising rasp of friction. He added a cherry to her drink and set it down with a smile. "Cheers."

"Thank you."

When he stepped away to fill a water glass, Hannah took a sip of the drink. It was strong, but the hint of citrus cut through the whisky. "Mmm. Amazing."

He threw her a smile as he topped off the water and set it down in front of her. "I'm glad it hit the spot."

"What do you recommend for food? I think I'd better get something in my stomach before I finish this."

"The burgers are great. We buy beef from a local ranch. The fish tacos are my favorite. I make the crema myself. Jicama slaw on the side."

"The tacos sound perfect."

"I'll get them started for you."

She took another sip and eyed his ass as he pushed through the kitchen door. He looked lean and strong, and she was thankful his blue plaid shirt was tucked into his worn jeans, because the view was heavenly. Good Lord, he must get hit on all day. He wasn't pretty like a model, but his large nose balanced the hard edge of his jaw.

The second sip hit her stomach, and heat flowed in little rivulets through her body as the alcohol kicked in. Hannah closed her eyes to savor it. Once she was sufficiently warmed, she unzipped her jacket and set it over the next chair to dry; then she did her best to finger comb her hair. For once, she was glad it was flat instead of curly. God only knew what her sisters might look like in this moisture.

She was thinking she should dab on a little lip gloss, but then the kitchen door swung open at the exact moment she realized why she couldn't. She'd left her purse in the cabin. Along with her credit cards. Hannah gulped in a panicked breath as she met Gabriel's eyes.

"What's wrong?" he asked, suddenly serious. "You okay?"

She shook her head. "I'm so embarrassed. I left my purse in my room."

"I guess I just bought you a drink, then."

"No, I'll go get it! I'll be back before the food is ready, I think. I'm just across the road."

"Relax. You can pay me later."

She jumped up from the bar stool, horrified down to her Midwestern bones. She probably looked like a hitchhiker grifting her way through Big Sur. "No, I'll be back before you know it."

"Sit. I mean it. If you go now, the ice will melt, and you'll ruin all my hard work."

She glanced at the drink. "Really?"

"Really. Anyway, you look trustworthy."

Relief pushed a laugh from her throat. She dropped back into her seat. "That's where you're wrong."

"A woman with secrets?"

"You have no idea."

"Oh, I bet I could hazard a few guesses. I've heard some amazing stuff from behind this bar. A lot of people come to Big Sur running away from things."

"God bless them," she murmured, raising the glass to her lips again. When she set it down, only half was left.

"Another?" he asked.

She really wanted another. She normally didn't drink every day. Far from it. But she deserved to spiral this week. Down, down, down. She cleared her throat. "I'm not going to abuse your generosity."

"Maybe I like a little abuse." His wink made her grab the drink and take another sip. He reached for a new glass. "One more old-fashioned coming up."

She liked watching him work. He looked calm and centered. His fingernails were cut short. Too short. As if he had to pare them down to keep from biting them. But they made his hands look rough and ready. No-nonsense.

"I'll leave you my phone when I get my wallet," she suggested. "As a security deposit."

"Nice try. Your phone is as useless as everyone else's here."

"My room key, then?"

He shot an unreadable look over his shoulder, and Hannah flushed.

"Right," she said quickly. "If I leave my room key, I couldn't get into my room. Plus that might be a little forward."

"You seem like a pretty up-front woman."

Hannah laughed. "That's a truly lovely way to put it."

"Just doing my job, miss."

"Ah. 'Miss.' You *are* good at this."

"The more you drink, the more charming I seem. It's one of the advantages of the job." He slid the second drink to her and settled a hip against the bar as if he meant to stay awhile. "So what are you doing here in Big Sur, Miss Hannah Smith? Hiking? Biking? Seeing the sights?"

She finished her first drink and melted into the buzz of it. She was spiraling in style. "No. None of those things."

"That's right. You've got a secret." He glanced at her left hand, possibly looking for a tan line to indicate a ring's recent removal. She impulsively rubbed her ring finger, as she'd done thousands of times since her separation. The indentation had faded months ago. There was no sign of her marriage now.

"Divorce?" he asked.

"I'm working on it." She looked at his bare hand. "You?"

"I came out on the other side seven years ago. Big Sur turns out to be a great place to lick your wounds."

She shrugged. "I'm not really licking anything." As soon as the words left her lips, she yelped with laughter and covered the sound. But covering her mouth didn't help. She laughed harder. Snorted. Guffawed until tears rolled down her cheeks.

When her vision finally cleared, Gabriel was shaking his head. But he was grinning, showing off a pair of adorable dimples. "Maybe you should get some food in your stomach before you start that second drink."

"Oops." She lifted the new glass. "Too late."

"Incorrigible," he scolded. "Let me check on those tacos."

As soon as he disappeared, Hannah tried to give herself a serious talking-to. "You're not here to flirt. You're not on vacation. This isn't a pleasure cruise." But damned if she didn't feel like herself for the first time in years. Confident and fun and a little reckless. It was likely just the whisky. Or maybe not *just* the whisky, she corrected mentally as Gabriel pushed through the door with a plate.

And the best thing about him wasn't even his looks. It was that he'd grown up here and probably had information. Okay, the cocktail skills and the food didn't hurt anything either. Her mouth watered as he set down the plate in front of her.

"Thank you. I'm starving."

He winked before he disappeared again. She was glad he'd gone, because she wasn't going to be ladylike about this. One bite of taco and she was groaning with pleasure. The tangy crema was the perfect contrast to the blackened fish and spicy salsa, and the tortillas were obviously freshly made. She polished off the first taco in half a dozen bites, and when she saw that Gabriel was safely occupied in the dining room, she licked the leftover crema and tomatillo salsa off her fingers. She knew she was slightly tipsy, and maybe that was affecting her opinion, but damned if the slaw didn't offset the glory of the taco perfectly. Gabriel Cabrillo was only getting sexier.

"Danger, Will Robinson," she whispered to herself before setting into the second taco with a bit more restraint.

The problem was that she'd never been afraid of a little danger. What she'd always feared was safety.

Of course, that made her think of Jeff, which sobered her up a tiny bit. She still wanted to call him. It wasn't just that she missed his friendship. She missed his mind, his insights. He was quick and logical, and he saw connections between past and present. That was his job. She wanted to lean on him and let him help. And he would help. Or he would have in the past. If he looked at all the evidence, he'd see something she couldn't see in all of this.

Shit. This damn whisky. She was stupidly flirting with one guy and idiotically missing another. But idiocy didn't ruin her appetite.

She'd always envied those women who couldn't eat when they were stressed. Whoever her mom was, the woman hadn't passed along that gene. Hannah finished the second taco with a wistful sigh, glad there wasn't a third, because she would have finished that one too.

When the door began to swing open, she snatched up her napkin and wiped the evidence of the massacre from her face.

That sexy black eyebrow of his arched as he glanced at her plate. "Should I take that as a good sign?"

"You should. It was amazing. All of it."

"Save room for dessert?"

She picked up her drink and smiled. "Already on it."

"A girl after my own heart."

"Funny that we'd meet at a bar." She nudged her phone toward him. "Are you sure you won't keep this as collateral? This bill is getting pricey."

"Oh, I think I could track you down pretty easily if it comes to it. You're at the Riverfall?"

"I am."

"Nice place."

"Do you know anything about it?"

He whisked her empty tumbler away and reached for a pitcher to refill her water. "Tucker's a good guy. One hundred percent sincere about that place. That's not always the case with newcomers."

"I heard it used to be a commune."

He paused in the act of setting the pitcher back down. "The bed and breakfast?"

"The land, yes. There were cabins and a garden."

"You know . . . I seem to remember some talk from when I was a kid. But there were a lot of hippies around back then. My mom was always warning us to stay away from them."

"Do you remember anything about the group at Riverfall?"

"I don't think so. I mean, there were a ton of hitchhikers around back then. There still are. You know what? I do remember the cabins, but that was later. Late '70s, after the place was abandoned. We used to sneak back there and poke around. But things get overgrown quickly around here. There wasn't much to see."

She wasn't giving up yet. "Do you think anyone who lived there is still here?"

Gabriel shrugged. "It's possible. I could ask around if you want."

"Really?" She grinned at the possibility of having a local on her side.

"Sure, but why the curiosity?"

She wasn't sure how much to say. She was tempted to blurt out the whole sordid story, just to tell *someone*. Someone who didn't know her parents or need to protect them. He wouldn't deny that it was possible. He wouldn't warn her that other people might be hurt by the truth, no matter how much she needed it.

But she wasn't buzzed enough to lay her worst secret out on the table like that. Not yet. "My parents lived there," she said, stripping the whole story down to the barest of bones.

"At the *commune*?" He stopped his busywork and tossed the rag over his shoulder as he turned to face her straight on.

"That's right. You're looking at a genuine love child."

"Wow. So you're a native too."

"I guess I am."

"Well, then." He reached beneath the counter and brought up a bottle and another glass to pour himself a shot. "Welcome home, Hannah." They clinked glasses.

She watched his throat work as he downed the shot of whisky. She sipped her drink. It was nice to be distracted. Really nice. "Thank you," she said.

"For what?"

"For making me feel better."

He leaned against the bar again, tightening the little circle of quiet around them. "So this isn't just a walk down memory lane?"

"No. Not by half." He watched her, his gaze steady. Maybe he was enjoying being distracted too. She decided to add a little flesh to the bones. "I don't know who my mother is. We left California. She stayed here. I'm hoping she could still be around."

"It's not a big community. What's her name?"

Hannah cringed and raised one shoulder.

"Ah. Secrets, indeed."

She hid her embarrassment behind a smile. "I don't suppose you know an old, incorrigible hippie woman with a taste for whisky and trouble? If so, send her my way."

"I'll keep my eye out."

"Thanks." Smiling couldn't hide her embarrassment anymore, so she finished her drink and stood. "I'll be right back with my wallet."

"Don't bother. It's on the house."

"Oh, come on!" she protested. "I don't want your pity meal. Or drinks."

Gabriel laughed, showing off slightly crooked bottom teeth that she found charming. "Pity didn't even come to mind. Consider it a welcome-home gift."

She tilted her head suspiciously. "Are you trying to keep me from coming back to pay? Want me to get out of your hair?"

"Definitely not. I already promised information to lure you back, didn't I?"

"Ah. A devious plan. Tonight?"

"I can't promise anything, but I'll call around and see what I hear this afternoon."

"Thank you again," she said, not promising anything herself. "For everything."

"You're welcome."

She took a few steps before remembering her jacket and cringed before she turned back to grab it. She was almost through the door when he called out.

"Hannah?"

"Yeah?" She stopped in the doorway and met his warm eyes.

"We close at nine."

Her neck tingled as she pushed through the door, his gaze prickling her skin. Yep, she was coming back tonight. No doubt about it.

CHAPTER 10

Nancy Drew had never had to deal with the internet.

It should have given Hannah an advantage, shouldn't it? All that information at her fingertips in an instant, just waiting to be found. But Hannah suspected the internet had only made her soft. When it failed her, she could only sit dumbly and stare at the screen.

She'd found only the same few stories about hippies in Big Sur. Plus, far too much information about people named Smith who lived in California. And although she'd found a hopeful link to Monterey voter registration records, the files only went to 1944. Not even close.

She wished she were back at the roadhouse, having another drink.

But all hope wasn't lost. She discovered that she could access voter files at the Monterey County registrar's office. She'd drive there tomorrow and check into it.

But property records. There had to be an online database somewhere. She tried several searches before she stumbled upon it. The database wasn't user-friendly. Or intuitive. But it would do. She didn't have a parcel number to look up, but she did have a name. Unfortunately, Peter Smith didn't come up with any hits in fifty years' worth of records.

"Okay," she whispered. She could do this. She typed in "Tucker Neff." And there it was. A deed granted to Tucker Neff from Jonathan

Worley seven years before. Satisfaction at this small victory made her growl.

She typed "Jonathan Worley" into the search and found the deed that had moved the property into his hands. And so on. Six owners back, she tried one more search. The result punched her in the gut.

Smith. Her own name right there, lit by the glow of her computer screen.

It wasn't Peter Smith. It wasn't her father. Instead, it was a man named Jacob Smith, granting the deed to a new buyer in 1972. "Jacob Smith," she whispered.

My God, was this man a relative? An uncle or a grandfather or a cousin? Smith was a common enough name, but it couldn't be a coincidence that he'd owned the land where she'd been born. Had it been a family farm? Had the commune come later? After 1972?

She searched his name and saw that the deed had been transferred to him in 1967 by an Abigail Freya. Hannah wrote down the names and both document numbers so she could see the actual deeds if she needed them.

And then she sat back and took a deep breath. She finally had something real.

Grabbing her phone, she saw she had no signal, so she sent Becky an email instead. Have you ever heard of Jacob Smith? I think he's a relative of ours.

While she waited for a reply, she tried searching for "Jacob Smith" and "Big Sur." Nothing came up. So she tried "Jacob Smith" and "Peter Smith," leaving off a location.

And it worked. It *worked*. There were a few hits from random genealogy sites that had nothing to do with her family, but the fifth entry down was a link to a Santa Cruz newspaper.

She licked her dry lips and clicked on it.

The site was a scan of the front page of an old newspaper, and right there in the middle was a picture of her father. And this was the '60s version of her father she'd expected. Glasses. A suit. Short hair receding halfway back on his head.

But no. That couldn't be right. She glanced at the date of the paper. 1966. Her father had only been twenty. How could—

Then she saw the second man in the picture. A boy, really. Skinny and shy-looking. Wearing a short-sleeved dress shirt and a tie, but no jacket. He held a book in his hand, and his head was turned toward the older man.

Hannah scrolled down, and a caption appeared. "Preacher Jacob Smith and his son Peter Smith hosted a revival meeting at the Santa Cruz fairgrounds for a crowd of hundreds before moving on to Watsonville."

Preachers?

She reached a careful hand to the screen and touched the shape of Jacob Smith's jaw. Her *grandfather's* jaw. It wasn't the answer she'd been looking for, but it felt important. A clue for her to follow, yes, but it was more than that. Her father had claimed his parents had both been dead by the time he was eighteen. Here was his father, still alive in 1966, and owning land until 1972.

Why would he have lied about his own parents?

Her email chimed.

> Where are you? Are you okay? I just tried to call and I couldn't get through. I don't recognize the name. How did you find him? Is he a cousin? Please call.

Hands shaking, Hannah wrote back.

> I can't call. I'm on Wi-Fi but there's still no cell signal. Jacob Smith is our grandfather. Dad said he died, but he was still alive in 1972. I found him through property records. Are you sure you don't remember anything? Maybe you could ask Rachel.

She attached a link to the newspaper article and hit "Send," trying to ignore the stab of guilt over revealing another of her father's lies. It felt wrong, but what the hell else was she supposed to do? She wasn't the one who'd lied. These weren't her secrets to protect.

Her computer chimed in a tone she didn't recognize, and she jerked back from the keyboard. Her eyes traveled around and around the screen until she spotted an icon bouncing at the bottom. A video call.

"Oh, crap," she groaned. Becky had found a way to make contact.

She waited for a few heartbeats, then a few more, seriously considering rejecting the call. But in the end, her love for Becky won out and she opened the application.

"I've been so worried!" Becky said as the screen opened to reveal her face far too close to the computer. "Are you okay? Is everything . . . I mean, good Lord, Hannah. Is he really our grandfather? Is this serious?"

"Get your nostrils out of the camera, Becks."

Becky pulled back a little, revealing her face and a wild mass of blond waves. She looked as if she'd been literally pulling her hair out with exasperation. "I thought you were looking for your mother!"

"I am, but I found him too."

"Like . . . he's there?"

"No, of course not. He'd be ancient. But we were born on land he owned. I'm on the property right now. He was here. You must have known him."

"I was three."

"Still, you must remember having a grandfather!"

"Why are you yelling at me? Do *you* remember anything from when you were three?"

Hannah sat back and bowed her head, waiting for her temper to pass. "I'm sorry. It's just that this is all so crazy. What was Dad hiding? Somebody must remember something."

"If his father was a weird traveling preacher, I'm going to assume that growing up with him wasn't easy."

"I guess." She made the video window smaller and looked at the newspaper picture again. "He married Mom the year this picture was taken. And then they moved with Jacob Smith to Big Sur."

"Are you sure?"

"I think so. They had Rachel here. Then you. And then I came along. How did that happen?"

"I don't know."

"Becky, there's something else."

Her sister groaned. "Of course there is."

"This place was a commune."

"A *what*?"

"A commune. Young people. Hippies. Free love."

Becky stared into the monitor for a long time before she burst into laughter. "Oh my God, Hannah! You can't be serious."

"I am. There were a lot of them out here. And it explains where I came from."

"Well, it doesn't explain anything else! Mom and Dad as *hippies*? You're insane."

"They lived here. There was a big communal garden. Cabins. A bathhouse."

"Hannah, I accept that you want to find your mother, but this is ridiculous. Mom and Dad were never hippies."

"But—"

"You just called to tell me we had a grandfather who was a preacher and owned the land. How does that fit into this tale of free love and socialism?"

Hannah had opened her mouth to argue, but she snapped it shut. Becky was right. Jacob Smith had been a Christian preacher, so the truth must be more complicated. Maybe Jacob had bought the farmhouse and shown up to find a bunch of hippies living in the woods. Maybe he'd even let them stay. From what she'd read online, they'd all been squatters and rebels in those days, camping out on grand estates or in state parks. Refusing to leave. Claiming it was America and they had the right to go anywhere they liked.

So maybe there had been a commune, but the Smiths hadn't been part of it until Peter had been drawn into sin and love with some dark-haired nymph. That certainly made more sense than the Smiths participating in LSD-fueled orgies.

"Maybe you're right. I'll know more soon. A local guy is helping me out."

"Just some guy? Is he a weirdo?"

"He's not a weirdo." Feeling a blush rise to her cheeks, she changed the subject. "How's Mom?" The word hung in the air for a moment. A lie. A mistake. But what else could Hannah call her?

Becky slumped a little. "Not great. She got another UTI."

"Oh, no."

"She spiked a fever yesterday. Got panicky. I think she was coming down with it before you left. That's why she was acting strange."

"I don't think that's why," Hannah said dryly, but she swallowed her bitterness. "They've got her on antibiotics?" She'd spent her whole life with no idea of how dangerous urinary tract infections were for the elderly. A quiet, hidden illness that could kill them before anyone realized what was happening. But now she knew all the details and dangers because her mother got an infection every six months or so.

"Started them last night."

"Once she's better . . ." Hannah cringed before she could even get the words out. Her conscience tried to keep them in, but she pushed hard against it. "Once she's better, maybe you could ask her about Jacob Smith."

"I'm not doing that." Becky sounded as hard as Rachel in that moment. As if Hannah were asking the unthinkable.

"Right. Okay. I've gotta go."

"Hannah, just—"

"Bye. Love you." She hit the button to end the connection.

She didn't need their judgment. How could they possibly understand? She was upsetting their comfortable, cozy lives, and they hated it. Fine. But she'd never felt cozy at all. She'd felt *strange*. And now she knew why.

Until now, the lie had only been about her. But now her sisters were involved too. They'd had grandparents they'd known nothing about. A family they'd been denied.

Good. Now she wasn't alone. They were all in this. They could feel a little of what she was feeling.

She closed the video window and got back to work.

CHAPTER 11

She was going to have to call her ex. Not for emotional support, but for actual, concrete information. Jeff was a professor of American history, and the 1960s was history, wasn't it?

Granted, his area of specialty was the industrial revolution and nineteenth-century trade, but he covered classes right up through the modern age. And loved it all, really.

But even if he had little knowledge of 1960s California, he'd know where to get it. *If* he still cared enough about her to help.

That was a damn big if.

Her stomach tightened and rolled at the idea of reaching out. She was trying to move on, and she hated looking back. The past was so much easier to deal with when it was getting smaller and smaller in the rearview mirror.

She didn't want to reach back, did she? Or was she actually using her grandfather as an excuse to bring Jeff closer again? No. She needed him gone. She *wanted* him gone. Probably.

"Shit," she groaned, glancing at the clock. It was already ten fifteen in Chicago, and she couldn't call from here anyway. She'd try tomorrow when she got to civilization. But now that she'd decided to do it, she couldn't just lounge around and live with it. She needed to take action. It was her way of coping with life. Better to make a mistake than spend days rehashing the same questions and doubts.

Hannah opened an email window and typed in his personal address. In the subject line, she wrote a simple "Hi."

"Shit," she groaned again. But then she dove right in. I'm sorry to bother you. I know things are . . . complicated. But I don't know who else to ask.

She typed, "I'm sorry," again, then deleted it with a grimace of disgust. She'd opened with her sorriness, and she wasn't going to pepper it throughout the note.

She was sorry, though. For a million things. For everything.

Flexing her fingers, she stared at the screen.

She ran from problems. That was her standard MO. Maybe because early in life she'd convinced herself that leaving Coswell, Iowa, behind would be her key to happiness. That if she could just get far enough away, she'd find the right place. She'd transferred that belief to relationships too. So she ran, and that meant she had to live with regrets instead of facing consequences.

A fair trade. So Hannah ignored her guilt and sorrow and typed up the facts instead.

She didn't reveal all of the truth. Just some of it. The part about her father, but not her mother. She wrote:

> But the story feels all wrong. I don't understand why my dad would have lied about his own father. And I don't understand some of the things I'm hearing. But I'm running into a dead end online. Do you have any suggestions for finding more information about this man? If you're willing to help . . .

She added a link to the photo she'd found, hoping he wouldn't be able to resist looking into this mystery whether he wanted to or not. Despite their recent differences, she knew him. Knew what he liked. What he loved.

Blowing out a long breath, she nudged the mouse up and clicked "Send" before she could second-guess herself.

When she looked up, she realized how dim it was in the cabin and glanced at the clock. Eight thirty. Hannah slammed the laptop shut and jumped up. She wanted to at least brush her hair and put on lip gloss before she saw Gabriel again.

Thank God she had something to do tonight; otherwise she'd sit around incessantly checking email.

She brushed her hair and rubbed a face wipe over her skin so she'd feel slightly less old and tired. After putting on powder, blush, and a little gloss, she changed from tennis shoes into boots and chose a different shirt. Then she grabbed her black leather jacket and headed out.

The old-fashioned key didn't seem secure enough to her. It was charming, sure, but it felt like there could be dozens of them floating around with the cabin number written in giant font on each of them. But she locked up tight anyway. She'd lived in the city too long.

As she stepped off the wooden platform into the dirt, she caught movement from the corner of her eye and swung to the right. Cabin four was there, and she thought maybe the quick rush of movement she'd seen had been someone ducking between the two cabins. Frowning, she crept forward, eyes locked on the edge of the wall, hands fisted in defense in case someone jumped out at her.

The key bit into her hand, and she was happy for the damn thing now as she twisted it around to stick out between her fingers, just as she'd learned to do at eighteen when she'd gone off to college.

She moved slowly, even as she wondered why, what difference could it make, why bother when whoever it was knew she was there? But her internal argument didn't bolster her courage, and it didn't quicken her steps. It felt like her heart raced through a thousand more beats before she drew even with the corner of the cabin and peeked around it.

There was no one there. Not anymore, at least. Anyone could have easily escaped by now along the shadowy dirt trail that snaked between the two buildings.

Feeling braver now that she knew no one was pressed up against the wall, waiting, Hannah moved along the path. She strained her ears, but something was humming in the cabin to her left—the water heater, maybe—and combined with the rush of water from the river, she wasn't sure if she'd hear footsteps or not.

Raising her makeshift weapon higher, she slid between the cabins and into the yard area behind them.

She was almost on him before she saw him. Hannah froze, then jerked backward into the space she'd just walked out of.

A man sat on the patio of cabin four. His back had been to her, thank God, because she'd caught both the glint of a wineglass in his hand and the murmur of soft conversation. She'd almost sneaked up on a couple having a romantic evening.

Hannah spun and rushed back to the front before she let herself suck in a loud gulp of air to fuel her racing pulse.

The shadow had probably been the neighbor, coming back from getting firewood or maybe a bottle of wine from the car. And she'd almost stabbed him with her cabin key.

Hannah hurried past the cabins and the parking area until she was moving downhill toward the inn and the highway beyond. The sun was somewhere below the trees, and everything around her felt blue and peaceful, calming her heart rate despite her rush to leave the cabins behind.

She wasn't used to being quite so alone in her solitude, that was all. In Chicago she was surrounded, even when alone in her apartment. And in Coswell there were neighbors everywhere. But here in the coastal forest she felt cut off from everything, and it had made her jumpy. "And stupid," she assured herself.

But before the words had even faded from her ears, she heard the sound of a small motor, and as she watched, that ancient ATV she'd seen earlier zipped out from the trees ahead and sped toward the inn. The same old man was driving. She could see his white hair waving in the breeze as he drove off.

She looked at where he'd emerged from the trees, then followed the motion of her head around until she was facing the cabins.

It didn't mean anything, surely. And hell, even if it had been him, it was his job to take care of the place. The grounds, the cabins, maybe even the trails. He worked here. Of course he'd be around.

But Hannah still crossed her arms tight and increased her pace toward the highway until she was almost jogging.

By the time she opened the door of the roadhouse, it was nearly nine, and guilt bit into her as she stepped inside. Gabriel had offered to help, but he likely hadn't planned on hanging around after closing to do it.

She was relieved to see that there were still two tables full of diners and a pair of men at the bar. She wasn't too late.

When she glanced behind her toward the window, she realized how dark it had already gotten. And she still had to walk home after this. A late stroll home was something she could handle with aplomb in Chicago. But here? She didn't even know what lived in these woods.

Hannah sat at the bar and slipped off the jacket to reveal the tank top she'd worn underneath. She wasn't flirting, per se. She just wanted Gabriel to know she didn't always look like a drowned rat, a form of wildlife she *was* familiar with even before seeing it in her bathroom mirror today.

She was just glancing down to check her cleavage when Gabriel said, "Hi."

Jerking her gaze up from her breasts, she saw him ducking under the side entrance of the bar with a big smile. "Are you having dinner?" he asked.

"No. I don't want to keep you. I just thought I'd stop by and se—"

"A drink, then."

"No, you're wrapping up."

"It'll be at least a half hour. Can you wait?"

Her smile relaxed. She wasn't keeping him. Instead, he was asking her to hang around. "No problem."

"Another whisky?"

"Maybe just a glass of white. Whatever you like best."

He winked again, probably an impulsive gesture in this job, but damned if she didn't enjoy the hell out of it. And she was happy for the drink after that weird episode of panic.

He quickly poured a glass of wine, then set the half-empty bottle down beside the glass. "Knock yourself out." He took two steps away, then paused. "Not literally, though."

"No passing out. Got it."

She was grateful for the chance to decompress for a minute and let the adrenaline drain from her body. Tomorrow she'd ask Tucker about the old handyman. Tonight she just had to get home safely. And find out what Gabriel had discovered. And see what was waiting in her inbox when she got back. Maybe an angry email from her ex. Maybe stony silence.

Okay, she was terrible at decompressing. But she was pretty decent at drinking wine, so she took a sip and smiled. It was good. Bright and golden on her tongue. She could get used to this Gabriel guy.

And everything was going fine. She was getting information. Closing in on an answer. Now that she was here, it was seeming less and less likely that she'd actually find her mother still living on this coast, but she might find her *somewhere*.

One of the tables got up to leave, and the two men at the other end of the bar rose too. They were dressed in high-end bicycling gear, and she wondered if they were going to ride somewhere on the highway in the dark. Concerned, she watched them leave, heading toward two bikes parked outside. As the door cut off her view, she shook her head.

"Everything all right?" Gabriel asked. She swung around to see him carrying a stack of clean glasses from the kitchen.

"I can barely enjoy driving on that highway. I can't imagine how people enjoy biking on it."

"They don't."

"Don't what?"

"Enjoy it. I know people who've biked all over the world, and when they get to Big Sur, they white-knuckle it the whole way."

"I honestly can't believe they don't all get hit by cars. Everyone who's driving is looking at the ocean!"

"It seems unwise to me."

"So why do they do it?"

Gabriel shrugged. "A lot feel it's something they have to do. Same reason you're here. Most of the others don't realize just how harrowing it will be."

Just like me, she thought but didn't say aloud.

Gabriel glanced up and lifted a hand toward the last table. "Excuse me for a second, Hannah."

He said it as if he were at dinner with her instead of running a business. The guy was adorable, and she had no room for adorable on this trip. Or in her heart.

If she even had a heart. Jeff had claimed otherwise at one point, and she'd suspected he was right.

She finished the wine and poured herself a half glass more.

The last table left. Someone turned up the background music until it wasn't background anymore. She closed her eyes and enjoyed the '70s rock. She'd always had a weakness for '70s radio hits. The memory of being in the family car rolled over her once again: windows rolled down to the summer heat because they didn't have AC, sisters crowded too close, making them all sweat more, her mom singing along, everyone bored but mostly happy.

She knew her life hadn't been bad. It hadn't even been mediocre. She'd had a great childhood, maybe just not the *right* one.

Her sisters had been so close, and the dozens of interests they'd shared with their mom had created a little blond trio. It felt as if half of Hannah's childhood memories involved passing the three of them as they chatted and laughed over baking, crafting, gardening, or any kind of busywork they could find. They'd never excluded Hannah. Not intentionally. But maybe something ancient and instinctual had kept her from joining in.

Or maybe . . . maybe she'd felt a secret resentment from a mother who'd loved her—really loved her—even while hating her a little. Dorothy had raised a child her husband had fathered with another woman. The love had been there, but surely it had been steeped in something subtle that even now Hannah couldn't identify.

"Ready?"

Hannah opened her eyes in surprise to find Gabriel tucking a stack of clean towels beneath the bar. She could hear dishes being washed behind the kitchen door. "Aren't you still cleaning up?"

"The benefits of being the owner." He shrugged on a leather jacket that was similar to hers and tipped his head toward the door. "Walk you home?"

"Oh, thank God," she breathed as she bounced off the stool and grabbed her stuff. "It's really dark here. And I think there are mountain lions."

"There are, but they're super shy."

"Funny."

"That's not a joke." He locked the door after she followed him outside.

She glanced around the lot. "Where's your car?"

"I live in a bungalow behind the roadhouse. There's a garage apartment too. A couple of my employees share it. Land is crazy expensive here."

"It seems like most people who have houses here have owned them forever."

"Exactly. It's a little like apartments in New York City. Once you've got a place, you never give it up."

Hannah couldn't see his wink, but she could feel it. She shivered a little, even though she'd tugged her jacket on, and pretended it was a delayed reaction to the mountain lion talk.

"So where are you from?" he asked.

She used to be embarrassed by the question, but she'd lost that a long time ago. Still, it felt more complicated than just saying Iowa. "Until recently I was in Chicago, but now I'm home taking care of my mom in Iowa." It wasn't so dark that she couldn't see him turn his head. "The mom I grew up with," she explained.

"Ah. She's sick?"

"She has dementia."

"I'm sorry. That must be hard."

"It is hard. It's exhausting in ways I never imagined. She's in a home, so mostly I just sit with her, but it's like having your heart broken every day. And then this happened . . ."

"What?"

Right. She hadn't told him that part. They stopped at the edge of the highway, and she used the distraction of looking for traffic to think for a moment. They hurried across the road, and when they stepped up the driveway into a spooky patch of fog, Hannah felt so thankful for Gabriel's presence that she threw caution to the wind and told him the truth.

"I didn't know before now. I thought my mother was my mother. They were married when I was born."

"Ah."

"Yeah. I found out the truth because of some medical tests. And now I'd like to know who my real mother is, so I really appreciate the help."

He drew closer in the mist, and she resisted the impulse to loop her arm through his so they wouldn't get separated in the darkness. If she veered into these woods, she might never be seen again. A ghost daughter to wander the land with her ghost mother.

"Did your mom tell you anything?"

"Not really. Either she can't or she won't. There's no way of knowing the difference at this point. And I'm angry either way. How awful is that? I'm angry at my mom for having dementia."

"I think that's pretty normal."

"I don't know. It doesn't feel normal."

"And your dad?" Gabriel pressed.

"He died a few years ago."

"Mine too. Back in '95, actually. It's been a long time, I guess. Doesn't feel like it."

"I'm sorry," she whispered.

"Me too."

"I still miss my dad so much. I wasn't ready for him to go. I mean, sometimes it felt like he was the only one on my side. My mom loved me, but . . . Now this. God, if he could just *tell* me what happened. If

I'd found out ten years ago, I would've asked my questions and gotten my answers. The end."

Gabriel's teeth flashed in the night, and she realized they were heading up out of the fog now. She could see the cabin lights ahead. "Somehow," he said, the low note of amusement in his voice gliding over her skin, "I doubt it would have been that simple."

Hannah laughed too loudly at that. He was right. It would have been an emotional, dramatic mess. She would have thrown at least three tantrums. "Already got me pegged?"

"You don't seem the type to accept things quietly."

"No. No, I guess I'm not. I would've ended up right here regardless, but at least I might have had her name. A way to find her."

"Any chance your mother will be able to answer questions in the future?"

Hannah shrugged. "I suppose anything is possible. But these days, her lucid moments are few and far between. And as soon as she gets stressed, she's gone again. That's the problem. Even if I catch her at the exact right moment on the exact right day, asking her that question will probably send her spiraling. I guess I could have stayed and tried, though."

"Or stayed and driven yourself crazy."

"That was what it felt like." She stopped at the entrance to her cabin. "Want to start a fire? Sit out back?"

"Sure."

She let him in through the front door, but crossed immediately to the back so he wouldn't think she was inviting him to her bed. Not that there was any room on the bed. It was covered with her laptop, a notebook, and her open suitcase. "Sorry about the mess," she said automatically, because she was used to saying that to anyone who stopped by her place. She could almost hear her mom saying, *If you were sorry about it, you'd clean it up!* True. She didn't really care that much about clutter.

Gabriel followed her out back with no comment. She grabbed the box of Riverfall Inn matches and lit one against the striker. The fire was already laid out with paper and kindling, and she had a flame going in just a few seconds.

Gabriel watched with his hands stuffed into the pockets of his jeans. She should've asked him to light it, she supposed. That was the kind of thing that made men feel useful. But she liked feeling useful too, and there was something incredibly satisfying about watching a fire she'd set herself grow and lick higher on the logs.

"Keep an eye on it?" she asked, trying to give him a little responsibility in case he needed it. She went back into the cabin to grab wineglasses.

He was in the same pose when she returned. Relaxed, his shoulders curving down in a way that would have been a slouch on another man, but somehow made him look solid. He was only an inch or two taller than she, but so wiry he looked longer.

Like any man, Gabriel could be the very nighttime danger she should be protecting herself from. He was stronger than she was, they were in the woods, and he could silence her with barely any effort. But she trusted her instincts. They'd been honed during her reckless college years of trying to talk herself into trusting men who gave off the wrong vibe.

Instincts were important. All women learned to trust fear.

But with him, she didn't feel any fear. He didn't stare at her too hard or get in her space or make proprietary gestures he had no business making. He flirted, yes, but he watched for her response and then let her reaction be the last word.

Hannah liked that. A lot.

She'd already finished her free bottle of wine, but there was another with a little handwritten price tag of twenty dollars. "I hope this red's okay. It came with the room." She handed him the bottle and the corkscrew, making him useful after all. The fire was blazing happily, and she dropped into the wooden chair with a sigh.

"Looks good. And thanks for the invitation." He poured them each a glass of wine and took his seat. *"Salud."*

She stretched out a little in her chair until the heat of the fire branded her knees with warmth.

"So I called Mom to ask her about this place," he said. "She's lived in Big Sur her whole life. Figured she'd know."

"Did she?"

"It was definitely a commune. She was very disapproving."

Her heart beat a little harder, still excited about the idea even though she had her doubts. "What did she say?"

"That they kept to themselves. That they didn't belong here. She said they all left a long time ago."

"All of them?" Her new hopes fell. "No one stayed?"

"She said they were here a few years, and then all of them cleared out. I asked if she knew anyone, any of the women, and she denied it. But she said there were a lot of women."

"Too many, apparently," she joked, but then the defeat hit her. "Well, damn it. I guess my little fantasy of finding her in Big Sur was pretty far-fetched. What were the chances she'd just be sitting here waiting for me?"

"Most people come for a season or two and then move on. I'm sorry."

"What about your family? You've stayed."

He smiled. "We've stayed and stayed. My mom's family goes back eight generations. They were ranchers here back when it was horses and wagons, and few enough of those."

"Do you have a big family?"

"A sister and two brothers. Lots of aunts and uncles. You?"

"Just two sisters."

"Hannah and her sisters?" he drawled.

She groaned. "Oh, God, no! I hate Woody Allen."

"I don't believe it. You're the first white person I've ever met who doesn't love him."

She tried to smother her snort of laughter but failed. "I honestly don't get it! His movies are about ancient, anxious men who are somehow irresistible to beautiful young women. And the weirdest part is that no one in the movie even comments on how weird it is. No one asks him if he sold his soul to the devil to attract this woman. Pure middle-aged male fantasy if you ask me."

"No doubt."

"Let them have their fun, I guess." She tipped her head back and stared up at the few stars she could see past the branches of the redwoods. "Did your mom remember anything else?"

"She called it Jacob's Rock."

That stopped her reverie. She looked at Gabriel. "The commune?"

"Yes."

Jacob's Rock. On land owned by Jacob Smith. She was closer to some kind of truth, but she still had no idea what it was. "Do you think I could talk to her?"

"I'm happy to ask."

"Thank you. I'm looking into land deeds tomorrow. And voter rolls. That might be my best bet for tracking down other adults who lived at this address. I'm hopeful."

"Good. I'll keep asking around. See if any of the other old-timers know more."

"That's really sweet, Gabriel. Thank you."

"It's no trouble."

She closed her eyes and breathed in the turpentine scent of the billions of evergreen needles waving on the wind above them. They shushed and shook hundreds of feet into the sky.

She wondered if her mother had ever slept out in the open here, with no walls to keep out the world. With no roof but the back of the man above her as they made love.

Hannah should probably hate her own mother for being some sort of betraying jezebel, but the truth was that she loved the idea. And she shouldn't love it. She knew that.

It must have hurt Dorothy Smith terribly. It must have hurt her father too, to be torn between two women. To have betrayed his wife.

Being a love child wasn't something Hannah should be proud of, so she'd pretend she wasn't.

"I should go," Gabriel said, and for a moment she wondered whether he should. It wouldn't take long to clear the mess off her bed, and then she could lose herself in another body for a night, the way she'd done throughout her twenties and well into her thirties. She wasn't too old for it. She still felt restless and alive and solid. Hell, she still felt twenty-five and just starting her real life.

But she wasn't. She was on the downhill slope now. Descending into wisdom.

The lie made her smile, and she opened her eyes to watch Gabriel rise to his feet. He set the wineglass on the wide wooden arm of his chair.

She stirred and leaned forward, but stopped when he held up a hand. "Don't get up. You look way too relaxed to move."

"What if you get lost on your way out of here?"

He grinned, his eyes sparkling in the faint light. "Then you might wake up to find me sleeping on your front step."

"I could take you to breakfast, get the rumor mill talking." She tipped her head. "Are there a lot of rumors about you?"

"Not much talk in the past few years. I'm old and boring." The sexy rumble of his voice belied the words. She imagined that sexy voice in her ear in the dark and was shot through with sudden arousal.

She stood and stepped into his space. He didn't back away, so she eased closer, slipped her hands inside his jacket and around the heat of his waist. When she tipped her chin up, he kissed her. A soft brush of lips. The faintest pressure. Another kiss. Another. Until she parted her lips for him and he gently settled in.

Mm. He tasted nice and felt even better.

His kisses promised slow finesse, but she suspected he was old enough to know when it shouldn't be sweet anymore. There was kissing and then there was sex, and she suspected he'd be as good at one as the other.

She hooked a finger into a belt loop of his jeans and tugged him closer, and he groaned a little as she opened her mouth for a deeper kiss.

He was a stranger and she didn't care. A stranger was what she needed. Someone totally new. Someone she'd never see again after this week.

His hand curved over her hip, just holding her, not taking anything more. His palm felt hot against the little gap between her jeans and her shirt. She wanted to feel that heat everywhere, shaping her body, discovering all her curves and angles.

She hadn't had a man in . . . Damn. *Damn.*

Hannah suddenly remembered the laptop on her bed. The email that might be waiting. The almost-ex-husband she was asking for help. The only man she'd slept with in the past nine years.

Gabriel must have sensed the change in her mindset. He lifted his head. Held still.

She didn't want to open her eyes. She really didn't. She just wanted to tug him down and hope he could drive all her problems away. It would work for a few minutes. Maybe a few hours.

"We're a little old for this," she whispered.

"You want to let the kids have all the fun?"

Accepting that she was going to make a responsible choice for once, she forced her eyes open and found him watching her closely. His mouth tipped up into a pained, lopsided smile.

She laughed. "Don't look at me like that! I was seriously thinking about it."

"I thought you might be. That's why I'm looking at you like this."

She tucked her head and laughed against his shoulder. "You're definitely a good kisser, Mr. Cabrillo."

"Well, shit. If I haven't at least gotten good at kissing in forty-eight years, I should hang up my spurs."

"Spurs?" she squealed, laughing harder as he shook his head.

"Just an expression."

"I would hope so! I think." He pressed a quick kiss to her neck that made her shiver and pull away. "No going near my neck. I won't be able to think."

He let her go easily, but his smile promised more fun anytime she wanted it. "That's valuable information."

"I hope you'll use it for good and not evil."

"A lot of good. Promise."

"Can I come by tomorrow?" she asked, instead of just saying screw it and leading him inside.

"Absolutely. I'm looking forward to it. Sleep tight."

He rounded the cabin instead of going through her room, and she listened to the soft scuff of his boots fade into the dark before she dropped into her chair.

It was nice to think he would've stayed if she'd asked. Nice to know she'd be here for little longer and she'd have the chance to reconsider. And it was nice to just lounge here and pretend she didn't need to go inside and check her email.

The fire cracked and popped. A puff of wind sent a tail of smoke toward her for a brief moment, and she held her breath and let it whisper over her, marking her with its scent. Tiny flakes of ash coated her jeans. The trees still shushed above her.

This place was beautiful. Peaceful. It was a fantasyland, and her father had lost himself for a few months or years. Real life had awaited him in Iowa just as it did Hannah, but God, she wanted to lose herself here too.

She closed her eyes on the idea of it and listened to the flames eat hundreds of years of wood away in minutes. The last of that chopped tree rose up into the sky and soared away.

CHAPTER 12

She could have taken Gabriel to bed after all. There'd been no email from Jeff. No intrusion of real life into her hideaway. So Hannah had somewhat grumpily shoved her mess to one side of the mattress, stripped naked, and fallen into bed.

When she woke, she was thankful for the isolation of the cabin, because she was sprawled nude across the sheets with all the curtains wide open. Hopefully Mr. Creepy Old Man hadn't been around to fix any broken screens this morning.

Despite her initial chagrin, she didn't jump up to cover herself. Once she'd looked around to be sure she wasn't entertaining the neighbors, Hannah stretched hard and relaxed back into the bed. The sun slanted through leaves and dappled her body with shifting light as if she were floating underwater.

She slid her hand onto her stomach and spread her fingers wide. Her skin was soft. Her blood warm. She liked the way her pulse thumped against her palm. Proof of life.

She was here. Real and solid, even without a career and a husband and a home. Even if she ran from everything, she was really still *here*.

Stretching hard again, she reached up and pressed her fingers to the cool wood of the headboard, sucked in her stomach, felt her nipples tighten in the cold. She was kind of happy she hadn't asked Gabriel to stay. And really happy she wasn't in Chicago with Jeff.

When she got up, the heated floors warmed her feet as she padded to the bathroom to shower the smokiness from her hair.

She knew it must be chilly outside, but in here it felt warm and perfect. A little womb. She stood under the spray for a long time, letting the water shape her body, the waves of liquid like hands that wanted nothing in return. She felt more at ease here than she had anywhere else in the past year. Was this the sense of homecoming she'd been searching for? Maybe the land had finally recognized her and taken her in.

Once the hot water ran out, Hannah wrapped herself up in a fluffy robe and climbed back into the bed to check her email.

He'd written back.

She stared at the Re: Hi. for a long time without clicking it. Right now everything was peaceful and lovely and there was the possibility that Jeff would be kind. Right now he might express worry and maybe even love for her. But once she clicked it, that possibility would cease to exist.

"Schrödinger's ex-husband," she murmured.

Breath trapped in her throat, she opened the email. It only took a few seconds to read.

> Is this why you called the other night? A genealogical
> search seems like a strange reason to get in touch
> when you've asked me not to contact you.

Damn. That was it. No sympathy. No understanding. Probably because she hadn't been willing to ask for it. She'd left out the truth about her mother for fear Jeff would respond to her bruises with more blows.

Still, they'd been married for years. Shouldn't he have picked up on her vulnerability?

"No," she muttered to herself. "You're an idiot."

Emotional clairvoyance was what she'd always hoped for. That he'd see past her walls and armor and understand the fear underneath.

He'd admired her toughness at first, and she'd waited and waited for him to discover her truths. But he wasn't a superhero. He couldn't see past walls. And she hadn't been willing to take his hand and show him the places where she hurt, so eventually she'd just floated away, adrift on her own invulnerability.

Story of her life. At least now she could see that it was her and not the men she'd chosen.

Well. Not some of them.

She wasn't sure when it had started, her separateness. Had she been born with it, or had she learned it growing up? Certainly Midwesterners were great at keeping their emotions locked down tight. It was almost explicitly encouraged. But more than that, her family had been bewildered by Hannah's needs and feelings.

Her sisters had rarely argued with their parents, and they'd never rebelled, even as teenagers. Only Hannah had caused trouble, pushing boundaries and asking for more, more, more. More answers and respect and freedom. She'd fought back hard against rules and restrictions and refused to go to church. She'd run off, walked away, skipped obligations.

She'd caused chaos, and when they'd resented her for it, she'd hidden her feelings of rejection behind more defiance. It felt like only her father had ever truly forgiven her for the years of tension. He'd accepted her in his quiet, steady way, and she'd needed him more than she'd ever admitted to anyone.

Now she knew why he'd felt like such a solid link compared to her mother.

Finding another firm connection, another parent, felt worth the risk, so Hannah set her teeth and girded her loins and typed out an honest reply to Jeff, hating every sincere, unguarded word she wrote.

By the time she'd dried her hair and dressed, it was nine and she was starving. She tugged on her leather jacket, the smell of wood smoke puffing over her as she slipped her arms in. The leather was warm from lying on the heated floor, and she was thrilled to take a little of the room's comfort with her as she grabbed her purse and stepped outside.

The sun was out somewhere in the east, but the coastal haze filtered its rays to a dull glow that didn't add any heat to the air. Despite the chill, she felt silly ducking into her car for the drive to the inn, but she planned to head straight to Salinas from breakfast. Her car rocked and bounced down the path, and she watched for any sign of the handyman as she drove. He didn't appear.

When she walked into the inn, the smell of bacon made her stomach twist with hunger. There'd be no noble refusal to eat Tucker's food today. Today she'd devour it.

Two couples were at the table. The same middle-aged pair she'd seen yesterday, along with a gay couple who looked to be in their late twenties and were already dressed in hiking gear. Was she the only person who'd ever come to this place alone? It was beginning to feel like it. But screw that. She didn't need someone else to help start a fire or to enjoy it with. Gabriel had been an admittedly nice addition, but she'd been smart enough to send him home and watch the fire die on her own.

"Morning!" Tucker called as he bustled in with a fresh pot of coffee. He held it up in question, and Hannah nodded thankfully as she slipped into an empty seat. "We've got maple bacon and French toast. Fresh fruit."

"That all sounds perfect, thank you."

He seemed genuinely pleased with her answer and headed straight back to the kitchen after pouring her coffee. Feeling much more clearheaded than she had the day before, Hannah chatted idly with the other guests about the anticipated weather for today. "Afternoon sun," the other woman said, "though that's the promise every day."

The two young men, both bearded and muscled, were a little more serious and quickly got back to plotting out a hike on an honest-to-goodness paper map. They were heading up into the hills as soon as they left. When Tucker popped out of the kitchen with a large white sack, they stood and gathered their things.

"Two roast beef sandwiches," Tucker said, "some fruit and cheese. You've got water bottles?"

"We're covered," one of the men said.

"Enjoy your lunch!"

Maybe she'd come back and do Big Sur right one day. Hiking. Beachcombing. A leisurely lunch overlooking a mountain view. But this time she'd settle for French toast.

When Tucker brought it out, she slathered on butter and real maple syrup, thinking how cruel it was that stress didn't burn as many calories as it felt it should. In a just world, she'd be able to eat like an Olympic swimmer during weeks like this. She certainly felt as if she were swimming through miles of water.

She shoveled an oversize bite into her mouth and enjoyed every second it took to chew it. Then she bit off half a slice of bacon and let the salt flood her tongue. The world felt vivid for the first time in a long while. It felt right.

The other couple finally decided which part of the coast they'd drive to today, and Hannah waved a goodbye as she chewed another thick bacon slice. It was only after she'd finished her French toast and dutifully started on the sliced melon that she remembered she was here for more than breakfast.

She wiped her hands and sipped the last of her coffee just as Tucker returned. "Find any juicy details yesterday?" he asked.

"Not much yet. But I wanted to ask you about an employee. The white-haired guy?"

"Joe?"

"I think so. He's the handyman? Groundskeeper?"

"Bit of both."

"Has he been around Big Sur for a while?"

"I'm not sure how long. He doesn't talk much."

"I thought maybe I could ask him a few questions. If he's a native, he might remember my family."

Tucker shrugged. "Sure."

"Is he around?"

"He usually is, but I don't see him often, to be honest. Checks in in the morning and gets straight to work. Moves fast for an old guy. I'll let him know you'd like to chat."

"Thanks." She wanted to ask his last name, just out of curiosity, but that felt like something she shouldn't ask about a man's employee. And if his name wasn't Smith, it wouldn't mean anything to her anyway. Still, she could see if he'd ever been a suspect in a string of motel murders.

But labeling him creepy wasn't fair. If the man had been hanging around the cabins, the best explanation was because he worked here. "I'm driving up to Salinas, but I'll be back this afternoon."

"Drive safe," he said with a wink that was nothing like the winks Gabriel gave. This one was blithe and promised nothing more than another cup of coffee.

A few minutes later, Hannah was pulling onto the highway and craning her neck to see if she could spot Gabriel's apartment behind the roadhouse. As with most potential sights in this part of Big Sur, her view was blocked by trees.

She drove up the coast, easing around curves and white-knuckling past cyclists while praying she didn't spot an RV coming before she could edge back over. The sun emerged with a suddenness that surprised her, and the ocean was instantly a glinting sea of jewels, all the grays blasted away in the light.

She passed the sandy beach just visible at the bottom of that steep cliff and kept going this time until the wilderness ended with an abruptness that startled her. If there was some natural dividing line between habitable and inhabitable, she couldn't see it, but one minute the land was wild and the next there were houses climbing the hills again.

After only two days in Big Sur, it felt strange to be back in traffic, caught at a stop sign next to a huge grocery store. Like stepping from the past into the present. Her phone dinged and buzzed, stirring to life after its slumber. She ignored the dozen notifications that popped onto the screen and continued on.

It felt great to use her amazing parallel-parking skills once she'd found a spot on the narrow streets of the town. And the place was beautiful, bursting with all types of flowers she'd never seen before. Nothing that would grow in Chicago. And nothing that people had even seen in Coswell. Hell, she was tempted to take a picture of the lime tree she'd parked next to, but she refused to be that obviously Midwestern.

"Fruit grows on trees," she muttered to herself. "You know that." But she still found citrus trees kind of magical.

Despite that she'd spent years manipulating accounts and creating paper trails, she'd never done any footwork, so she wasn't sure what to expect as she walked into the county offices. Would they be suspicious about her requests? Would she fill out forms and then sit waiting for hours? Would they glare at her and tell her to come back between two and three next Friday?

The offices were simple and had obviously been built in the '70s, but she was surprised by the welcoming smile of the middle-aged Asian woman who sat behind the desk at the recorder's office. Hardly the stereotype of an unhelpful government employee. "Can I help you?" the woman asked as if she were excited to be of use.

"Hi! I'd like to get copies of a couple of deeds. I have the record numbers and the physical address."

"No problem."

That was it. Ten minutes and forty dollars later, Hannah had copies of two deeds in her hand.

"Oh," she said, just as she was turning to leave. "Are voting records in this building? I was hoping to see who was registered to vote at this address."

The woman winced. "Sorry. Voting records aren't public. I mean, you can look up a name and see if they were registered to vote, but that's it. No address. Nothing like that."

"Shit," she muttered, then winced to herself. "Sorry. Thank you for the information." There went her best guess at how to find all the adults living at the commune. But maybe hippies didn't register to vote anyway. Back to square one. Or maybe square two. She was making progress.

She took the deeds to the hallway and sat on a bench to look them over.

They both seemed to be standard documents with unfortunately no mention of the gang of misfits Jacob Smith may have brought along with the deal. But his signature was there, and the overly large *J* and *S* in his name somehow made him less a figment of her imagination. He'd been a real man. One with an ego, probably.

Her phone dinged, and she remembered the messages she'd ignored earlier and pulled it from her purse.

Two missed calls. One from Becky and one from Jasmine. Jasmine had left a message, and Hannah smiled as soon as the recording started. "Hey, chick! I'm calling from Planet Earth with some great news. Not about me. Well, I went out on another date with Terrance, and he was pretty great, but that's another story. I mean I have great news about this whole Iowa situation. Are you intrigued? Call me!"

Instead of calling Jasmine back, she clicked over to her texts to see what the other alerts had been. Both texts were from Becky.

Mom's feeling better today. She's more lucid. I told her you'd gone back to Chicago for a visit.

Hannah was simultaneously happy that her mom was doing better and pissed off that Becky was adding more lies to the situation.

She typed out, If Mom is more lucid, maybe you could ask her about Big Sur instead of lying about where I am. Then she stared at the sentence for a full minute before deleting it. Becky wasn't going to ask. She never would. There was no point throwing punches over it.

Plus Becky's second text was a bit of an olive branch. Have you found anything new? Are you doing ok?

Hannah decided not to slap the branch from her sister's hand. Nothing new so far. I'm good. Glad Mom is better. I'll be back in Coswell as soon as I can. Tell Mom I love her. Give her a kiss for me.

"But better not tell her it's from me," she muttered as she hit "Send." "She might hide."

After responding to her sister, Hannah couldn't avoid her email icon anymore. She clicked it, and there was a new email from Jeff, waiting in bold at the top of the list. Her heart fluttered like a crippled bird as she opened the email.

> Holy crap, Hannah. What is going on? I didn't know your dad that well before he died, but . . . this is kind of mind-boggling. And your mom is just so . . . I don't know. I'll check out the link you sent me and see what I find. Call me when you can.

Hannah felt a rush of relief so powerful that a sob fell from her mouth before she even realized she was crying. No one else in her family had tried to help her. Her mother couldn't. Her sisters would rather not be emotionally inconvenienced. But her ex-husband . . . Was he even considered family now? Maybe he was, since the divorce wasn't final.

She drew a shaky breath and wiped her eyes. He was going to help. He still cared. She hadn't ruined everything quite as thoroughly as she'd thought.

Reading his email one last time, she saw that he hadn't signed his name, which was a blessing. If he'd left off the "Love," it would have hurt. But if he'd used it, that would have been worse. Hannah backed out of the email and tried to steady her breath so she'd sound normal when she called him.

As she stood to leave, she glanced at a paper taped to the county recorder's glass door. It listed all the documents that were available. Instead of leaving, Hannah stepped back inside the office. "It's me again. Can I get a copy of my birth certificate while I'm here?" She'd ordered one online, but why wait?

The woman cheerfully handed her a short form. "It's twenty-five dollars."

Hannah filled out the paper and handed over her credit card. Five minutes later she had a copy of her birth certificate stamped with the seal of the state of California. But it wasn't any more legitimate than her other copy. Same information. Same lies. At least her parents hadn't been secret forgers. The state had the exact information on file that she'd found at home. Another dead end.

As she folded the certificate to fit it into her purse, her gaze caught on a name near the bottom. Maria Diaz. The woman who'd claimed to have attended Hannah's birth. She had obviously lied about the birth, but if Hannah could track her down, maybe she'd be willing to tell the truth now.

It was one more name she could look into. One more person to ask about. This trip to Salinas wasn't a total loss.

She walked outside into the smell of fresh flowers and thought about stopping at the oceanfront to have lunch. She could pretend she was on vacation. A confident, carefree woman with something wonderful to return home to.

But first, she'd call her soon-to-be ex about her adulterous dead father and pretend they weren't fighting over her money. "Good times," she whispered as she sat on the curb beneath the lime tree.

She called Jeff's number and listened to the phone ring as she nudged a tiny, desiccated lime around with her foot.

"Hannah?" he said as soon as he picked up, and tears filled her eyes again. Clogged her throat. Her mind.

"Hi, Jeff. I-I'm sorry to bother you, I just didn't know who else to call."

"Hey, are you crying? Don't cry. Please. It's fine."

But of course, his soft "don't cry" only made her cry harder. And she hated crying. Stupid vulnerability. She could count on one hand the number of times she'd cried in front of him during their marriage.

She lifted the hem of her shirt and scrubbed her eyes dry. "Sorry. I'm fine. It's just been crazy, you know?"

"I know. Or actually, I don't know. Because I still can't get my head around it."

"Neither can I. But it looks like my dad had an affair during some hippie-crazed fever dream of a summer. And I have no idea who my real mother is."

"What about your birth certificate?"

"It names Dorothy, but it was issued weeks after my birth. A home birth. At a fucking *commune*, Jeff."

He blew out a long sigh, and she could practically see him dragging a hand through his wavy brown hair. "I looked at that picture you sent. I'm just starting to track down more information, but I've verified that Jacob Smith was a traveling evangelical preacher. Traveling preachers were pretty common back then before cable. How else were people going to find God?"

"Right. Makes sense."

"The records on him are scarce, but it looks like Jacob was originally from Arkansas."

Hannah's lashes fluttered. Arkansas? She'd never heard word one about Arkansas from her father. "Okay. So how did an itinerant preacher from Arkansas end up in a hippie commune in Northern California?"

"I'm not sure," he said, but she could hear the hesitation in his voice. He wasn't sure, but he suspected *something*.

"I'm running into dead ends here, Jeff. There were so many people congregating in Big Sur around that time. There's an actual commune still in existence, if you can believe that. But no one seems to remember my family. Or my mother. And I just . . . I'm running out of time. Mom is getting worse. She can't—or won't—tell me anything. But if I can just get a name, maybe I can find the woman who gave birth to me."

"Even with a name, you might find nothing. Or she might not want to be found. I think you're investing too much into this, Hannah."

It was so strangely familiar. The sound of her name on his lips. No one said it like him. Like a sigh. An endearment. She missed being dear to someone. Or she hated it. She wasn't sure anymore. She couldn't stay in a relationship just because she wanted someone around to help her through periods of stress. That wasn't fair.

"I am probably investing too much," she finally said. "It's just . . . It's always felt like something was wrong. Like *I* was wrong. But maybe it wasn't me, Jeff. Maybe I was sensing *this*. All of this boiling just beneath the surface."

"Maybe," he agreed, and tears burned her eyes again, because he hadn't reassured her. *There's never been anything wrong with you, Hannah.* A lie, of course, but one she wanted to hear. Just for a moment. She'd laugh and tell him to stop trying to comfort her with flattery, and then he'd chuckle and tell her she'd be fine.

But he wouldn't do that for her. Not anymore.

She cleared the sorrow from her throat. "I want to know where I come from. Who I really am. Why I'm . . . like this."

A pen tapped against a desk on his side of the line. Another old sound she hadn't realized she missed. "Okay, I have a suspicion."

"What?" she pressed.

"These traveling preachers were a popular attraction in small towns and at fairgrounds, that sort of thing. They would set up a big tent on county land and preach for a week or two. Then they'd move on. Which meant they were on the same roads the hippies traveled."

"Okay."

"It was a strange mix of people who were searching for something more and people who were there to promise it. Have you ever heard the term *Jesus freak*?"

"Sure. Of course."

"We use it today to mean someone who's a rabid evangelical, but that's not what it meant then. Back then a Jesus freak was a weirdo, long-haired hippie who'd found Christ and was happy to tell you all about it."

"Really? There were *Christian* hippies?"

"Yep. And I'm thinking this intersection of your preaching grandfather and the young people in Northern California might have resulted in a group of Christian hippies settling down for a little while."

"Oh," she said as the idea sank into her. "Oh my God! I think you might be right! I couldn't imagine my mom and dad as hippies, but maybe that's because they weren't. They were just trying to convert them!"

"Exactly. And maybe your dad got a little *too* close to one of the women. He, uh, probably hadn't been exposed to much free love before then."

"Wow. That's crazy. But it makes sense. I think. Maybe?"

"I found a reference to a place called Jacob's Rock in Big Sur. Have you heard that name?"

"Yes! I heard it yesterday. Where did you see it?"

"It was mentioned in passing in an evangelical newsletter in 1969. There were no details aside from it being in Monterey County, but I'm thinking that could be your grandfather's place."

"That's what I assume too. I'm just . . ." She dropped her head and stared at the dried lime resting against her shoe. "This is so crazy. I found her blood type, and then my world exploded. My sisters didn't want me to come here. They wanted me to just leave it alone. Accept it. Do you think you could just accept it and never look for answers?"

"I have no idea. I don't think anyone could know unless it happened to them."

"It's why I'm so different from them, Jeff."

"I guess it must be."

She didn't want to get off the phone, which was as good a reason to hang up as any. "I'm really sorry I had to involve you. I couldn't think of anyone else to call, so . . . thank you."

"It's nothing."

"No. It's something, and considering the circumstances . . ."

The pen tapping stopped abruptly, and an uncomfortable silence dropped into place like a slamming door. "We can talk about the circumstances later."

"All right. Can you email me if you find anything else? I won't have cell service."

"Sure. I'll see what I find."

She sat under the lime tree for a long time, phone in hand, heart on her sleeve. Anyone who passed would see right away that she was going through a breakup. She'd seen heartbreak a hundred times on women's faces. Just not on hers. Not since she was young and throwing herself into bad relationships with gusto.

By the time she got out of entanglements with men, she'd long ago moved on in her head. But with Jeff it was different. This was a dull ache waiting to blossom into scalding pain with only a little prodding.

They'd had what anyone else would have been satisfied with. Love, respect, fidelity. Hannah felt as if she were the only woman in the world who couldn't be happy and fulfilled with those three things.

She still loved him. She did. She just wanted more than that. Or less. Even she didn't know. All she was sure of was that walking out of their condo had let her breathe easily for the first time in years.

Finally pushing up to her feet, she opened the map on her phone and mapped out driving directions to the main library, hoping they'd have more old newspapers than the ones she'd found online.

They did. The library was in Monterey, and it was surprisingly small for a wealthy little town, but the local history area was rather sprawling. She searched the microfiche files for her father's name, then her grandfather's, but she found nothing. Then she tried "Jacob's Rock" and got a hit.

"Nice," she breathed, and set off to the cabinet to pull the correct file.

After ten minutes of scrolling, Hannah felt seasick. And discouraged. None of the hundreds of articles rolling by had been about anything called Jacob's Rock, much less *her* Jacob's Rock. She'd found the location referenced on the computer, but there were only three articles on that page. One was about an auction of a property in Carmel. One was about two new school buses. And there was a tiny, one-paragraph story about a partial lunar eclipse that she suspected had been written by someone who'd failed science class.

She backed up two pages, then forward two, then went back to the page it was supposed to be on. Finally, she sat back and let her eyes roam over the ads on the page. And there it was. A tiny square in the middle-right column of page six.

Welcome, brothers and sisters! An invitation to join in the worship of Christ, Our Everlasting Lord and Savior. Save Your Eternal Soul from Damnation! Worship services at 9:00 a.m. sharp each Sunday. Prayer and song every night at 7:00 p.m., weather permitting. Jacob's Rock, Big Sur, mile marker 49.

"Holy shit," she breathed. She let out a sharp laugh at the appropriateness of the curse, then quickly hit the "Print" button before the damn thing slipped through her fingers.

Jeff had been right. They hadn't been hippies after all. The date of the paper was April 10, 1967. Only a few weeks after Jacob Smith had purchased the property. Perhaps tired of wandering, he'd started his own church. And a few little lost hippie lambs had found a shepherd.

She wasn't sure this led her any closer to finding her mother, but it satisfied at least a few of her questions about who her father had been. He'd been exactly who he'd seemed. A quiet Christian man, albeit one who'd been led astray at some point. But whatever mistakes he'd made, he'd obviously tried to atone for them by living an uneventful life afterward.

She paid for her copy and headed back toward the wild coastlands with a sense of triumph. Rolling down her windows, she turned up the music and slipped on her shades. The forecast had been right for once. It was sunnier than it had been since she'd arrived.

A curve took her out over the ocean, and she spotted the little crescent beach ahead, all golden sand lapped by white foam. The water was still painfully blue, nearly as turquoise as the Caribbean. When she reached the turnout, she slowed and pulled in.

Screw it. She wanted to walk on that beach.

Ignoring the couple taking a selfie at the other end of the turnout, Hannah headed toward the sandy trailhead she'd parked next to. Fortunately, she'd worn her tennis shoes. Unfortunately, she hadn't brought any water to drink, and even as she started down, she knew she'd regret all of this on the long hike back up. But hell, she was an expert at dealing with regret. She'd sail through with flying colors.

Seagulls squawked somewhere down below, but the birds that circled on thermal currents overhead were black. When a shadow glided over her, she stopped to shade her eyes and look up. Condors?

She wondered if she was imagining the red color of the birds' heads. She'd thought condors were all dead or dying, but here were some right above her.

Taking the rare bird as a good sign, she worked her way down the switchbacks of the trail, trying to keep her eyes on her feet despite the beautiful lure of the ocean.

When she finally reached the bottom, she looked up to a private world. She could hear the cars whizzing by far above, but she was the only soul on this beach. The only set of eyes seeing the high cliffs and raucous waves and blindingly blue water.

The beach was rockier than it appeared from above, the sand strewn with surf-smoothed stones, but she took off her shoes and walked barefoot anyway. The sand was warm and shifting beneath her toes. Crabs scuttled at her fearsome approach, and she grinned at the way they waved their claws in threat.

After jumping over a pile of old kelp, she rolled up her jeans and edged closer to the water. For a moment she indulged a fantasy of skinny-dipping. She might be visible from above, but surely she'd be too small to gawk at. And if someone had binoculars, well . . . she'd make their naked-middle-aged-lady dreams come true. Her ass wasn't in quite the same place it had been at nineteen, but it was passable.

When an ambitious wave climbed high on the sand and lapped over her bare feet, she shouted out a bark of laughter. No skinny-dipping for her. The water was absolutely freezing. She might lose her nipples to frostbite.

Still, it felt good to put her feet in the sea, even if her toes went a little numb. What was it about water that drew people to it generation after generation? Was it the mystery of a vast expanse of liquid they couldn't conquer? Couldn't survive? Was it compelling just because it was dangerous?

She stared out over the waves for long minutes, wondering if her mother had ever done the same. On a hotter day, in a gentler surf, maybe her mother had been brave enough to skinny-dip here. Maybe Hannah was brave like her.

She turned and walked back toward the cliffs, glancing at the ridge above until she could no longer see the guardrail. When all signs of civilization had disappeared, she reached for the hem of her shirt and tugged it up and over her head in one quick motion. Then she shucked her jeans and stripped off her bra and panties.

Hesitating for a moment, she wondered about the sand flea situation. Was it a bad time of year? Would she have to explain bites all over her bare ass? But then she remembered there'd be no one to see them, no one to explain to. Probably.

"Right."

She carefully eased down onto the warm sand. Stretching out, she closed her eyes and smiled. If this was what it felt like to be a hippie, she had no idea why they'd been searching for religion. What else did you need to find when the sun was covering your whole body like a blanket and lighting your eyelids into red fire? The sea breeze crashed over her and then receded, a different rhythm than the surf. Little tendrils of air licked at her like flames.

She spread her fingers in the sun-warmed sand, each shift finding coolness just beneath the surface. Lying there, it occurred to her that it didn't matter who her parents were, what they'd done, how they'd raised her. *She* got to choose who she was. If she wanted something different, it was up to her.

But what did she want?

She'd always denied wanting to be like her sisters, her mother, but if that were true, why couldn't she find peace with it? Why had she tried to be a loving wife when she'd known she would fail? Why did she feel guilty about not having kids when she'd never wanted them?

Or had she? Were those things she actually wanted and was afraid to ask for?

She took a deep breath. Another gust of wind slipped along her nude body. "What do I want?" she whispered into the sky, hoping some sea god or Mother Nature or hippie magic would give her an answer.

But no. She couldn't decipher the angry calls of the seagulls or the whisper of the surf. She did, however, detect the crunching sound of footsteps coming down the trail.

"Crap!" she yelped, and rolled quickly to her knees to brush off the sand. Voices drifted down, and she decided to risk the sand and tug on her panties. "Crap, crap, crap."

She slipped on her bra, then struggled to fasten it. Just as the hooks caught, she realized she should have gotten her other clothes on first and dealt with the bra later. Too late, though. She yanked the shirt over her head, then spent precious seconds turning her jeans right-side out.

"You are the worst—" She shoved one sand-covered foot in. "Hippie—" Hopping, she yanked the jeans up one leg, then balanced on her other foot. "Ever."

Two men jogged down the last ten feet of the trail. One of them glanced at her just as her jeans caught on the plumpest part of her butt.

She tugged hard. Sand scraped her ass cheeks. That was the exact moment it hit her: she was having a midlife crisis. What other explanation was there for a woman her age to try to pitifully recapture the wild, free spirit of youth?

The other man turned to see what his friend was looking at just as her jeans gave in to the struggle and slid the rest of the way up. Now that her crotch was covered, she smiled wildly and waved. *Nothing to see here, gents. Move along.*

Apparently there really was nothing to see, because they each raised a hand in greeting and turned to walk toward the water.

Thank God. Maybe they'd assumed her black panties were swimsuit bottoms and she'd been out here sunbathing like a normal person.

Or maybe they didn't give a shit what she did and she was the only one feeling awkward.

Lightheaded from the frantic fight with her clothing, she dropped to her butt and stared out at the view.

Was this whole trip just a midlife crisis? Was she another sad, average sap fighting an unwinnable battle against aging?

They always said that people who were going mad never suspected madness. That was the insidious magic of insanity. She'd been under a lot of stress. Divorce. Job loss. Moving. Those were all gigantic stressors. Maybe learning her whole life had been a lie had finally broken her, and now she was another pitiable fool flirting with every sexy server who delivered a cocktail.

"At least he's not a twenty-five-year-old blond," she muttered. But she honestly had considered renting a convertible for this adventure.

The panic had finally worked itself from her system, so she pulled on her shoes and headed back to the trail. She had to stop every hundred feet or so and catch her breath from the steep climb, but that gave her a nice break from the chafing sand, so she didn't mind. She was getting exfoliated in places she'd never dreamed she even needed it. Maybe it'd be a good time to sleep with Gabriel after all. Or maybe she'd need a salve.

By the time she got back to her car, clouds were moving in. By the time she reached her cabin, rain was falling. A perfect excuse to get back into her warm little womb.

She didn't want to get sand everywhere, so she stripped down in the shower before turning the water up high to blast away all the grit. Remembering the mad scramble with her clothes, she laughed into the steam. Then she laughed harder.

Screw it. If she was having a midlife crisis, at least it was in a beautiful place with an ocean, a forest, and a hot silver fox. At least she wasn't sitting in her childhood bedroom weeping and drinking herself into a stupor every night.

Her afternoon played out exactly as her morning had. She stayed in the shower too long, then climbed back into bed to check her emails.

It was as good a place as any, especially with the rain dripping and driz-
zling along the windows.

There was no note from Jeff, so she sent him a picture she'd snapped
of the Jacob's Rock notice to push him along. As she was typing, an
email arrived from Jasmine. She should have called Jasmine back when
she had cell service, but she couldn't seem to get excited about Chicago
gossip at this point. Still, she opened the email.

> I know you're crazy busy in Iowa (that was sarcasm,
> in case you don't have that sort of thing there), but
> call me back! I'm serious!

Jasmine ruined the seriousness by ending with several eggplant
emojis, but Hannah wrote back immediately.

> On an emergency trip to the boonies. No cell ser-
> vice! Can you give me the news by email?

Apparently she could, because while Hannah was doing an online
search for anyone named Maria Diaz in California, her email chimed.
It was a welcome distraction from the pages and pages of online phone-
book hits and background-check offers. The name Diaz seemed to be
the Smith of California.

> Ok. Delete this and you didn't hear it from me. But
> Frank Wells is floating the idea of hiring back some of
> the layoffs. And your name came up. Ok, I'm the one
> who brought your name up, but he seemed excited.
> I think they're trying to wrest back a little control from
> the new bosses. YOU COULD COME BAAAAAACK!
> He might be giving you a call soon, Hannah! Get back
> to civilization so you can say yes! For meeeeeee!

"Oh my God," Hannah whispered.

Her old job. Her old city. Her old life.

She didn't even know what to think. Her fingers were numb. Her face tingled. She could have it all back. The life she'd walked away from. *If* her old boss called.

"He might not call," she cautioned her leaping heart. They'd paid her a big settlement just two months ago. It would be stupid to bring her back right away. But those were sunk costs. And Frank had always liked her. And she was good at her job.

Then again, she'd also been tired of her job when she'd left. She'd been a little sad to go, but mostly she'd been relieved to be getting out. To *escape*. Sugarcoating that relief had been the overwhelming rightness of what she was doing: going home to take care of her mom.

But of course, Dorothy wasn't her mom. Did her sisters still expect her to stay?

Hannah groaned aloud. Of course they did. She expected herself to stay. Regardless of this secret past, Dorothy had loved and raised her, and Hannah owed her the same kind of care.

But Chicago called to her. The familiarity of its streets and people and *life*. She could change things up with a new neighborhood and a new place. Or she could slip right back into what she knew. Live near her favorite pubs and restaurants and shops. She could even make peace with Jeff.

Her heart clenched at the thought, and what did that mean? Did she want him back?

No. Definitely not.

She glanced at his last email and remembered that lightning strike of emotion when she'd realized he truly still cared.

So *probably* not.

"I can't do this right now." Her words sounded angry in the tiny cabin, but they felt like fear.

She typed a quick reply to Jasmine. OMG! I don't even know what to think. I'll call you as soon as I can! Then she slammed her laptop closed and got up to dress.

There was no reason to even think about any of this crap right now. She didn't have a job offer yet, and Jeff certainly hadn't invited her to talk about anything other than her family. She had enough stress without inviting more in.

She got dressed and pulled her hair up into a damp bun, though she suspected it might never dry here. Worst-case scenario she'd dry it before she went to bed tonight.

"Yeah, right," she scoffed. She knew damn well that the worst-case scenario involved her falling into bed with wet hair and dealing with the mess in the morning. But for now she was heading to the roadhouse, so she put on a little makeup and lip gloss and double-checked her look in the mirror. Deciding it was somewhere between "good enough" and "pretty all right," she grabbed her purse and opened the door.

And stopped in her tracks.

The old man was staring right at her. Joe. His ATV was parked directly in front of her cabin, and he stared through the windshield as if he'd been sitting there awhile. Had he knocked and she hadn't heard? Or was he just . . . waiting?

She pulled the door closed behind her, then locked it before he could approach and shove her into the cabin.

It probably didn't matter. He likely had some sort of master key. But she wanted him to see her locking up.

When she turned back to him, he was standing next to the ATV, arms crossed. "You wanted something?" he asked.

"I just had a few questions." She moved forward so they'd be in view of anyone driving through the grounds or looking out from the other cabins. "I'm checking into the history of this place, and I wondered how long you'd been working around here."

He shrugged. "Pretty long time."

"Were you here in the 1970s? Maybe '72?"

"Off and on," he acknowledged, clearly not interested in being helpful. The washed-out blue of his eyes studied her warily.

"Can you tell me about Jacob's Rock?"

His hooded eyes widened for a split second, though nothing else on his face gave away his surprise. But that was enough. He knew. She'd seen it.

Maybe that glimpse of her own knowledge had nudged him into curiosity, because he asked, "What do you want to know?"

"Were you part of it? A member or a . . . um, congregant?"

Joe snorted, his cheeks creasing as a bitter smile flashed and then disappeared. "I was never much for religion."

"So how did you know them?"

"Well, back then we all took care of each other. Traveled together. Helped people out. I stayed here off and on at the beginning."

"The beginning?" she pressed.

"It was a place to crash for a while. Me and my woman camped here for a few months. Then shit started to get too religious, and I wasn't interested."

"So you moved on?"

His mouth flattened until she couldn't see it through the beard. "I went to crash with some friends up the coast. She stayed."

"Oh." Wait, did that mean . . . ? Was it possible this man's ex-girlfriend was Hannah's *mother*?

"I was . . . um . . . I was born here in '72. Would you happen to know who had a baby around then?"

"Babies are women's business."

"What?" she snapped. Oh, sure. Pregnancy was women's business, no matter that there was always a penis rather critically involved in the process.

He seemed to sense that she was about to lose her temper and pushed up from leaning on the hood to shift back toward the driver's seat of the ATV. "Look, lady, I wasn't living here in '72. I came by sometimes, yeah, but there were always big bellies and lots of half-naked kids running around." Dropping into the seat, he immediately popped the brake.

"Wait—"

The engine roared to life, and he backed out. When she held up a hand, he paused just long enough to shift. As he pulled out, he tossed one last revelation over his shoulder, his eyes glinting and hard. "You sure do look like your daddy, though."

"Wait!" she yelled, but he didn't hear or didn't care, and the ATV tore down the lane and around the curve.

It was only then that it hit her. She knew she was her father's child, because she was nearly a clone of him. But her father and grandfather looked exactly the same.

Could she really be sure of anything at all?

CHAPTER 13

No. She wasn't going to wonder about this bullshit all night. She was already dressed and ready to go, so Hannah jumped in her rental and followed the road toward the inn, unwilling to let that little Rumpelstiltskin scurry away with her past.

Pulling into the narrow driveway that ran alongside the farmhouse, she spotted Joe shutting up the doors of a shed, closing the ATV inside. He was apparently wrapping up for the night, but she wasn't done with him yet, and surely she was faster than he was on foot. He wouldn't escape so easily this time.

"Did you know my father?" she demanded as she got out of her car.

His white head jerked up, mouth twisting into a scowl. "Lady, I'm just trying to get my work done."

"I know, and I won't take up much more of your time. Just tell me. Please. You knew . . . ?" She swallowed and decided to hope for the best. "You knew Peter?"

"Yeah," he said without hesitation, and the sick, heavy knot in her stomach untangled itself. At least her father was real.

"My dad," she rasped, then cleared her throat to try to make it work again. "My dad was a good man."

Joe shrugged. "He was all right. Better than the old guy, at any rate."

"How so?"

He locked the shed and grabbed a box of tools from the ground, his eyes sliding over everything but her. "This was all a long time ago. It was none of my business then, and it's none of my business now."

"My mother . . . she was one of those people who came here to crash? A friend of yours, maybe?"

He stared a long time, his gray eyebrows sinking lower and lower. In the end he shook his head and spun on his heel to head toward the back of the house.

"Just tell me her name!" Hannah called. "Please! Do you at least know her name?"

Joe stopped. His shoulders dipped a little lower, and he shook his head again, as if he were reminding himself not to answer. But then his back rose on a deep breath, and he lifted his head to stare toward the trees. "She called herself Rain. That's all I ever knew about her. She wasn't part of my group, and I didn't come over here much at the end."

He started walking again, but Hannah stumbled after him. "Do you know when she left?"

"No!" he snapped, waving a hand as if she were a horsefly that needed shooing. "Now leave me the hell alone before you really piss me off."

She did. She stopped, locking her knees so she rocked a little as she watched him hurry away. But she wasn't really seeing him. Instead, she pictured a beautiful, willowy woman named Rain with a gaze that followed Peter Smith too closely. A mouth that smiled easily. Skin dark from the traveling sun.

"Rain." The name made her laugh. Of course it was Rain. It had either been that or Butterfly or Clover or something, right? Rain. Short for Rainbow, maybe. Hannah's real mother.

It was perfect, aside from the fact that it probably wasn't her real name. Oh, well. Fake or not, it was a hell of a lot more than she'd had before.

After a day like today, Hannah needed someone to talk to, so she drove her car back to the cabin and left it there to hike to the roadhouse. Joe was weird and pissy, but he didn't seem too dangerous, even if his styling choices were a little too close to Charles Manson's.

When she walked into the roadhouse, she couldn't stop her stupid grin at the sight of Gabriel at the bar. It was really, really good to see a friendly face, especially one that smiled back when he spotted her.

It was just past five thirty, so a few people had gathered at the roadhouse for dinner already. She'd noticed that Big Sur shut down pretty early, probably because the highway's dips and turns were a menace in the dark. Despite the early dinner crowd, her seat at the bar was open, as if it had been waiting for her. "Hey," she said as she slid onto the stool.

"Hey, yourself. Did you find any good clues today?"

"Maybe. If you buy me a drink, I'll give you the juicy details."

His eyes crinkled with amusement as he reached for a glass. "Old-fashioned?" he asked.

"Definitely. Thank you."

Today the plaid of his button-down was white and pale blue and gray, and the open collar glowed against his skin. She stared at the hollow of his neck for a moment, imagining that she could tuck herself just there in bed. Listen to his heartbeat, the steadiness of it drowning out everything she didn't want to know about her life.

Damn. She made herself look away. He might be the right man, but this wasn't the right time. She'd save him for her next midlife crisis. Drive back to Big Sur with new tits and a red convertible and sleep her way through all the hot bartenders from here to San Diego.

"The band is playing tonight," he said, "if you want to hang around awhile."

"Are they good?"

"Good enough that I pay them. Mediocre enough that it's only for one night a week."

"Ha. Well, unless there's a better show in walking distance, I guess that's good enough for me."

He slid the drink to her, then slipped an extra cherry into the glass before popping another into his mouth. "Pay up," he ordered.

"Okay. Have you ever heard the term *Jesus freak*?"

"Of course. Christian hippies."

"Am I the only one who didn't know that? We don't have those in the Midwest! Anyway, apparently Jacob's little commune wasn't so much about free love as it was about bringing hippies back to the Lord."

"Ah. That makes sense."

"How so?"

"There seemed to be some ominous notes in what I was hearing. Fire and brimstone kind of stuff."

Hannah leaned forward, both hands wrapping around the drink as if it were an anchor. "Really?"

"Yeah. In fact, I saw my mom this morning, and she said she felt bad for those poor sinners who'd strayed from the word of God."

Hannah smiled. "Oh, and does she feel bad for you?"

"Definitely. She thinks if I started going to church, I might give her grandchildren."

She almost choked on her sip of whisky. "Seems more likely if you skip church and stay in bed."

"I'll float that theory by her."

"I have to say, it's a relief to know I'm not the only one who's a procreative disappointment."

"Hey, at least the expectations end for you at a certain age. I'm close to fifty, and my mother still assures me I have plenty of time."

"Don't worry. You do."

He snapped a bar towel in her direction. "Bite your tongue."

"All right, but then you won't get the juiciest tidbit of all."

Gabriel leaned a hip against the bar and stared down at her. "Spill it."

"Her name was Rain. My mom."

"Rain." The name made him smile too, and she liked that.

"I know there were probably a hundred girls named Rain who passed through here, but it's something."

"It's great. How did you find it?"

"I made that old handyman at the inn tell me. Joe. Do you know him?"

"Not really. Seen him around. He's not exactly the social type."

"I definitely got that feeling. You don't think he's dangerous, do you?"

Gabriel shrugged. "Not that I've heard."

"Anyway, he admitted that he crashed at Jacob's Rock for a few months before things got too churchy. And he gave me Rain's name. After I chased him down. I'm pretty proud of myself. It was a great Scooby-Doo moment."

"Maybe you should tug on his beard and see if he's really Rain underneath that mask."

"Good tip. I'll try it next time."

She noticed his gaze wander toward the dining room and tipped her head. "Go on. I've taken up too much of your time."

"No, but I should go make the rounds."

"Of course. But, oh!" She dug in her purse for the stiff sheet of folded paper. "I'm sorry. Just one more second?"

"Absolutely." He leaned against the bar, waiting for her to unfold the paper and slide it toward him.

She pointed at the signature. "Do you know a woman named Maria Diaz? She supposedly witnessed my birth."

He went still, looking down at the name she'd indicated. His eyes tightened in something that almost looked like anger.

"I'm sorry," she said quickly. "I didn't mean it like you'd know anyone with a Hispanic last name. I just thought there was an off chance she might still be here."

"No." He shook his head and flashed a tight smile. "No, it's fine. The name sounds a little familiar, but there are quite a few Marias around. I'll check into it."

"Thank you. She obviously lied about my birth for some reason. I'd love to know why."

"Absolutely. Excuse me."

He disappeared into the kitchen, and Hannah spun the birth certificate around to stare at it. When her stomach growled, she realized Gabriel hadn't taken her dinner order. At least she had the drink to keep her company until he returned.

CHAPTER 14

Ninety minutes later, she was stuffed full of fish and chips and drunk enough that she was pretty sure the house band was the best cover band in America. They were playing one of her favorite Elvis Costello songs when she glanced out the front window and saw Gabriel in the moonlight, staring at the highway.

If she'd been sober, she would have left him alone, but she had too much false bravado dripping into her veins to pass up the opportunity. She slipped out the front door to join him. She was surprised to see him raise a cigarette to his mouth and take a long drag.

"I didn't know you smoked."

He glanced over with a flat-mouthed smile before he blew out a long stream of smoke that hovered in the heavy air for a moment before curling toward the stars. "I don't. Quit a few years ago."

"Now it's a guilty pleasure?"

"Something like that. I give in about once a week."

"Seemed like a good night for it?"

"Must be the music. Makes me feel young again."

She reached for his cigarette and stole a drag herself. "I smoked in college. I give in about once a year."

"It can't possibly hurt, can it?"

Hannah shrugged, closing her eyes as the nicotine hit her hard. "No more than a thousand other things."

"How's the band?" he asked.

"They're amazing, actually. Or your drinks are amazing. Either way, tonight feels good, thanks to you."

"I'm glad." He went quiet after that. Even over the muffled music and the soft whir of insects, she could feel his silence.

Hannah opened her eyes and flushed at the way he was staring at her.

"I like the way you look when you feel good," he said.

Her heart thumped hard. Once. Twice. When he lifted a hand to stroke it along her jaw, her heart surrendered its attempt at strength and raced to a fluttering speed. Damn, damn, damn.

Her lips parted to draw more air, and his gaze fell to her mouth, and she felt so damn glad he was going to kiss her. This day had been too long, and she wanted something sweet to cap it off.

When he leaned in, she smiled and he smiled back, so the kiss started light and happy. But it didn't stay there.

He shifted closer, taking her more deeply, and he tasted like her youth. A teenage boy behind his father's barn, stealing smokes from his parents and kisses from a girl. Hard liquor and fresh cigarettes and cold outdoor air.

She'd lost her virginity in a barn just like that, on a crisp autumn day, with a boy who'd been thoughtful enough to bring blankets and condoms. She'd loved him for a little while, and then she'd moved on. It could be the same with Gabriel.

A car blew by, kicking up air, and she didn't give a damn. She was standing drunk beneath the stars, kissing a hot man next to a midnight highway. The breeze smelled of the ocean and strange trees, and everything felt so new.

She heard Gabriel flick the cigarette away, and then both his hands were framing her face, tipping her head to open her up for him. She did.

When she slid her arms around his waist, her thumb found the edge of his shirt, and she slipped beneath it, pressing her hand to the searing heat of his back. He inhaled sharply, and the power of that spiked through her veins. She slid her hand higher, reveling in the curve of his spine under her fingers.

He turned her body, and Hannah let herself be eased toward the side of the restaurant. If she'd seen Gabriel smoking out here, then people could see them kissing. She didn't want to be seen. She wanted darkness. Eyes closed. Lights off. Neither of them looking, just feeling, touching, tasting.

His mouth left hers and moved to her neck. Hannah gasped. She panted. Gravel scuffed under her feet. She felt the wall of the restaurant against her back. She arched her neck, and Gabriel made a deep noise of approval as her fingernails dug into his back to pull him closer.

"Oh, God," she whispered when his teeth scraped the sensitive skin beneath her ear.

There were a hundred reasons not to do this, but there always were. Sex wasn't supposed to be logical, and God, she'd missed the desperate, clawing need of doing this the wrong way. The right way. The only way worth doing.

She dropped her jacket in the dirt, and then his hands were on her just the way she'd wanted, sliding beneath her top, his fingers rough and rasping on her skin.

Hannah reached for the button of his jeans, fingers fumbling between the denim and the heat of his body. He cursed against her neck. Shook his head. But instead of saying no, he growled, "My place."

She nodded and grabbed her jacket, and he wrapped his hand in hers to lead the way along a dark path that circled the roadhouse. A small, high window cast a little glow and a lot of kitchen noise as they hurried toward a porch light twenty feet away.

He opened the door and, as if he'd read her mind, didn't bother hitting any light switches. They made it about two feet in before she was against the wall again. He dragged her top up and all the way over her head. She helped him tug his off too. In the dimness of the moonlight, she saw his wallet, heard the crinkle of a condom wrapper. She pulled his mouth back to hers, then struggled to strip out of her tight jeans.

Afraid that he might be slow or gentle or something else she didn't need, Hannah wrapped one leg around his hip and dug her nails into the back of his neck. "Yes," she growled as he stroked over her, and then he was inside her, hard and deep as she hissed in satisfaction.

Neither spoke after that. Their mouths were too busy. Their hands. Their bodies.

Within minutes, they were on the floor, and how long had it been since Hannah couldn't even make it to a couch? Ten years? Twenty?

She felt the marks she'd left on his skin, and she didn't care. There had been a spark between them since that first meeting, but tonight it was something frantic and dark. She closed her eyes and let herself feel every second of it. The climax hit her fast and hard, almost before she was ready, as if her body were trying desperately to escape her mind and its endless worries.

She let herself go. Let herself feel nothing but pleasure.

Afterward, Gabriel panted above her, his sweat-slick forehead pressed to hers, their rapid breaths tangling together. "Damn," he rasped.

She huffed out a laugh. "Just what I was thinking."

"I thought we were too old for this."

She curved her hand around the nape of his neck and eased him down for a sweet kiss. "We are. Your knees might never be the same."

"True. But worth it."

She kissed him one last time before letting him go. He rose, and a light came on somewhere as she grabbed her panties and jeans and tugged them back on. Laughing quietly, she shook her head as she wiggled her jeans up her thighs. God, she felt so much better. Maybe this midlife crisis thing wasn't so bad after all.

He stepped back into the hall, and she watched his silhouette button his fly. "I'm sorry." His voice rumbled through her, and she shivered. "I have to get back."

"I know. It's fine."

"Stay," he said. "I'll be back in an hour or two."

Hannah sighed. She wanted to. Wanted to grab a beer from his fridge and stretch out on his couch and wait for another round. "I can't."

"My bed is comfortable, and I make a damned good chorizo hash. Stay."

She shook her head and sighed again, letting him hear her disappointment. "I really can't. It's just . . . too complicated."

He watched her for a long moment, then offered a hand to help her to her feet. "All right." He pressed a kiss to her forehead, her nose, her mouth. "I've gotta run. Take your time."

He grabbed his shirt, and then he was walking out, his boots crunching on the gravel, the taste of him still on her mouth.

She stood against his wall and wondered if she should change her mind and stay. She'd only be here for a couple more days, surely. And after a few nights back in Coswell, Iowa, lying alone in her childhood bedroom, she would regret not getting a little more of Gabriel Cabrillo.

Her life felt as fragile as cracked glass right now. There might be relief in throwing caution to the wind and breaking it wide open just to get it over with. Jump right into chaos and risk and damn the consequences.

But no. The sex had been enough risk for now. She couldn't add emotion and romance to the mix.

She got dressed and walked away from Gabriel's bed and the roadhouse and back to all the shit waiting for her at the cabin. But she also walked back to the fire, the quiet, and her own company. It wasn't the worst choice she'd ever made.

CHAPTER 15

She fell asleep in a T-shirt and underwear like a normal human, and that was a damn good thing, because someone was pounding on her door when she woke up. Hannah sat straight up, bleated a quick "What?" in confusion, and then stared at the door as her heart did its best to tear its way out of her chest.

"What?" she asked again more loudly, but it was still just a croak.

The knocking came again, slightly less booming now that she was awake and not filtering the sound through a dream. Light trickled in from the opposite window, and judging from the watery grayness, she'd woken to another cloudy morning.

Still blinking, Hannah jumped from bed, tugged on a pair of yoga pants, and opened the door.

She was met by the irritated face of a sullen teenage girl.

"Hi," Hannah said, surprised to see the girl who'd checked her in. Somewhere between jumping from bed and opening the door, she'd decided it was the old groundskeeper coming to confess another memory.

The girl raised her chin in greeting. "Somebody called the inn looking for you, and Tucker wanted me to let you know."

"Someone called?" She felt a sharp spark of alarm for her mom. "Who?"

The girl looked down at the palm of her hand where she'd scrawled a name in black ink. "Jeff Wessing. He said he sent an email and wants you to call when you can."

"Oh. Okay. Thank you."

The girl was rolling her eyes as she turned away, but Hannah was already closing her door and didn't give a damn. She grabbed her laptop and logged in, her mind racing with possibilities. Was something wrong? Was he okay?

A glance at the corner of the screen revealed it was only eight in the morning, but that meant it was ten in Chicago, and when the mail screen popped open, she saw that he'd already sent two emails.

She felt a stab of guilt as she remembered what she'd done last night and grimaced with relief that she hadn't stayed at Gabriel's. What if the hotel had passed on the message that her bed wasn't slept in?

So she'd made a good decision. She'd now racked up several in a row and felt damn proud.

Hannah opened the first email. Hey, I found more information. Can you call me this morning?

He'd sent it at 5:00 a.m., 7:00 his time. The second email he'd sent two hours later. At work now. Give me a call. I think this is important.

She wrote back immediately. Sorry, I just woke up. What's going on? Is everything ok? Do you have an app for video calls? You can just use my email address.

She'd only had time to pee and wash her hands before her computer made that chirping alert. Hannah glanced in the mirror to be sure she didn't have any visible hickeys—that would just be rude—then bounded back to the bed and answered the call.

And suddenly Jeff was right there. For the first time in months. That pair of worry lines between his brows. The jaw he only bothered shaving every third day. His nose too big on the screen but just fine in person.

"Hi," she said, smoothing down her bedhead. Hopefully he couldn't see the guilt on her face. It was worthless anyway. No doubt he'd been dating for months now.

"Hey!" he responded. "Sorry if someone from the inn woke you. I was going a little stir-crazy sitting on this information, and I started to wonder if you'd already checked out or . . ."

"Or you were being super single-minded again?" she asked.

He smiled that familiar sheepish smile. "Was I? Okay, probably I was. But from here it all seemed a little dire."

"It's fine. I probably didn't need a full nine hours of sleep. But why dire?"

"Well . . . I sent out some feelers last night, and I woke up to a note from a colleague at UC Berkeley who does some work with local history. A lot of people in that area wrote memoirs about their exploits during the '60s and '70s. They all thought they were on a unique adventure, you know? But the truth is most of the memoirs read pretty much the same. Lots of drugs and free love with no consequences, that sort of thing."

"Let me guess. They're all men?"

Jeff laughed, leaning too close to the camera so his smile filled her screen. "You got it. How would you even know if you'd knocked someone up when you're all on the road and constantly moving?"

"Bastards," she said, an old joke between them, and his smile softened before fading altogether. She cleared her throat. "I guess maybe it's a miracle my dad stuck around. Or she did."

"Well, that's the thing . . ."

"What?"

"I think she might have stuck around for other reasons."

Hannah made a hurry-up gesture. "What other reasons?"

Jeff ran a hand over his face, the stubble rasping against his fingers in a way that made her throat a little tight. He took a deep breath. "I think maybe your grandfather was running a cult."

"A *what?*"

"A cult."

"Like Charles Manson?" Her voice rose a little too high. "Jim Jones?"

"Not on that level, of course. But there were lots of little . . . bubbles of personality back then. And if you find lost people and give them drugs and new ideas . . . it's not so hard to manipulate them."

Hannah had no idea what to think. She shook her head hard. "You're saying he was giving them *drugs?*"

"No, that was just an example. One of the memoirs mentioned a couple of communes in Big Sur, plus a place called Jacob's Rock. Hold on, I'll quote it." He lifted a paper. "'Jacob's Rock, run by a crazy old preacher with a wife and two concubines. They fed us well, but we moved on after two days.'"

"Holy shit," she breathed. "Two *concubines?*"

"Yeah."

"But that doesn't . . . that doesn't mean it was a cult, does it?"

Jeff leaned back in his chair, his face soft with sympathy. "I suppose not. But we're talking about vulnerable young people and an evangelical preacher who could apparently talk them into accepting a little old-fashioned polygamy."

"But . . . Good God. Is that all this guy said?"

"I'm afraid so. Frankly, he didn't even seem that shocked. We have no idea how many people were running places like that. You've only heard of the big ones, and those were because innocent people died. But there was a huge commune of Christians in Tennessee that practiced polygamy without much trouble. Thousands of them. The commune is still there."

"*Really?*"

"Yep. So a small group that didn't make much fuss before it faded into oblivion . . ." She watched him raise a shoulder; then her eyes drifted to the office behind him. The stacks of books and pictures of his favorite historic sites. How many times had she been in that office with him? A hundred? A thousand? Last night felt strangely far away now.

She cleared her throat. "And my father?" she asked, hating to even let the words out of her mouth.

"I don't know. Oftentimes it's only the leader who gets to live with special rules."

"But . . ." She closed her eyes. "But maybe his son too."

"I'm looking into it," he promised. "But it's just as likely it was a friendship or an affair."

"God," she groaned. "I can't picture any of this. You knew my dad! This is crazy. He was . . . he was boring. Steady."

"I know. And regardless of what happened in Big Sur, that's still who he was, Hannah. He was your dad. A deacon at his church. A member of the Kiwanis Club."

"And a guy with a harem."

"Come on. I'm sure that's not how it was."

She looked through the window that faced her fire pit, but all she could see were the dark boughs of the redwoods blocking out the sky. "I thought this was a happy place."

"Maybe it was. Jacob Smith could have just been an old guy who tried to fit free love into his idea of Jesus."

He was only saying what she'd been trying to convince herself of for the past few days. But it didn't seem quite as possible anymore. "I think I need some coffee," she murmured.

"You do. You look tired."

She blushed and smoothed her hair down. "I'm sure."

"I just meant you look like I rudely woke you up."

"You did!"

"Sorry. And sorry to be the bearer of weird news."

"Don't apologize. You didn't have to help with any of this. And . . ." She looked up at the ceiling, hoping to gather her thoughts, but she didn't spot anything except one cobweb in the rafters. "I'm sorry we couldn't just talk out all that other stuff."

"Maybe when this is over," he suggested.

"Yeah. That's a good idea. We'll figure it out, okay?"

"That'd be good. I can't really afford the legal fees."

She felt a stab of bitterness that it was all about money, but she shoved that down beneath her feelings of gratitude and hid it there.

"Watch your email," he said. "I'll be in touch if I find out more. And I'll try not to sic the inn on you again."

"It's all right. I know historical research is sometimes an emergency to you."

He winked and signed off with a smile, and that was the image of him frozen on her computer for a few seconds. Amused at one of her jokes. Easy and happy. She hadn't seen that for so long, not during the whole last year of their marriage. Mostly because she'd been grumpy and starting fights. Or just avoiding him.

Hannah had come here looking for a way to blame that on her real mother, really. Validate that it was her genetics and not Hannah's own shortcomings. It had been a relief to imagine her mother as a free spirit who couldn't be held down by love and commitment. But what if it had nothing to do with a free spirit?

"Then that would really suck," she said to the empty cabin.

She could pack up now and leave these sticky questions behind without ever finding the real answers. She could blame her faults on genetics or fraud or all the lies her family had told and be satisfied with that. The perfect defense.

Or she could stay and find out the truth.

Her email dinged like she'd gotten a quiz question right. Damn it.

She didn't recognize the name, but she clicked on the email and immediately realized it was from the daycare woman next door.

My mother-in-law is coming down today if you
want to stop in! She should be here by ten, and
she loves to gossip. Come on over!

Okay, the universe was obviously telling her to stay. So she'd stay.
Even if it entailed braving the halls of toddler hell.

She meant to go straight to breakfast, but instead Hannah found
herself taking the trail that veered toward the meadow.

Tucking her hands into her pockets to keep them warm, she looked
out over the grass. Condensation had deepened the grass to dark, wet
green, so the meadow didn't seem quite so light and magical. Maybe
the garden hadn't been tended by peaceful hippie girls. Maybe they'd
been near servants, bent over in the mud and wet to feed the men of
the cult.

Hannah turned away and trudged toward the inn. She watched
for Joe as she walked, rehearsing the questions she'd pepper him with if
she found him. He'd clearly left out some very important details during
their conversation. Would he call it a cult if she pressed him? He obviously had negative feelings about the place.

In the end, the questions she practiced didn't matter. Joe didn't
appear on her walk, and when she got to the inn, Hannah saw the shed
locked up tight. He could be off today. Nobody worked seven days a
week.

Disappointed, she went inside and slipped quietly into a chair
at the far end of the table. Two new couples were at breakfast today.
Hannah offered the barest smile she could manage, and they all smiled
back and left her to her breakfast.

Tucker didn't make an appearance either. Instead, a young, heavyset
woman Hannah had never seen popped in and out of the room and
laid dishes on the sideboard. Hannah served herself and ate enough to
silence the gnawing worry in her gut.

Both of the couples were quiet in that way people were after many years of marriage. Hannah had never been sure if it was contentment or boredom. Maybe a mixture of both. Whatever it was, it held no appeal for her.

She escaped as quickly as she could and walked toward the river, listening for the sound of Joe's vehicle the whole way. But all she heard was water and birdsong as she moved along the trail and edged around the daycare fence. She'd assumed it was for privacy, but now she saw that it was meant to keep the kids safe. Safe from the river and from the endless march of the woods going up and up into the hills.

Kids could disappear here. She wondered if they ever did. Maybe she'd had more sisters. Or brothers. Maybe some of the kids had never made it out.

Hannah shook her head as she rounded the fence and stepped onto the dirt road. She was getting dark and maudlin, imagining her past as something sinister when it was just sad.

This time when she rang Jenny's doorbell, she was ready for the squeals from inside. She braced herself and pasted on a smile.

"Hannah!" Jenny said as she opened the door, same braid over her shoulder, same baby attached to her hip. Hannah assumed it was the same baby, at any rate. It was white and plump and bald. Other than that, who could tell?

"These kids must give you quite a workout," she said.

"They definitely keep me moving all day. Come in! Mom's in the kitchen."

"Thank you so much for the invitation."

"It's no problem. The more the merrier. Plus, I might get some good new gossip."

Hannah tried not to wince. These women were being generous and had no idea how serious this was to her. And hell, if it was anyone else's family, Hannah would be just as invested in the entertainment of it. A secret baby? Sex with hippies? A possible cult? It was delicious.

Speaking of delicious, she smelled baking cookies before she even got to the kitchen. The shy kid peeked around the doorway, then turned and raced away when Hannah tried a smile.

This was all reminding her of Rachel's home, populated with nurturing women and so many kids. Her nieces and nephews and various neighborhood children, because why not? The more the merrier!

She stiffened her spine and tried not to feel inferior. She wasn't like them. And that was fine.

It was *fine*.

"Did you wash your hands?" she heard a woman asking just before she stepped through the door.

The little boy who'd stalked Hannah the last time nodded solemnly up at an older lady who was wiping a bowl with a dishcloth.

"Good boy," the woman said. "The cookies will be ready in ten minutes."

He nodded again, then raced away into another room. The woman, whose silver hair was cropped close to her head, reached to put the bowl away on an open shelf when she noticed Hannah.

"Hello! You must be Hannah. I'm Ruth Schwartz." She slid the bowl into place and turned to grasp Hannah's hand. Her fingers were calloused, as if she spent a lot of time working outdoors. Hannah felt immediately more comfortable.

"Hannah Smith," she said. "Nice to meet you."

"Let's grab a cup of tea and sit down for a chat."

Tea wasn't normally her thing, but it sounded perfect today. Cozy, comforting, gentle. Ruth poured water from a pot into three mugs and dropped tea bags into each.

"I'll just hover," Jenny said, rocking back and forth as the baby in her arms began to lose its battle with sleep.

Ruth set two of the mugs on the kitchen table, and Hannah took a seat. "So your family used to live *over there?*" Eyebrows raised, she tipped her head slowly toward the Riverfall property.

"They did. A long time ago. Until 1972."

"Well, we didn't buy this house until '79, but there were still stories, let me tell you." She leaned closer, dipping the tea bag slowly up and down in the steaming water. "When we first moved here, my husband traveled quite a bit, so I spent a lot of nights alone. And it was so creepy. I mean, it was creepy enough just being out in the middle of nowhere alone, but we'd heard stories about the scary old man next door."

"He still lived there?" she asked in shock.

"No, he was long gone. Somebody was trying to make it take off as a guesthouse, but he didn't have money to fix the place up. So everything was normal and fine, but I heard rumors. You know?"

"Rumors about what?"

Ruth glanced at Jenny, but Jenny just shrugged.

"Were they your family?" Ruth asked. "I don't want to be disrespectful."

"Please don't worry about that. I'm trying to figure out the truth. You won't hurt my feelings."

Jenny brought a plate over for the tea bags and offered honey. Hannah scooped a large teaspoon into her mug and waited.

"Okay." Ruth's voice dropped. "I heard he loved to preach about hell and damnation. He had a big tent and invited everyone, but the services were so dark that people around here stopped going. But the young people who lived there . . . they'd take drugs and moan and wail through the sermons. And then . . ."

Jenny had stopped rocking, and Ruth's voice dropped even more as Hannah leaned closer. "Then he started saying God was speaking to him."

Despite the warm cup in her hands, Hannah shivered.

Ruth nodded as if she'd seen. "Like, *really* speaking to him. People told me the stories like they were funny, but I didn't think they were funny when I was here alone at night. Some man just a stone's throw away had been calling up God and the devil, and even though I didn't believe, I didn't like it."

Hannah didn't like it either. "I get it."

"And then one day he just disappeared. No word to anyone around here. He and his people were just gone, and someone else owned the place. But where did he go?"

"You don't know?"

"No one knows. I'd hear animals scratching around at night and think, what if he's out living in the woods somewhere?"

Hannah grimaced. "Oh, God."

"I mean, he wasn't, obviously. But late night isn't the most rational time of the day. My imagination ran wild. But then I had the kids, and I got too tired and busy for ghost stories."

The oven timer dinged, and Ruth got up to check the cookies. Jenny left to put the baby down for its nap, and Hannah was alone with her tea. She closed her eyes and sipped it, but the spicy sweetness couldn't cut the bitterness on her tongue.

Suddenly, her idyllic childhood seemed idyllic again. If she'd been taken away from her roots, maybe it had been for a damn good reason. Instead of a free, beautiful hippie, maybe her mother had been more like Squeaky Fromme and the other Manson girls. Screaming about an apocalyptic future. Wild-eyed with madness. Maybe Hannah had inherited *that*.

The toddlers ran in, looking for cookies, but Ruth shooed them out so they wouldn't be tempted near the hot metal sheet. Hannah took another long sip of her tea and looked up to find that her tiny stalker hadn't been chased far enough away. He stood in the doorway, staring at her. Then he barked.

Hannah blinked.

He barked again, then put the ragged stuffed animal he was carrying—a roadkill raccoon, maybe? between his teeth before he dropped to all fours. Hannah watched in confused horror as he crawled to her feet and dropped the matted animal on her shoes. He barked again. "Ruff, ruff!"

"He wants you to throw it!" Ruth said with much more cheer than Hannah was feeling.

"Like . . . he wants to play fetch?"

"Yep."

"Isn't that a little demeaning?"

"It's pretending. It's good for his brain."

Hannah nodded, but she just stared at the boy until he barked again, prompting her to reach for the toy. She picked the furry thing up between two fingers and tossed it into the next room.

He took off so fast that she jumped in alarm. And sure enough, he retrieved the toy with his teeth and brought it back to her.

Hannah was almost sure this qualified as child abuse, but she tossed the animal again. And again. As if he were a dog.

Ten tosses later, he seemed to wear himself out and came to sit at her feet and rest his head against her legs. Hannah patted his hair. He panted and snuggled closer, so she stroked his soft brown hair and murmured, "Good doggie."

Maybe she wasn't so bad with kids after all. Or maybe she just needed a dog. Whatever the reason, she didn't really mind him wrapping his little arms around her legs and settling in. She didn't even mind when Ruth brought him a cookie and he rested it on her jeans, though she knew the warm chocolate chips would leave stains. Instead of extricating herself, she just ate her own cookie and petted his head.

Ruth sat back down and dropped her voice to a whisper. "There were rumors he married one of those young girls. Wanted to start his own Eden." Hannah remembered her mother's strange words. *We left the garden.* Is that what she'd meant? The Garden of Eden?

"He was already married," Hannah clarified.

Ruth shrugged. "Maybe it's just a rumor, then."

No, it wasn't just a rumor. It was a rumor based on him taking concubines. Jesus, this was all insane.

Jenny returned without the baby and grabbed a cookie.

"I hope I didn't say too much," Ruth said.

"Nonsense. I'm so grateful to you for telling me. I can't seem to find many people around here who saw this stuff firsthand. Did all of his followers leave Big Sur?"

"As far as I know. I mean, none of them were from around here."

"I don't suppose either of you recognize the name Maria Diaz?"

"No," Jenny said. "I'm sorry."

But Ruth frowned. "Maria Diaz? I think that was Maria Frank's name! Before she remarried!"

Hannah sat up straight. "Really? You know her?"

Ruth nodded. "Does she still run the bakery, Jenny?"

"As far as I know."

"Yes!" Ruth said, lighting up with excitement. "She runs a bakery out of her house! She used to make rolls and bread for most of the restaurants around here, but I think she's slowed down to only supplying one or two. She makes the most amazing herb rolls with herbs from her own garden. They're the best."

"Was she part of this church?"

"Maria?" Ruth gasped. "Absolutely not. I can't even imagine it."

"Do you think she might talk to me? I think she may have known my mother. If you have her address . . ."

"I don't know the address, but I'll draw you a map. I'm sure she'd be happy to help. And grab some of those rolls while you're there. In fact, I think I'll stop by on my way north tonight and grab some myself."

Hannah nodded, but the rest of the chatter flowed right through her. This was it. If this Maria hadn't been part of Jacob's Rock, she had at least been called in whenever women gave birth. She'd known the women. She'd seen whatever tide of darkness had eventually swallowed them. She'd known Rain and Dorothy.

Hannah reached down to pet the little boy's head as she swallowed hard against the gritty dryness suddenly coating her mouth. Maria was the key. An eyewitness to the "women's business" part of Jacob's Rock.

She'd finally have the truth whether she wanted it or not.

CHAPTER 16

The little house was the opposite of the inn. The opposite of Jacob's Rock. As if the owner had decided she could bear no more trees and darkness and shade in her life.

Far north of the tourist haunts of Big Sur, the house sat above the road in a rocky meadow that angled down past the highway until it ended in stark cliffs. It was tiny. Just a cinderblock square with a faded, hand-painted sign that read **MARIA'S BAKERY**, but it was surrounded by tufts of green and gold plants. An herb garden instead of a lawn.

Did Maria live here alone, a hundred yards above the highway, watching the world and the waves from her kitchen window? Was Jacob's Rock one of the things that had driven her here? Or had the bright peace of this spot washed away all that darkness? What if she barely remembered it at all?

Hannah got out of her car and climbed a long path that wound through the miniature garden toward the front door. The entry had an air of disuse about it; a few pebbles littered the steps, and a spider had woven an elaborate web on the porch light. The driveway had led around the side of the house, and she imagined that was the entrance that Maria used. This door was probably rarely opened. There were no neighbors to come knocking for an afternoon chat.

But Hannah knocked.

She hadn't realized there'd been singing until it stopped. A soft, low sound from inside the house that had blended into the distant surf. Hannah clutched her purse and waited.

The door stayed closed for so long that Hannah finally decided it wouldn't be opened. If Maria was inside, she didn't want to talk. Maybe it was wise to be afraid of strangers off a highway like this. Or maybe she'd heard Hannah was poking around in the ashes of the past and wanted to avoid her.

Given any other circumstance, she'd respect the woman's obvious desire for solitude. Hannah understood that need deep in her bones. But this was the end of her journey in Big Sur. She might move on to trying to find her mother elsewhere, but Rain wasn't here. That much was clear.

She knocked again, a faint panic beginning to fizz through her veins. What if Maria wouldn't talk to her? Hannah couldn't just move on knowing the answers were here. But what else could she do? Break in and demand a conversation?

Just as she'd decided to give up and try knocking at the side door, the lock clicked. The knob turned.

She wasn't sure who she'd expected Maria Diaz to be, but it certainly wasn't this cherubic grandmother. She only came up to Hannah's shoulder, and her round face was free of wrinkles aside from the deep smile lines around her eyes. Her short wavy hair was generously shot through with silver. "Can I help you?" she asked.

"Mrs. Frank? I'm Hannah Smith."

At first it seemed as though the name meant nothing to her. She stared at Hannah, her head cocked, eyes steady. But then Maria dipped her chin and opened the door wider. "Come in, Hannah."

Hannah hesitated. "Do you know me?" she asked. Her voice sounded pleading and weak, but she didn't care. She needed to know.

Maria's smile was faint, but even that small acknowledgment creased her eyes into happy crescents. "I do. Though you look a little different from the last time I saw you."

"When I was born?"

"Yes. You were strong. And loud."

"I still am. Loud, at least." Her throat closed, and she didn't want to frighten this woman with unexpected sobbing, so Hannah swallowed hard and stepped into the house. It was no surprise that the air was infused with the smell of baking bread, but it still settled over her like a warm embrace. The scent was the embodiment of comfort, and there were framed pictures of small children on every surface of the living room she stood in.

This woman had lied about something very important all those years ago, but Hannah couldn't summon an ounce of fear now. Naive, maybe, but surely Maria wasn't a threat. Hadn't ever been a threat.

"Would you like a cup of coffee? I'm afraid I don't have any treats to offer. My blood sugar . . . The doctor says my dessert days are over."

"No, I'm good, thank you. I just had a cookie, in fact. Another might be overkill."

"Please," Maria said, gesturing toward a delicate floral couch. Hannah wondered if it had once been covered with plastic to keep it safe from sticky hands.

"This is a beautiful place," she said as she took a seat.

"Thank you. It's getting too cold for me these days, but I can't seem to leave it." Maria settled herself in a chair and smoothed her simple brown skirt down.

Hannah wasn't sure where to start, so she withdrew the birth certificate from her purse and took her time unfolding it, trying to figure out what to say. After a dozen thumps of her heart, she still couldn't find the right words, so she held the paper out to Maria without comment.

Maria sighed. "I knew it was a mistake when I did it."

"Why did you sign it? What happened? I just . . . I just need to know."

Maria smoothed a finger over the names. First Hannah's. Then her father's. Then Dorothy's. "They asked me to sign it. Begged me, actually. They said it would be better for you, and I believed that. Your mother was gone. Your father loved you. And I knew Dorothy would love you too. I'm sorry if I was wrong."

"No. You weren't wrong. She did love me."

Maria's mouth went flat. "Has she passed?"

"No. My father died six years ago. My mother—Dorothy—has dementia. And I didn't know about any of this until a few days ago. The medical records . . . There was a discrepancy."

"I'm sorry," Maria said.

"Do you know where my mother went? My real mother?"

She was shaking her head before Hannah even finished the question. "The last time I saw her was at your delivery. A month later, they said she'd run away. I wasn't surprised, really."

"Why not?"

Maria pressed her lips tight together, her eyes darkening with sadness.

"I . . ." The syllable emerged as a sick croak, so Hannah cleared her throat and tried again. "Please. I know it wasn't a good place. Will you tell me what happened? What happened to all of them? No one else seems to know."

The stiffness in Maria's shoulders didn't promise much, so Hannah tried again. "I know I'm a stranger. You don't know anything about me. But I promise I'm not here to get you in trouble. I just need the truth, whatever it is. *Please.*"

Maria sighed and seemed to shrink even smaller. "Every child deserves to know where she comes from," she said, but then she crossed herself, as if even saying it was a curse. "Someone owes you that."

Hannah had to refrain from reaching out to the woman in gratitude. "Thank you."

"It wasn't a bad place at first," Maria said. "I tried out a few of the sermons. I was raised Catholic, but even I felt a little lost back then. The world was changing so fast. But I only attended a dozen times, if that. Your father was a good man, and his sermons were interesting, but I didn't like Jacob Smith's preaching."

"I've heard he was . . . harsh."

"He was indeed. And I didn't see any sign of the devil in Big Sur. It felt like fearmongering to me. Manipulation. Regardless, Jacob asked for my help, and I gave it. Your mother was almost ready to give birth to Rachel, and someone told them I used to assist my mother with women."

Her mouth tipped up in a faint smile. "There weren't so many laws then, or at least no one around to see they were followed. My mother was a midwife for women who needed help. I learned a little from her. Nowadays I'd be in prison, of course. No formal training. No license."

"So you delivered Rachel and Becky?"

"I did. Dorothy was healthy. Things seemed fine. But then she didn't get pregnant again."

"Oh. Was that a big deal?"

Maria's mouth twisted. "It was. Jacob had started preaching a new kind of Christianity. Telling people they should live like the holy men of the Bible. Be fruitful and multiply. Populate the earth with God-fearing Christians."

That wasn't as much of a shock to Hannah as it might have been when she'd first started this quest. "I heard he'd taken a, um, concubine."

"He did that. But then he married her. And then another. Not legally, of course, but there were ceremonies."

"He married two more girls? What did his wife think?"

"To be honest, I think she liked being in charge of these new wives. Maybe it kept Jacob out of her bed too."

Hannah winced, and the wince turned into a grimace as she squeezed her eyes shut. "And my father?"

"Your father disagreed with it, to be honest."

Her eyes popped open. "Oh, thank God."

"I saw the tension when I was over there delivering babies. There were a few other married couples, part of the flock, and someone was always pregnant. Your father seemed *uncomfortable*. Unhappy. But then his daddy turned him."

"Turned him how?"

"Jacob said he'd had a vision from God that Rain was ready to marry and she was meant for Peter. Just like in the Bible when Abraham's wife could bear no children. Peter had to marry to keep the flock growing. It was his duty to God."

"And my father bought that?"

Maria shook her head. "I don't know. But Jacob said he'd give Rain to one of the other men, and maybe Peter thought he'd at least be a kind husband. He was."

"But what about Dorothy? And Rain? They went along with this?"

"I'm not sure they were given a choice. Jacob moved Rain up to the big house, and he conducted the marriage ceremony, and Rain moved into a room with Peter and Dorothy."

"Jesus! They all lived *together*?"

"There wasn't much space. There were lots of children and only so many beds."

Hannah's mind reeled. Her parents, her Midwestern, conservative, modest parents had moved another woman into their bedroom. Another *wife*. "This is insane," she whispered.

"I know."

"You don't understand. I grew up in Iowa. In a small town. My parents were . . . they were just so average. Kind. Quiet. Never any trouble."

Maria reached out to squeeze her hand. "If you live with a madman long enough, I guess anything starts to sound sane. He had them so mixed up they didn't know right from wrong."

She squeezed Maria's hand so hard she made herself let go to stop from hurting the older woman. "Well, I guess I know what happened next."

"Yes. Nine months later, you were born."

"My God." She clasped her hands together to pretend they weren't shaking. "I thought I was a love child. I thought I was coming here to find a wild, sweet story."

"I'm sure Rain loved you."

"But she left."

"She was probably scared. Confused."

"Do you know where she went?"

"No. I'm sorry. I came by a month later to check on one of the pregnant women, and Peter said she'd run off."

"Just like that."

"Hannah," Maria said softly. "She didn't run away to leave you. I'm sure of that. She was living in a harsh, strange situation, and she was too young to deal with any of that. Especially with all those hormones shaking through her body. She got scared and she ran. That's all."

"How old was she?"

"She was eighteen when you were born."

The blood left Hannah's head in one fell swoop. One minute she was seeing and hearing, and the next her ears were full of static, her vision a wash of red, the top of her head buzzing, angry at the lack of oxygen. "When I was born?" she whispered.

"Seventeen when they married."

Her father . . . her married, adult father had moved a teenager into his house. His room. His *bed*. He'd had sex with a damaged teenage girl in the same room with his wife.

Rain had been a lost child. She must have been. Perhaps discarded by one family, then manipulated and dominated by another. Rain hadn't been a free spirit at all. She'd been abused.

"You've got to understand," Maria said. "All those girls were young. The boys too. Oh, they had beards and drugs and guitars, but they were seventeen, eighteen, nineteen. Living on the streets. Finding their way. Seventeen was a lot older than most of the girls who hitchhiked their way through here."

"But my *father*. How could he have done that?"

"He thought it was right. Reading about all those men in the Bible with wives and handmaidens . . . He let himself believe it. And she was a pretty girl. Sweet. Alone. I'm sure he thought she was better off with him than going back to the streets of San Francisco."

"Well, she didn't think that, obviously. She left him. Left me."

"She did."

"Good," Hannah spat. "Good for her. She deserved better than that. She deserved a life of being a lover and a friend and a *person*, and not some young whore he could order into his bed!"

"Hannah." Maria took her hand again, and this time Hannah held tight.

"I can't believe my father did that. How could he have . . . ?"

But how could *Hannah*? She'd so desperately wanted to be *more* than she'd thought she was that she'd been excited by the thought of her father falling in love with another woman. Of betraying Dorothy in some fantastically romantic way just so Hannah could know that her origins were more magical than the cornfields of Iowa.

But Dorothy hadn't only been cheated on. She'd been forced to witness it. To watch. To sanction. One day she'd had a marriage and two beautiful daughters, and the next she'd been forced to share her love and pretend it was God's will.

Maria shifted to the couch, sitting beside Hannah. "Shhhh," she murmured, her hand rubbing warm circles into Hannah's back.

Hannah was crying and she couldn't stop. She couldn't imagine being seventeen and surrounded by grown men telling her what the rest of her life would be.

Poor Rain. No wonder she hadn't wanted Hannah. A baby born as a reminder of something awful.

"I'm sorry," Maria said. "I shouldn't have told you."

"No." She sucked in a deep breath and immediately lost it to a sob. "No. I . . . I needed to know."

"They made mistakes. All of them. But they thought they were doing it for the glory of God."

"Or the glory of a madman!"

"Your father had a good heart. I promise. Even through all of this."

She shook her head, but she couldn't reconcile her denial with the man she'd loved. He'd always been her rock, through all those years of her fighting with her mother, fighting with everyone. He'd always been calm and steady and good.

And Dorothy had loved her too, in her own quiet way. She'd loved Hannah even though just looking at this other woman's child must have hurt.

She finally managed to take a breath that didn't end in a sob. "And the birth certificate?"

"Once your mother was gone for a month, they convinced me she wasn't coming back. And that you needed your family. It would be simpler, they said. No questions. No complications. Dorothy meant to raise you, and she was a great mom, and I let myself be talked into it. But I shouldn't have. I'm sorry."

For some reason, her apology made Hannah cry again. Maybe because she sounded as if she meant it, and Hannah just wanted someone to feel bad about what had happened to her. She shook her head and wrapped her arms around Maria. "You don't have to be sorry."

"I do. She might have come back."

Hannah made herself let the poor woman go. "But she didn't."

"No. Not as far as I know. It wasn't long after I signed your birth certificate that your family left. Your father had finally seen that it was all so wrong. I'm not sure what set him off, but he took all of you and walked away. Others started leaving then too."

"Really? That's good, right?"

"Yes. Your father's defection seemed to fracture Jacob's control of his flock. By September, only a few were left. His wife and two of his young women, one of whom had had a son. One young man remained too, but his brain was pretty burned out on LSD. That was it."

"Where did they go?"

"I have no idea. South, I heard. Could have been Los Angeles. Or the desert. That's all I know."

Hannah nodded. "Did you know Rain's name? Her last name?"

"No. I'm sorry."

"I can't imagine how I'd ever find her. Her real name couldn't have been Rain."

Maria didn't answer, but she didn't need to. This was the end of it. Hannah didn't get a prize of a new mother or a new family, but she had some sort of explanation, albeit a damned heartbreaking one.

"Thank you so much for telling me the truth," she said. "And don't worry. I won't tell anyone else about your role. You did what you thought was best."

"Perhaps everyone did," Maria said.

But that wasn't true. If her grandfather had been a madman, her father hadn't done his best. He should've known better. Should have *done* better.

"I'd never have gotten answers without you. I can't thank you enough. But I'll let you get back to your day." Hannah stood. "You're a bit of a legend around here. I heard your herb rolls are amazing."

Maria smiled and rose easily to her feet despite her age. "Let me get some for you."

"Oh, I didn't mean—"

"Not another word. The least I can do is offer you a bit of bread. Just give me a moment." She bustled into a kitchen that was visible through a narrow doorway. Hannah let her eyes wander, allowing the end of her journey sink in. But it wouldn't. Already her mind was wondering about those DNA tests. Even if she didn't have a name, she might be able to make a connection to a family. She might eventually even find her mother. But would Rain want to remember such an awful time of her life? Would Hannah be hurting her if she reappeared?

The framed pictures of children that decorated the room didn't help Hannah's nerves any. They all looked so happy. So loved and wanted. Laughing, sleeping, smiling for the camera. Each one of them belonged exactly where they were.

Hannah wandered toward a shelf, rubbing her neck in a hopeless effort to loosen the tension there. When her eye first fell on a small picture in the center of the shelf, Hannah thought the man only reminded her of someone. His arms were slung around two women who shared his black hair and brown eyes, though his face was leaner. And his temples didn't have nearly as much silver as they did now.

Her eyelids fluttered a little in shock. Her heart fluttered a lot. She let her gaze fly over the other pictures, but he wasn't in any of them. She moved to the wall next to the door and looked over those photos. And there he was again. Holding a little girl wearing a princess T-shirt and a tiara, a birthday cake on the table near them.

"I added a few jalapeño rolls as well," Maria said as she returned with a white paper bag. She stood beside Hannah and followed her eyes to the picture. "Gabriel was right to send you here. I told him I couldn't talk to you, but I was being a coward. He made the right choice."

Hannah made herself nod. Yes. Sure. Everything was fine.

"Sometimes the child knows better than the mother. Tell him I'm not angry."

"I will," she murmured. "Of course."

Maria pressed the bag into Hannah's hands. *"Vaya con Dios, querida."*

"Thank you," Hannah said automatically.

She felt Maria hug her again, and she must have hugged back, but Hannah was in too much shock to know what she was doing. She left the house, walked to her car, opened the door, got behind the wheel. But she didn't dare drive.

Maria was Gabriel's mother.

The night before, that strange look on his face when she'd shown him the birth certificate, that hadn't been confusion or irritation; it had been deceit.

Had he known more the whole time? Had he feigned ignorance about Jacob's Rock from their very first meeting to protect his mother?

Hannah had been relying on him. Leaning on him as a new friend willing to help, and he'd been preventing her from learning the truth.

And then last night. "Shit," she whispered. They'd had sex. *After* he knew she was looking for Maria. He'd asked her to stay at his place. Nearly insisted. Why? So he could keep an eye on her? So she would trust him and tell him more?

She touched her mouth. She'd slept with a liar.

"You're okay," she said aloud. And she was, wasn't she? She'd slept with plenty of liars in her lifetime. And hell, her own parents had lied to her about everything, and she'd survived it. Gabriel had lied, and that didn't mean he was dangerous. Everyone lied.

Except Jeff. He hadn't lied. He'd told the truth, and she'd believed him, and it had still been all wrong.

She needed to call Jeff. Tell him he'd been right about it being a cult. She needed to call Becky too. Tell her what had happened. What their family had run from. And surely Rachel must remember some of it. A new mother suddenly showing up in the family. A new sister. All of them living in a house with a cult leader.

Maybe Rachel had suppressed it. Or maybe her mind had decided the river and the garden were the only things worth remembering. But to be fair to Rachel, Hannah could only remember two things from early childhood: getting a cast for a broken arm and a vague, warm recollection of her kindergarten teacher that was likely bolstered by the class photo she still had.

That was it. The rest of it was a blank.

Finally steady enough to drive, she started the car and headed down the steep drive toward the highway. She turned right toward civilization and drove numbly up the coast, for once not caring about the blind curves and steep drop-offs.

The tourists standing at the side of the road to stare out at the ocean looked dumb to her now. Stupid. The world wasn't a beautiful place. That gorgeous landscape would kill you in just one day if you were left exposed. The cold, the current, the jagged rocks. This place wasn't meant to be inhabited. Nobody could thrive here.

When she reached the boundary of the first town, she breathed a sigh of relief despite that her phone came alive and began chiming with texts and messages. She ignored the alerts and drove through Carmel and into Monterey, following the signs toward the touristy area. It was past noon. She was hungry. All that other shit could wait.

She found a glitzy seafood restaurant at an oceanfront hotel and ordered paella and sourdough bread along with a glass of wine. A propane heater kept her warm as she glared at the dark blots of otters floating on the sea.

She wanted to be home now. Not in Iowa, but in Chicago. She wanted to have never left. If she'd stayed put, none of this would exist. She'd just be the same fucked-up Hannah she'd always been, instead of this new confused version who no longer even had a foundation to push off from.

She was flotsam now. Adrift. No mother. No father she recognized. Half sisters who would hate her for digging these stained skeletons up.

"Couldn't I have just been a hippie love child?" she asked her glass of wine.

What a naive little fairy tale she'd been weaving, pretending she could strip naked at the beach and know what her mother's life had been.

She downed the wine and picked up her phone.

There were the usual texts from Becky, working to keep the peace. Hannah ignored them and checked her phone messages. An old one from Jasmine. And one that had come today from a number at her previous employer.

Hannah blew out a long sigh, trying to keep her excitement in check. It could be anything. It could be nothing.

But it wasn't. It was a job offer.

She listened to the message, but she was too revved up to take in what her old boss was saying. She listened a second time and a third.

He wanted her back. Same salary. Same position. "I can't offer you a raise, but I hope keeping your settlement will help make that more palatable." His familiar wry humor made her smile. Just nostalgia, surely. She'd been burned out when she'd left. Relieved to get the hell out of Dodge.

Working the tax system on behalf of greedy billionaires had started feeling dirty. But why? If she didn't do it, someone else would. It was all legal. She'd never stepped outside the law. But the laws were shit.

And she was really, really good at working the system. Far better than she was at being a good daughter. A good wife.

She wanted to call and say yes right away. She could pack up her suitcase, buy a plane ticket, and be in Chicago by midnight. She could stay with Jasmine or rent a gorgeous hotel room overlooking the city lights. She could wake up and take a walk along the lake. Grab a hot coffee and a warm doughnut. She could have real sushi for lunch. With Jeff, maybe. They could talk about Jacob's Rock in person.

The paella and sourdough arrived just in time to save her from herself. The impulse to answer immediately faded as she sliced the tiny loaf of bread and spread butter into each slice until it melted.

She couldn't say yes today. Even she, flawed as she was, recognized that this was yet another impulse to run away. Her life was an ugly mess, and she wanted to turn her back on it. Instead of fleeing, she needed to take a little time to think even if she didn't want to.

Sliding over to her email app, she pulled up her old boss's contact and wrote a quick note to let him know she'd received his message. To be honest, I'm stunned and excited by the offer. But I'll be off the grid for another 24 hours. Ok if I call you tomorrow to discuss at length?

She checked flights to Chicago, but didn't purchase a ticket. Not yet.

After turning down a second glass of wine, she let herself savor the food. This was her last full day in California. The last full day of this part of her life. For today, she'd sit with what she'd learned. Tomorrow was time enough to decide about the rest of it.

So instead of breaking the news to her sisters, she sent Becky a meaningless reassurance. I'm doing well. Wrapping things up here. More later! Let me know how Mom is doing.

And just like that she suddenly missed her mother. Not Rain, but Dorothy, the woman who'd loved and raised her. The woman who'd accepted her husband's child and done her best.

They had never seen eye to eye, and even now Hannah had no idea if that was because of her birth or her genes or just because they'd clashed the same way that millions of mothers and daughters had clashed over thousands of years. Did it matter? Their relationship hadn't been perfect, but it had been exponentially better than it could have been under the circumstances.

And Hannah missed her. The way she'd worked crossword puzzles after the dinner dishes were done. The little frown of concentration between her eyes when she watched *Quincy* or *Matlock*. The soothing little clucks when she fussed over a sick daughter.

The school lunches she'd packed in elementary school, always on the same schedule: PB&J on Mondays and Wednesdays, bologna on Tuesdays and Thursdays, tuna on Fridays. Nothing fancy. No crusts cut off. No little notes included. Just a sandwich and an apple and a thermos of cheap juice. But those three lunches had been waiting on the counter without fail every day, whether her mother was already gone to volunteer at the church or whether she was sick with the flu. Three lunch boxes. Pink Barbie boxes for Rachel and Becky, a red Wonder Woman box for Hannah.

That was being a mother. The everyday work, even when she didn't understand her daughter's tempers or moods or music or makeup. Even as Hannah had disappointed her over and over again, Dorothy had never stopped loving her. Hannah had always had a place to go for Christmas or Thanksgiving, and maybe that was what had made it so easy to stay away. She'd always known she was welcome. Loved. Cared for. Her little rebellions had been nothing but tantrums.

She watched the otters playing, and by the time she finished lunch, she'd found the beauty in that harsh sea again.

Whatever Rain had found in Big Sur, it must have been better than what she'd run from. For a time. Perhaps she'd gotten what she'd needed from that place, from Peter Smith, from Hannah, and then she'd moved on to something better.

Hannah hoped that was true. If Rain was anything like her daughter, she'd screwed up plenty of times in her life, but hopefully she'd found herself eventually. Hopefully Hannah would too.

A set of stairs led from the hotel down to a beach trail, and Hannah walked along it for a few minutes until she found a bench that she could settle on to call Jeff.

"You were right," she said as soon as he answered. "It was definitely a cult."

"What did you find?" The question was sharp with worry.

"I tracked down the woman who assisted at my birth."

"She was part of the cult?"

"No, she just played midwife for them. She seemed like a very nice woman."

His pen tapped the desk. "She was willing to talk about it?"

"She was. She said Jacob Smith started preaching about end times and repopulating with true believers. He said God spoke to him and told him it was time to live biblically. He took two more wives."

"Wow."

"My father was hesitant to accept polygamy, apparently."

"Wait. You're not saying . . ." His voice trailed into uncertain silence.

"What?"

"Was Jacob Smith your father?"

"No. No. In order to convince my dad . . ." She sighed and told herself to just say it quickly. "Jacob gave my dad another wife. A young girl. She was . . . she was seventeen. That was my mother."

"Holy shit, Hannah. Are you sure?"

"I'm sure. He took another wife. And they had me."

"Wow. That's . . . Are you okay?"

This time, she didn't cry. She wanted to, but she didn't. "I'm freaking out a little bit, but I'm glad I know the truth. I think."

"I can't wrap my head around it," he said. "It must be almost impossible for you."

"Yeah. I can't understand how he did that to Dorothy. Or to Rain."

"Did you get her last name, at least? So you can try to find her?"

"No. Maria didn't know it. She said Rain ran away after I was born. She never came back."

"She was so young."

"I know. I don't blame her. It was a really fucked-up situation. More fucked-up than anything I even came near as a teenager."

"I'm sorry, Hannah. I'm really, really sorry."

She closed her eyes to hold back tears. She was done with crying. But she wished he were here or she were there. Wished he could put his arms around her, even if it was for the last time. "Thank you."

"So after your real mom ran off, they faked the birth certificate?"

"Yes. They convinced Maria it would be better for me. And I guess it was."

"Then what happened?"

"I guess my dad packed up his family and left. Thankfully. God knows what would have become of us if he'd stayed."

"I, uh . . . I may have an answer to that. I wanted to be absolutely sure before I said anything."

"What?" she demanded, but he still hesitated. His pen tapped faster. "Come on, Jeff. Just tell me. I can't live with more suspense."

"It's something from a Mexican newspaper, and I'm still checking on the translation."

"A *Mexican* paper? What are you talking about?"

The pen stopped. His chair squeaked. "In 1974 the body of a white man was found in the Sonora region of Mexico. He was found with three women, a man, and a small child. All of them dead."

"That could—" she started past the thick fear in her throat, but her throat wanted to seal itself up. She swallowed several times until the dread loosened its hold. "That could have been anyone." But Maria had said he was down to one male follower when he left. Three women. One child.

"They'd arrived a year earlier. They bought a ranch. He started a church. His name was Jacob."

"Jacob what?"

"He called himself Jacob Christo."

"And you think it was him?" She was whispering now, as if someone might hear about this terrible crime and report her. "My grandfather?"

"The age seems right. And the timing. The paper said they all drank poison."

Poison.

"The women were named as Frances, Violet, and Cora Christo. Do you recognize any of those names?"

"I don't. I'm not sure I would. But you think that's him? And you think he killed them all?"

"That I'm not sure of. They might have taken poison willingly. It's happened before."

Right. Jonestown. They'd mixed the poison with Kool-Aid and served it to the kids too. "Maria said after my father left, a lot of others left too. He was down to just a few people when he sold the land and disappeared."

"He lost control. And that's one thing men like him hate. It might have pushed him over the edge."

"That's . . . Well, I was going to say that's crazy, but I guess that's pretty obvious."

"Yeah. I'll keep looking. I'm not sure there will be anything more to find, but I'll try."

"Thank you, Jeff. Really. Thank you for all of this. I'm sorry again. About everything."

"I know you are."

She wasn't sure she should ask, but she was going to. Screw it. "I've got some business in Chicago. I'm thinking I'll fly in this week. Could we grab coffee or something? Drinks? It's fine if you're busy."

"No, just let me know. It'd be nice to see you."

"Okay, good. We could talk."

"Sure. Give me a heads-up when you're coming. I'll make sure my schedule is free."

She hung up and walked to her car so she wouldn't sit there staring at the ocean and thinking about Jeff. He was her ex-husband. Soon to be, at least. She'd slept with another man. They still had a divorce to settle. And she wasn't going to stare dreamily out at the sea and pine for this man she'd walked away from.

She could pine for him while driving, like a reasonable person. Anticipating that there might be a little more pining tonight, she stepped into a corner convenience store for a bottle of red.

Halfway back to Big Sur, she remembered that she'd meant to grab some takeout while she was in town so she wouldn't have to go to the roadhouse for dinner. She ignored her panicked impulse to turn around. She could go to dinner somewhere else. Or if she was feeling as antisocial as she felt right now, she could eat the rolls his mother had given her.

His mother.

"Good God," she whispered to herself for likely the fifth time that day.

Her grandfather was a murderer or as good as one, her father was a polygamist, and the man she'd started an affair with had been trying to keep her from the truth.

She was definitely buying a ticket out of here as soon as she got to her laptop. She'd lock herself in her cabin, pack her suitcase, have herb rolls and wine for dinner, then get the hell out of Big Sur first thing in the morning.

By the time she got back to the Riverfall, she told herself she was fine, but the truth was that her heart stumbled with fear when she had to slow for her turn in front of the roadhouse. Was he watching for her? Did he know she'd seen Maria? She took the turn too fast, gravel pinging against the undercarriage of the car as she jolted up the hill.

Had it been nothing but deception from the moment she'd revealed her reasons for being here? Had Gabriel been encouraging her interest just to pump her for more information?

She laughed bitterly at her poor choice of imagery, then slowed as she drove past the inn.

Her mother had lived here. In this house. With her father and sisters and Dorothy. Hannah drove on but felt pulled back to the inn. Maybe if she'd stayed there this whole time, she would have felt more of the truth instead of getting lost in the fantasy of romantic hippies.

She parked at the cabin, but instead of heading inside, she left her things in the car and returned up the road, back to where she'd been born. She didn't go inside. She should, she supposed. It was just around check-in time, so some of the rooms must be vacant and awaiting new guests. One of those rooms was the one her family had shared. Her whole family. A father, two mothers, two sisters. And Hannah. The living proof of a terrible betrayal.

But she didn't want to go in. She stood on the lane next to the shed and looked up at the windows.

She should have asked Maria what her mother had looked like. What she'd *been* like. Maybe if she called in a few weeks, Maria would be willing to tell her more, but it hurt Hannah's heart that she'd finally found someone who knew her mother and she'd forgotten to *ask*.

Had Rain been funny and warm and happy-go-lucky? Smart and serious and dark? Quiet and sad?

Did it even matter?

Now she knew there was plenty of darkness and restlessness on her father's side to blame for all of Hannah's shortcomings. Certainly her grandfather had been unreliable and passionate. Restless enough to move from place to place and wife to wife and belief to belief.

Maybe her father would have been like that too, if he hadn't worked so damn hard for the rest of his life to settle down and never make a mistake again.

Hannah watched the windows for a ghost of her past, but she didn't see anyone. Not even a maid. Not until she heard footsteps to her left and turned to see Joe.

"Back to ask more questions?" he barked.

"No. I'm just looking around."

He grunted some sort of response, though there was no indication if it was positive or negative. But as he passed, heading for the shed, Hannah realized she did have a question.

"Actually. If you wouldn't mind . . . ?"

He didn't pause. "I'm not stopping work for you."

Fine. She followed him to the door of the shed. "The woman you came here with. What was her name?"

He shot her a glare before he turned back to hang a wrench on the wall. "Cora," he answered. "Not that it's any of your business."

Hannah squeezed her eyes shut to try to stop the shock of the horror. "Joe?"

"Yeah?"

"Did she leave with Jacob?"

"Yeah."

"Are you . . . ? Are you waiting for her to come back here? Is that why you stayed?"

His hand paused in the middle of sorting through a bin of loose bolts. "Why would you ask that?"

"It's just that . . ." Jesus, how should she say this? And did she even have any right? It might not be true. It wasn't verified. It was just a story that could be a coincidence. But she knew damn well it wasn't.

"Look, lady," he said, "I'm not hanging around here waiting for a long-lost love. She's obviously not coming back."

"Maybe she would if she could."

He shrugged. "Maybe. But I'm not dumb enough to think it might happen. Not anymore. It was a damn long time ago, and you're not going to find anything here either. Unless you're looking for a latte or gluten-free bread. We got both of those in abundance."

Right. He wasn't pining away for Cora. He wasn't still waiting. And she didn't have the right to pass on a rumor, did she?

But it was more than a rumor. She knew it was. She'd known it even before he told her Cora's name.

"Joe."

He glanced toward her before he crouched down to dig through a box of work gloves. "What?"

"I heard something. About Jacob. A friend was helping me look into the history here, and he found an article from a Mexican newspaper."

Joe grunted.

"A man calling himself Jacob Christo bought a ranch there in 1973. He lived there with three women, one other man, and a child. They were all found dead a year later."

Joe seemed to find the gloves he was looking for and stood. He slapped them against his hand.

"The article said one of the women was named Cora."

Joe nodded. He nodded as if he already knew, but she watched the color drain from his neck and leave ghostly white behind.

"The other women were Violet and Frances."

The gloves slapped into his palm again, then his head bowed. "Must be them, then."

"The authorities suspected poison. I just . . . I thought you should know."

"All right."

But it wasn't all right. His head was still bowed, the sides of his neck winged by tight tendons. She didn't know him well enough to reach out. She couldn't comfort him. "I'm sorry," she whispered.

Joe grunted again, and she thought that was all he'd offer, but then he spoke, his voice filled with gravel. "I told her he was dangerous. I told her over and over. But he had some kind of power over her. And she had fire in her eyes. I don't know why."

"I'm sorry," Hannah repeated.

"I hoped she would wise up soon enough."

"She would have. Given a chance, I'm sure she would have come back."

"Yeah," he said, but he didn't sound convinced.

"I'm not sure if I should have told you, but . . . I know how shitty it feels to be left holding loose ends."

"Thanks," he said. Then he slapped the gloves against his hand one last time and looked up to meet her eyes. "Thank you. I appreciate it."

"You're welcome."

"I thought you were nothing but trouble when you showed up here."

"Ha. No reason to change your mind now."

"You're all right. Just brought a lot of memories back, and I didn't like it."

"I apologize for that. But I've got the truth now. I know about the polygamy. I know who my mother is. I know she ran off after I was born and never came back. So I'll be out of your hair after today. I can keep looking for her as easily from Iowa as here."

"So you're going to keep looking?"

"I don't know. I shouldn't. But I'm kind of a restless soul."

He looked away, the gloves squeezed tight in his hand now, knuckles pale.

"Why?" she pressed. "Do you know something else? Anything will help. I mean, I don't even know her real name. That's not a good starting place."

Instead of answering, he moved toward her, tipping his head so she'd step out of the doorway. He walked to the ancient ATV and got in the driver's seat. Apparently he'd had enough conversation.

Hannah sighed, but she couldn't blame the man if he wanted to be alone. He'd just found out a woman he'd loved had been dead for decades.

Joe started the engine. "You coming?" he shouted over the rumble.

Hannah pointed to herself as if he might have been talking to someone else. Joe jerked his head toward the seat, so she scrambled in, trying to hide her nervousness. A few days ago, she wouldn't have gone anywhere with this man. But hell, if things got wild, she could always jump out of the ATV. There weren't any doors.

The vehicle leapt forward, so she grabbed the roll bar and held on for dear life. They couldn't be going over twenty miles per hour, but it felt more like fifty as they bounced over ruts and took curves. Once they got to the main drive that led to the cabins, it wasn't so bad. A straight shot. She'd probably survive. This really wasn't the way she wanted to go.

At some point on the short drive, she'd assumed he was giving her a lift back to her cabin to get her out of his hair. But instead of turning toward the cabins, Joe took a left and headed toward the meadow. At a slower pace, thank God.

He stopped at the edge of the grass and shut off the engine, throwing the world into sudden silence. She glanced his way, but he just stared ahead, so Hannah looked toward the meadow too. A crow swooped down and disappeared into the green, leaving only tails of wiggling grass behind to mark his progress.

"Are you going to be okay?" she asked, still hoping she had no reason to be nervous.

"Yep. I'm fine." Hopefully Cora had been so far away for so long that the pain was only a dull surprise, not something sharp and bright.

Joe finally hauled himself out of the ATV, rocking the whole thing in the process. Hannah waited for the shaking to stop before getting out.

"Come on," he said.

"Where are we going?" Not that she even expected an answer from the man. True to form, he just started walking across the meadow.

Hannah glanced around, looking for some sort of witness, but the secluded nature of the cabins worked both ways. You couldn't have privacy without isolation.

On the off chance that her revelation had snapped his sanity in two, she pulled out her phone and sent a quick text to herself as evidence. **Riverfall Inn meadow with Old Joe. Look for my body here.**

Then she took off after him, jogging through the grass and hoping she didn't step on any crows. He headed toward a corner and waited for her to join him there. Panting, Hannah squinted past the trees to the ruins beyond.

"The old bathhouse?" she asked.

"She's buried just behind it."

"What? Who is?" Was he talking about Cora? Had he lost his mind? She felt him watching and turned to try to gauge the look in his eyes. She didn't find any menace there. Only weariness.

"Rain," he said. "She didn't run off. She's been here the whole time."

"What?" she repeated, snapping the word at him in alarm. "What are you talking about?" Was he saying he'd killed her? Hannah took a step back, but Joe wasn't even looking at her anymore. He'd turned back to stare into the trees. "She's dead?" Hannah whispered.

"She is."

Her heart rate had spiked, and she felt dizzy with the rush of blood and half-deaf from the sound of it. Could she get away from him if he tried to grab her?

"Did you . . . ? Were you there?" She eased a foot back, ready to run as fast as she could. But Joe just stared into the trees.

"Nope. I wasn't here. I don't know exactly how it happened. She died two weeks after the baby was born. After *you* were born, I mean. They tried to say it was childbed fever, but . . . there were rumors."

"What . . . what kind of rumors?" she stammered.

"Poison."

Hannah gasped, then covered her mouth as if to hold in her horror. Poison. Just like the others. "No. She ran off. You weren't living here. You must be wrong."

"I'm not wrong. Cora told me. They didn't want to involve the authorities. Didn't want police sniffing around. So they buried her back here. I snuck back to see the grave myself."

"But . . . but Maria said . . ."

"They lied to her too, I'm sure. She wasn't one of them. No reason to trust her."

Fingers still pressed to her parted lips, Hannah shook her head. It couldn't be true. But of course it could. She'd disappeared. Death was as likely a reason as any.

"Who said it was poison?" she pressed.

He shrugged. "They were all whispering about it. Cora denied that part, but there was a new hardness in her. Stress. Fear. So I eavesdropped. People said Rain hadn't been sick at all. Worn out, yes, but fine. One morning she just didn't wake up. Her lips were blue. Eyes wide open. Hands all curled up into claws. That's it. They buried her right away."

Hannah kept shaking her head until Joe finally sighed. "Just thought you should know. Since you let me know about Cora."

He started to retreat, and Hannah's hand shot out to stop him before she could even form the thought. "Wait. Will you show me the grave?"

A stupid idea, asking this man to take her farther into the woods when she'd been worried he might kill her just a few moments ago. But she needed to *see*.

He looked down at her hand on his arm for a moment before nodding. "All right. But watch the poison oak."

She didn't know what poison oak looked like, and she didn't particularly care. Her real mother was dead. Had always been dead. And someone had *killed* her.

"Do you know who did it?" she asked Joe's back as he slipped into the bushes. She pushed through, keeping him in sight.

"No. Someone who wanted her dead, I'd guess. Or hell, maybe she did it herself. Plenty of people have taken that route."

Hannah couldn't wrap her head around it. Not yet. This beautiful hippie girl she'd been chasing was dead. The end.

She watched her feet, keeping an eye out for debris as they worked their way around the collapsing building. The redwood timbers were tilted this way and that, and the sheet-metal roof had collapsed. An open doorway revealed piles of brown pine needles and a broken toilet bowl.

"The cabins didn't have plumbing," Joe tossed over his shoulder.

"They had to come all the way out here for a bathroom?"

"There was already a water source here. Jacob didn't have the money to move it." He tapped a hand against the back corner of the building. "I helped build this when everyone first arrived. We were happy to have any kind of shower, frankly. It was nice here for a few months, even if I had to ignore all the Jesus talk."

"Why did people stay?" she asked.

Joe pressed through a thicket of immature redwoods that were barely eight feet high, their spindly branches easy to push aside. "There were drugs," he said. "And food. A place to sleep. A shower. Friends would hitch down and stay a few nights. Hell, it was a little like summer camp. The rules came later. And the crazy shit after that."

He stopped on a little rise. Hannah joined him, feeling the hollow thump of decades of pine needles beneath her feet.

"There," he said, tipping his head down the rise toward another clump of tiny redwoods. "We started clearing this area for more cabins, but never finished."

Hannah stepped down, trying not to slide on the top layer of loose detritus. She slipped once but found her balance again. When she reached flat ground, she looked around. "Where?"

"There's no marker. She's about three feet in front of you."

Hannah took one step forward and stopped. *We left her there.* Dorothy had said that herself. Still, Hannah didn't want to believe it. "You're sure?"

"I saw the turned soil. They tried to pack it down and cover it with leaves and such, but . . . I'm sure."

She winced at the idea of them packing dirt on top of that poor girl. Had her father helped? Had he thrown dirt on top of his eighteen-year-old wife?

Had he *killed* her? But no. Why would he have?

Hannah wished she had flowers. An offering. Anything. Just a simple wooden cross would have meant something to Rain, even if Hannah herself didn't believe.

Or maybe she should call the police. Call and tell them a girl was dead and maybe she'd been killed or maybe she'd done it to herself and maybe she had parents still looking and maybe she even had a real name.

Hannah scrubbed her hands over her face. Why the hell had she started this stupid search in the first place? Why had she wanted to know? Her sisters had been right. She should have kept her head down and shut the hell up and gone on with her life like a good Midwestern girl. She didn't want to know this, and she didn't want to make this decision.

She didn't even want to be here. And she didn't have to be. She could call the police from anywhere, anytime.

Hannah spun around and marched back uphill. "Thank you," she said as she passed Joe. "Thank you for telling me the truth."

"You gonna be all right?" Joe called over his shoulder as she scrambled back through trees and bushes and poison.

"Probably not," she shouted, because she should have stayed where she'd been meant to stay. Do what she'd promised. She should have loved her husband and her job and her life like other people loved theirs. Why the hell hadn't it been enough for her? She'd wanted something else, but not *this*.

Once she got to the meadow, she jogged toward the road. When she hit the path, she picked up speed and ran to her cabin. She burst through the door and slammed it behind her, then leaned over, hands on her knees, trying to catch her breath. But she couldn't get enough air. She was weeping. Sobbing. Her lungs seized up as if they needed to cut off oxygen to end her panic.

And she was panicking. For the first time, she'd done something really wrong. She'd looked at the dirt that covered her mother's body, and she'd just walked away. Left her there. Something terrible had happened, and Hannah was going to add to all the wrongs like every other person had done.

So many must have known. All the adults in the big house, at least. And they'd all agreed that Rain's life wasn't worth stirring up trouble over. Hannah had just made the same decision. Because there was no question trouble would be stirred. And for the first time in her life, Hannah only wanted calm.

She needed someone. She needed her *dad*. He'd been the only rock in her life, and now even her memories of him had crumbled to dust.

He'd been a good man. Her whole damn life she'd known that one thing. Her father had been a good, decent, hardworking man.

But he couldn't have been. He hadn't walked away from a lover who'd run out on him. He'd thrown a girl in the dirt and pretended she'd never existed.

Hands shaking, Hannah lurched into the bathroom and grabbed a towel. Even as she sobbed, she scrubbed the tears from her face. She had to get out of here. Had to get back where she belonged. She didn't have time to break down yet.

"Stop it," she ordered herself. "Stop. Stop."

She held her breath for a moment, then inhaled deeply. The sobs slowed. She got control.

As soon as she could see again, she fired up her laptop and searched for a morning flight home. She'd leave Big Sur at 5:00 a.m. if she had to. She'd run just as her father had forty-five years before. And like him, she'd never, ever come back.

CHAPTER 17

She was on her second jalapeño roll and her third glass of wine when he knocked. She knew it was him immediately. Who else could it be?

If Gabriel had shown up before glass number two, Hannah might have been scared. Instead, she felt only a hollow dread in her stomach as she stared at the door.

He couldn't get in. She just had to wait him out. Her suitcase was packed, her flight booked, and she was done with this godforsaken place. All she had to do was sleep through the night and she was out of here.

He knocked again.

Hannah set the wineglass down and crossed her arms. She didn't know who he was, really. Couldn't begin to suspect his motivations. Even now, she was the only one who knew what his mom had done. What if Maria had only been pretending to be a nice old lady? What if she'd called Gabriel and told him that Hannah was a problem? What if she actually knew Rain was dead and was just trying to keep Hannah quiet?

It belatedly occurred to her that the rolls could be poisoned. If so, she was already a goner.

He didn't knock again, but she couldn't tell if he'd walked away or not. Her heartbeat thundered, banging in her ears so she could hear nothing from the other side of the wall.

Craning her neck, she glanced toward the back door. Had that been a shadow in the window? Was he sniffing around, looking for an opening? She'd checked that back lock several times, but now she wasn't sure anymore. Was it secure?

She pushed slowly to her feet and turned to stare at the back wall. She took one careful step. The floor creaked. And suddenly his voice boomed behind her. "Hannah?"

She spun, hands flying to her mouth to hold in a shriek. The door was still closed. He hadn't broken in.

He knocked one more time. "Hannah?"

Glaring at the door, she felt her fear begin to freeze into something harder. "Go away!" she yelled.

"Hannah, please. I just want to say I'm sorry."

"You're *sorry?*" she ground out between clenched teeth. He'd been the one good thing she'd found here. Something easy in this sea of crap.

"I don't know what to say." His voice was more muffled now. Subdued.

She stomped to the door and yanked it wide open. "How about you say you're a liar?" Her words were too loud. She could hear that. And she could see it in the way he took a step back and held his hands up.

"She's my mother," he said, hands tipping up now, pleading for understanding.

"So you decided to screw with me and see what I knew?"

"No. That wasn't how it was."

"You were lying to me this whole time. Like . . . like some kind of scheming psycho!"

"That's not true. I swear it's not true. Last night was the first time I realized she was involved."

"Last night. When I showed you the birth certificate. *Before* we had sex."

Gabriel winced. "Yes."

She stepped out, put her hands to his chest, shoved him. Hard. "What the *hell*, Gabriel?" She shoved again. He barely shifted under her hands but stepped back off the small landing.

"I'm sorry. Can we just talk?"

"You're not coming into my room. You're a creep."

He grimaced again, but nodded. "We'll talk here, then." He dropped down to sit on the step, watching her with big brown puppy-dog eyes.

Hannah looked around, half hoping she'd suddenly see a lot of neighbors. But there was no one here. Only the constant presence of the river, chasing over rocks and roots somewhere in the forest. The gray light was turning blue, the invisible sun disappearing somewhere over the sea.

"My full name is Gabriel Antonio Cabrillo Diaz."

She crossed her arms and didn't respond.

"She was acting weird about all this," he explained. "Hurrying past my questions. I thought it was disapproval. That was all. Distaste for weird hippie stuff. She used to warn us all the time when we were kids to stay away from them. I thought that was why she didn't want to talk."

"And then?"

"Then you showed me the birth certificate."

"And you pretended you didn't know who she was."

He nodded. "She's my *mom*, Hannah. What did you expect me to do?"

"I expected you *not* to sleep with me just so you could keep an eye on me and figure out if I was a threat."

"That's not what happened."

"Oh, come on, Gabriel. You just suddenly found me irresistible?"

"Yes," he said. "No. I don't know. I was stressed—"

"Yeah, no wonder you needed a cigarette."

"I felt bad for you. I wanted to help, but . . . Shit, Hannah. It just happened, okay?"

"Why did you ask me to spend the night?"

"I don't know."

She snorted.

"I'm serious! It wasn't nefarious. I just wanted you to spend the night. That's all."

"You wanted to keep me away from your mom."

He tipped his head back to stare at the sky. Shook his head. Avoided her gaze. "That's not true."

"You wanted to ask a few more questions."

"Okay, that might be true. But that wasn't why I slept with you."

She crossed her arms tighter as a shiver worked through her. "Then why did you?"

He threw his hands up and finally met her eyes. "Because I've liked you since the moment you sat down at my bar! Because you were strong and hot and it seemed like something we both needed. That's why!"

She rolled her eyes.

"Come on. You wanted to sleep with me too. Did you know who my mom was and you were playing me for more information?"

She gasped. "No!"

"Then why think my motivation was any different? We were attracted to each other. That's what last night was about. That's it."

She was too tired to keep the anger fueled. It began to melt away, leaving a little hollow in her chest. Too drained to fight anymore, Hannah let her legs give out and finally sat down next to him.

"I'm sorry," he said again. "I'm sorry I wasn't truthful. But she was scared, and I haven't seen her scared many times in my life. I wanted to protect her."

"You have a right to keep your mother's secrets. I get that."

"She called me after you left her house. She told me about your mom. About you."

Her shoulders slumped. She let her head fall into her hands and cradled the weight of it. "I'm not going to get her in trouble, if that's what you're worried about."

"She told me that too."

"Okay. I accept your apology." She stared down at her boots, at the dried brown leaves and needles beneath them. He owed more allegiance to his mother. Of course he did. So why did she feel so betrayed? "I'm sorry I pushed you."

"It's fine."

"I don't know. I just wanted you to be something good in this. Not another awful lie."

"Last night wasn't a lie."

"Everything's a lie," she said, horrified even as the melodramatic words left her mouth. But they were true, weren't they?

"Are you going to keep looking for her?" Gabriel asked.

She tried to bite back her laughter. "No. I'm definitely done looking."

"I'm sure my mom would be happy to—"

"No," she interrupted. "I'm leaving tomorrow. I need to get back home."

"Oh."

The light faded as she stared at the ground. Gabriel was still beside her. Patient. She liked him. She really did. But she felt like she was miles away already.

His arm nudged her shoulder. "Come to the roadhouse. Let me feed you, at least."

"I already ate."

"I really don't want this to end on a bad note."

This time she didn't try to stifle her laughter. "I'm afraid that's the only way this story is going to end. It's not your fault. That's just the way it is. But I'm sorry for dragging you into this."

"I'm not."

Her smile was only a little bitter when she finally lifted her head. "The sex was pretty good."

"*Pretty* good?" He slapped a hand over his heart. "Way to wound a man's ego."

The bitterness faded and she reached over to pull him in for a kiss. It was simple. Sweet. Just what she needed. "Thank you," she whispered, "for making me laugh."

He kissed her again. "Anytime. I mean that. You know where I am."

"You probably take in a new stray every week."

"No," he said quietly, "I don't."

When she let him go, he nodded and stood, his mouth flat and grim. "Stay safe. And come back sometime."

She smiled, but that was a lie too. She was never coming back here.

Once he was gone, Hannah started one last blaze in the fire pit. She finished her last bottle of wine and sat staring into the flames until they were red-hot and licking at the highest log.

Then she dropped in her birth certificate. The copies of the deeds. The newspaper printouts. The notes she'd brought from home. She wished she could throw her memories in there too. Forget everything she'd learned.

Since she couldn't burn them, she'd stuff them down. Lock them up. Like any good Midwesterner would.

Rain was faceless, formless, nameless. Dust to dust. And Hannah was going home.

HOME

CHAPTER 18

She tapped the coffee stirrer nervously against the mug, tap, tap, tap, as if she were channeling Jeff. Did she need him here so badly that she couldn't wait with any kind of calm? Maybe, because she was as fidgety as a five-year-old, but she did her best not to scratch the itchy poison oak rash on her left forearm.

She would have preferred to meet him in a bar, but he was teaching a night class and had to head back to campus after this. When they were dating, she would have been able to charm him into a glass of wine before class, but they weren't close enough for flirtation anymore. Strange that people could be so distant after so many years of sharing a bed.

The late-afternoon meeting with her old boss had gone well, though she'd had to apologize for wearing jeans and a leather jacket that reeked of wood smoke. He looked like he'd lost an inch of hairline since her departure, and he'd been up-front about the offer. He was trying to reassemble a couple of the old teams. Some of their most important clients were dissatisfied with the lower level of service they were receiving. The new CEO had meant to cut costs by letting go of the highest-paid employees; instead, he was about to lose major clients.

Hannah hadn't accepted the job yet, but she imagined she'd say yes within a couple of days.

The city had rolled out its best weather for her. She wasn't fooled. She knew they'd just emerged from four days of thunderstorms. But God, the streets were clean and the lake sparkled with welcome. She was far from Big Sur and damn happy about that.

It already felt like a dream. She'd stolen out of there in early morning darkness so she had no last memories of the inn or the coast to take with her. She'd driven all the way to San Jose before she'd stopped for breakfast and coffee. She'd chosen Starbucks to be sure there'd be no visual clues she was still in California.

If she tried really hard, maybe she could pretend she didn't know about the grave. The body. The death. Maybe she'd eventually believe that it wasn't her responsibility and that running away had been the right thing to do for once. But for now she'd concentrate on fixing older mistakes. The fresh ones could wait.

The door of the little coffee place opened, and Hannah's head jerked to attention as it had with every whoosh of that door. This time she was rewarded with the sight of Jeff walking in. He wore a V-neck sweater she didn't recognize. He'd shaved. And he smiled when he saw her.

Pulse skipping, Hannah sprang to her feet, then hovered there, unsure how to greet him. She wanted to hug him. Because she'd missed him. Because he'd helped her. But that didn't mean he felt warm and cozy toward her.

Her arms had turned out on their own, though, and Jeff responded by opening his as well, and then he was hugging her hard. Her head tucked under his chin just as it always did when they embraced. She closed her eyes and listened to his heartbeat.

"Thank you," she said when she pulled away.

"It was nothing," he answered. "How are you doing?"

"I don't know, honestly." The waitress came over to get his coffee order, and Hannah took the opportunity to study his face. He looked good. A little more tan than normal, as if he'd gotten back into running after the breakup. It was something he used to do every spring before giving up in the heat of the summer.

He settled into his chair and met her gaze. "Still reeling?"

"Yeah."

"It'll take time to process."

He didn't know the whole truth. She wanted to tell him. Wanted to share the burden. But she'd also have to share the guilt. What if he told her she had to notify the authorities? What if she was never ready for that?

He reached out to pat her hand. "I'm looking for more in Mexico. I'll let you know what I find."

"It's all right," she said quickly. "I confirmed that one of the women with him was named Cora. I'm sure I could find a marriage certificate somewhere to verify my grandmother's name, but . . . I know Jacob Christo was Jacob Smith. I don't have any doubts."

He nodded. He'd obviously come to the same conclusion.

"Jesus," she huffed. "What a strange world."

"People reach out to weird things when society is in flux." The waitress brought his triple espresso, and Hannah winced. When Jeff looked up, they both smiled. He'd always been able to drink caffeine late into the evening and never have trouble sleeping. But every single time, she'd been convinced that this time would be disastrous.

Hannah held up both hands. "Drink away. I'm sure you'll be fine."

"I have a three-hour-long lecture to get through!"

"Better get another, then."

He clinked his cup against her decaf latte. "Welcome back to Chicago."

"Thanks. My meeting went well."

"What meeting?"

Hannah held her breath for a moment. "I've been offered my old position."

Jeff's eyebrows flew high. "Wow. I thought you were done with that."

"So did I. But I decided maybe I had more work to do." She was talking about the job, but that wasn't all she meant. She watched Jeff closely, but he only sipped his espresso and nodded.

"That's great. Did you accept?"

"Not yet."

"Well, congratulations on the offer, regardless." She knew he meant it, but there was a tiny edge to his words. A reminder that he'd asked for half of her settlement money. Now she was here talking about making more money and still pissed that he wanted what she had.

Hannah cleared her throat. "How's your brother?" she asked. "I saw some of the wedding pictures."

Jeff smiled. "Dan's great. Really great. In fact, Alisha is pregnant."

"That's wonderful!" she said brightly, her hollow response to anyone's pregnancy news. But it wasn't hollow for Jeff. He grinned in delight.

"It is wonderful. He's so close, I'll get to be super involved. She's due in September. I'm going to help them fix up the sunroom this summer. Turn it into a family room. Their place is a little small for all that baby gear. I can't wait."

He'd been nearly this excited the last time one of his friends had had a baby, but there was a new spark in his eyes now. His only nieces and nephews had been Hannah's family. He'd lost them in the split. And though he'd been nearly as awkward around older kids as Hannah was, he'd been great with babies.

"It's not too late for you, you know." She wasn't sure why she said it. As a test or maybe as a genuine wish for him. But after she spoke, her gut tightened into a painful knot.

Jeff sipped his espresso with no hint of tension in his shoulders. If it was a test, he wasn't worried about the grade. "Yeah." He set the coffee down slowly. "I've been thinking that myself lately. Maybe it's not too late for me."

And just like that, she knew. It was over between them. Really, truly over.

All her thoughts of whether she wanted him back or whether she should have given motherhood a shot . . . all of them flew out the window of that coffee shop and up into the bright blue sky above the city. She actually glanced outside as if she could see them disappearing.

It hadn't just been her giving up on the relationship. It had been him too. For all his reassurances and promises, he hadn't been content with their marriage either.

She almost laughed. She almost threw her head back and let the bitter humor spill out, but if she did that, her laughter would turn to tears. Not sweet, sad tears either. But tired, angry, *furious* tears.

Jeff had liked being married. He'd wanted children. And he'd loved Hannah. That had been her biggest crime. Letting Jeff fall in love with her. And letting them both believe that love would be enough.

He'd talked her into marriage not because it was right for her, but because it was right for him. When he'd assured her that he'd never cared that much about having kids, maybe he'd meant it. Or maybe he'd hoped that she would settle into marriage and get a little softer. More nurturing. Less selfish.

But that was the thing. That was the goddamn, giant, sparkling thing right in the middle of the room. Hannah had been agonizing her whole damn life about being selfish. Wanting life the way she wanted it. Needing the things she needed.

So she was selfish. And so was everyone else.

Jeff had wanted marriage and he'd gotten it. Her sisters had wanted husbands and children and houses and they'd had them. Yes, they put a lot of care into other people's lives, but they did it because they wanted to. Because caring for others made them happy and fulfilled. They thrived on it, and Hannah didn't.

She'd tried to tell Jeff that from the start. That marriage scared her. That she would fail at it, even if she loved him. But her fears hadn't dissuaded him from what *he* wanted.

Jeff started talking about the plans for Dan's sunroom, and Hannah let him talk, but she barely listened.

What was she doing here? Did she want this man back, or was she just afraid of her yearning to be alone? She could return to Chicago without returning to him. They could be friends, maybe. She could watch from a distance as he remarried, had a child, lived the life he wanted.

Pain lanced her heart at the idea, but it wasn't a mortal wound. It was only a relief of aching pressure. She'd walked away from him. Run away. But maybe she was ready to truly let him go.

She loved him. And they weren't right together. She'd tried it his way. Now she would try it hers.

Jeff had lapsed into silence, familiar enough with her moods that he knew she wasn't listening. She smiled in apology. "Sorry. It's been a long week."

"I get it."

"I know I was the one who cut off contact and I shouldn't have reached out to you, but . . . I'm glad I did. And I'm glad you gave me a chance."

"I don't hate you," he said, and Hannah's eyes filled with tears.

"I know that too. I do. But thank you for saying it."

Jeff took her hand, and she held tight for a moment, squeezing hard. She wished she could round the table and curl up in his lap and let him hold her, but when his other hand wrapped around her fingers and cradled her hand, she settled for that. It was comfort, at least.

"I guess this was good," he finally said. "If you're coming back to Chicago, we could be seeing each other around. It shouldn't be so damn awkward."

No. It shouldn't. "We should settle things," she offered, untangling her fingers from his. "So you can move on."

He didn't disagree. He was finally ready too.

"I can't give you half, Jeff. It's my money. I worked hard for it. I didn't even get that settlement offer until we'd already split! You have your own money, your own career."

"Yes. But I worked hard for your career too. The move to Chicago . . ."

"You wanted to be here too."

"I did, but I gave up a lot."

"You're tenured here now. Everything worked out fine!"

"It's expensive as hell to live here. And I would've been tenured five years ago if we hadn't moved so you could have your dream job. I could have earned a hell of a lot more. Taken time to write another book. We came here for *you*."

It wasn't exactly true. Jeff had fallen in love with Chicago during her interview process. He'd insisted they look at apartments even before she'd gotten her offer. He'd put in his time at his old college, but he'd hated that place.

She could make all those points. A week ago, she would have.

But he was right too. He'd sacrificed. For her.

"Half of the settlement," she offered. "Fine. But only a quarter of the IRA. None of the 401(k). You have a pension, and I need my retirement money."

He cocked his head. Watched her for a long time.

"Please," she added.

Finally, he nodded. "All right. Half the settlement. A quarter of the IRA. I'll accept that."

She reached out to shake, and they both pretended her hand wasn't trembling. It was over. Really over. And despite her resolve, she had a little trouble letting go of him.

"It's okay," Jeff said.

Hannah nodded and finally let her hand slide free. "It is."

"Let me know when you move back." He was already gathering up his things. He knocked back the last of the espresso and stood.

"I will. And let me know when your brother's baby is born. I'll send my usual gift."

"A bottle of good whisky?"

"You got it."

Laughing, he laid down a ten and waved goodbye. A few feet from the table, he turned back. "If you decide to track down your mom, drop me a line. I'll be happy to help if I can."

She forced a smile, but she was too aware that their life together was ending with a lie, and she looked down before he could see it in her eyes. Once outside, he waved again from the other side of the glass, and she waved back.

He looked relieved as he walked away. He was likely dating already. Maybe he'd met someone as excited about his brother's baby as he was. Someone softer and sweeter than Hannah could ever be.

She pushed the last of her coffee away, wiped her damp cheeks, and walked out.

She didn't have anywhere to go, really. She could look at apartments. Stroll through her old neighborhood and see what was there. But Jeff was still in that area. Maybe she could get something closer to the lake. She'd found the truth, and it was time to get on with the rest of her life. But somehow Hannah found herself wandering aimlessly for three hours before she finally knew where to go.

CHAPTER 19

Another rental car. Another highway. But here the sky was a blindingly crisp shade of blue and the clouds had sharp edges that didn't hint at any danger.

At long last, Hannah finally felt at home.

She'd driven straight through, unable to sit still and wait for a morning flight to Des Moines. She'd needed to move, so she'd rented a car and driven all night to get back to Coswell.

Her own car was still at long-term parking in Des Moines from her original trip. She'd need to drive the ninety minutes down later to return this car and retrieve her own. But she had more important things to do first.

She'd managed to snag five hours of sleep once she'd pulled up to her dark, silent house, but she felt as if she'd had ten.

For the first time in a very long while, she felt sure of who she was and what she was doing. No longer running on pure fear, she didn't clutch the steering wheel or face the coming meeting with dread. She was ready to take this on.

When she reached the care center, she picked up the book from the passenger seat and walked in. Her mother's favorite novel. Hannah had already read it aloud to her twice before she'd pretended to lose it, unable to bear the sugar-sweet family saga one more time. She preferred her novels with sex and maybe a few shootings. But this wasn't about her anymore. It never should have been. Her mother was dying and afraid.

"Hi, Hannah!" the nurse called in surprise as Hannah approached the station.

"Good morning, Tonya!"

"I didn't expect you today. I thought Becky said she'd be in this afternoon."

"Well, I'm back from my trip, so you're stuck with me." She winked and they both laughed. Hannah waved to another nurse down the hall as she opened her mother's door.

It was a good day. Hannah could see that right away. Dorothy smiled as she looked up, though her eyes didn't light in recognition. Still, the smile was good. Hannah smiled back.

"Hi, Mom."

"Hello, there! What a lovely skirt you're wearing."

"Thank you." She glanced down at the white maxi skirt she'd worn. Weary of jeans and boots after California, today she'd worn a skirt and sandals and a flowy blue top. "You look beautiful today yourself," she told Dorothy, though her dress was a worn green one that Hannah had seen a hundred times. "I brought a book for us to read."

She held up the novel, and Dorothy beamed. "Oh my! That's my favorite! I haven't read it in years."

"Yes, a little birdie told me it was your favorite. I thought we could read a couple of chapters today."

"That would be lovely!"

She pulled a chair close to Dorothy and patted her hand. Instead of pulling away, Dorothy smiled. "What's your name, dear?" she asked.

Hannah held on to her smile. Tricking her mother wasn't the point. She didn't want to be cruel. She didn't want to indulge some morbid fantasy. But she needed to put an end to this for all of them. To confirm her worst suspicions or lay them to rest.

She took her mother's hand in both of hers and held her gently. "I'm Rain," she said, and watched Dorothy's eyes flutter.

"W-who?" she hooted softly.

"Rain. From Big Sur. From Jacob's Rock."

"Oh, but . . ." Dorothy tugged her hand away and cradled it to her chest. "But that can't be."

"It is. I heard you'd been ill, and I came to see you."

"Rain?" her mother whispered, her thin eyelids trembling again as her face drained of color.

"That's right," Hannah said in a soothing voice. "It's been a long time, but I came to help take care of you. We always took care of each other, didn't we, Dorothy?"

Her mother's eyes pooled with tears. This time when her eyelids fluttered, two fat drops slid down her cheeks. Her chin trembled. "But, Rain? I thought you were dead."

"I'm not."

"They told me you were dead!"

Hannah shook her head. "I was sick for a long while, but I'm fine now. Right as rain." She realized the joke as soon as she said it and laughed.

A shaky smile crossed Dorothy's face. "Really? You're all right?"

"I'm fine. Don't I look fine?"

"Oh!" Dorothy gasped, and then she reached out to grab Hannah's hand with a startling quickness. "Oh, I'm so glad! I didn't mean to hurt you. Not really."

Hannah took a deep breath. She held her mother's hand and felt the weight of the truth settle over her like a smothering blanket.

She'd known this. She really had. After all, who was the one person who would have wanted Rain dead? She'd known it, but hearing it still filled her body with iron and tried to pull her down to the floor.

"The poison?" she managed to breathe.

"Oh, Rain." Dorothy's hands trembled around Hannah's. "I'm sorry. It was all so wrong. I knew it was all wrong. You were sinning, and I just had to get you to stop."

Hannah swallowed hard.

"I didn't want you to go to hell. I wanted to save you from it! I told Peter that. I explained. He said it was his fault. He shouldn't have put us in that situation. He said he buried you!"

Hannah twined her fingers into her mother's. "No. It was all a mistake."

"Rain, I'm so relieved! I shouldn't have done it. I just wanted it to stop. That's all. That man wasn't God. He was the devil."

"You're right. He wasn't a good man."

"He wasn't. Peter said we could leave. That we'd leave all that behind. But he said we could never speak of it again. He said it was his fault for letting us down. Oh, Rain, he was so sorry. So sorry for both of us."

"Not like his father."

"No, nothing like his father. Peter saw it then. He saw that it was all sin and evil, and we left. But we left you there. Oh, Rain, I'm so sorry. I'm sorry I hurt you." She was crying deeply now, hunched over Hannah's hands.

Hannah pulled free and scooted forward to embrace her. "It's all right, Dorothy. It's all right now."

This woman had killed her real mother. Lashed out in mindless anger and desperation and taken a young girl's life. But this woman had also raised Hannah. Loved her. Made her who she was.

All this time, Hannah had assumed her parents were perfect, simple souls who'd somehow managed to stumble into having a maelstrom of a child. Then she'd convinced herself that all her wildness had come from the faceless woman who'd given birth to her. But the truth was that Hannah had come from all of them.

They'd all been victims and perpetrators. All contributed something dark and complex to Hannah's soul. But what they'd passed on had been nothing more dark and complex than what they'd each nurtured in their hearts.

"It's all right," she whispered again, stroking the soft wisps of Dorothy's graying curls. "I'm here now."

"I'm sorry, Rain," her mother sobbed. "I'm sorry."

"Shhhh. I know you are."

"I just wanted it to stop."

"I know."

This was who she was. The daughter of a lost child. The daughter of a deeply flawed man. The daughter of a murderer.

But who she became now was up to her.

She held Dorothy close. Rocked her. Stroked her hair. Dorothy finally calmed, and her red-rimmed eyes traveled the room as if she wasn't sure what had happened or why she'd been upset.

"Why don't you lie down for a little while?" Hannah suggested. "I'll read to you."

"Yes, I want to lie down." She shot Hannah a suspicious look, the idea that she was Rain already lost. Maybe she'd lost it on purpose this time. That was fine. Hannah would never bring it up again.

Hannah helped her into bed, propping up her head a little and covering her with a light blanket. She read the first two chapters even though Dorothy fell asleep five pages in. Then she kissed her mom's papery forehead and took her phone to the garden.

"I'm back," she said as soon as Becky answered the call.

"Back where?" her sister asked.

"Back in Coswell. So you don't need to drive down and sit with Mom today. I'm here."

"What? You're just *back*? I thought you were still in California!"

"I flew into Chicago to take care of something last night, but I'm home now."

"Chicago? What were you doing there?"

"Nothing," she answered. Nothing at all. She'd turned down the job first thing this morning. Then she'd instructed her lawyer to draw up the divorce settlement. She wasn't needed in Chicago. She was needed here.

"Well . . ." She could almost hear Becky shaking her head. "What the heck happened?"

My real mother was Dad's second wife. They were polygamists. We all lived together, one big family in a little room. After I was born, Mom killed my mother, and Dad buried her in the woods behind the toilets. Then we fled before our grandfather could talk us into drinking poison. Pretty standard stuff.

That was what Hannah had to live with for the rest of her life. But she'd finally learned her lesson. Everyone had their burdens. She didn't have to make her loved ones feel her pain to make it real. It was real even if she never told another soul. It meant something even if she never lashed out or struggled or rebelled.

She didn't need to share it. And she couldn't run from it. It was hers forever.

"Hannah?" Becky asked, fear in her voice. "What happened?"

Hannah faked a smile for her sister even though she wasn't there. "Not much. They had a church there, and Dad must have gotten a little too caught up in trying to save a few souls, that's all. My real mother was a hippie girl who moved on after I was born. The end."

Becky sighed. "My God. I guess it must be true, but . . . Dad? I can't imagine him doing anything that crazy."

"Yeah, it's pretty bizarre."

"And Mom! She just accepted you as her own child? That woman is a saint."

"She is," Hannah agreed, keeping her voice as light as possible.

"So are you going to keep looking for your mother? I know Rachel and I discouraged you, but I've been thinking about it and—"

"No," Hannah interrupted. "No, I don't even know her real name. She could be anywhere. I'm done looking."

"Wow. Just . . . wow. I mean . . . God, are you okay?"

"I'm fine. Just tired. Will you let Rachel know?"

"Hannah, you should call her yourself. You need to talk."

They did need to talk. She needed to get to know her oldest sister again. Or maybe get to know her for the first time, with no feelings of inferiority or foreignness. "I'll call her tomorrow, all right? I need to get settled today."

"Maybe we should come down this weekend," Becky suggested. "Have a little sister time."

Eyes closed, Hannah nodded. "That would be nice. I love you, Becks."

"I love you too."

Hannah tucked her phone away and walked back inside. A display sat on this side of the nurses' station. A handmade sign and a can asking for donations for little Olivia Jensen. Hannah stopped.

"Tonya? Do you know who Olivia Jensen's parents are?"

"Willis and Patty. Patty is my second cousin. They think there's a good chance this treatment will work, but that poor baby is all worn out. They all are."

"I'm so sorry." Hannah knew who Willis Jensen was, but he'd been several years behind her in school. Hannah slipped a couple of bills into the can. "I'm not good at many things, but I'm great at accounting. Could you let Patty know I'd be happy to help figure out the reporting and taxes for them when the time comes?"

"That's so kind! Thank you! I'll let them know."

"All right. You know where to find me."

She returned to her mother's room. She sat in the chair next to her bed and flipped through her mom's favorite book. And finally, she wasn't restless. She wasn't out of place. She knew who she was. She was a woman taking care of her dying mom. It didn't feel natural, but that didn't mean it wasn't right. And it didn't mean she couldn't do it.

Her whole life she'd thought she loved people the wrong way. She'd been the wrong kind of daughter, sister, girlfriend, wife. She didn't have other women's gifts. She was just so *different*. But right now, different felt fine, and she'd take care of her mother in her own way. Dorothy belonged to her the same way she belonged to Dorothy. Not through blood, but through time. Sacrifice. Lies. Pain. And love. Years of love. Maybe it didn't make up for what had happened in Big Sur all those years before, but it meant something.

Scooting closer, she held Dorothy's hand and waited for her mother to wake up and need her again. She'd be here every day until her mother died. She'd offer the kind of care she could to Dorothy, not her sisters' kind of care, but her own, and that would be enough. And after that, there would be time to figure out the rest of her life. She could go anywhere. Be anything. But for now, she'd be a daughter.

ABOUT THE AUTHOR

 Victoria Helen Stone, the author of *Evelyn, After,* is the nom de plume of *USA Today* bestselling romance novelist Victoria Dahl. After publishing more than twenty-five books, she has taken a turn toward the darker side of genre fiction. Born and educated in the Midwest, she finished her first manuscript just after college. In 2016, she was the recipient of the American Library Association's prestigious Reading List Award. Having escaped the plains of her youth, she now resides with her family in a small town high in the Rocky Mountains, where she enjoys hiking, snowshoeing, and not skiing (too dangerous). For more on the author and her work, visit www.VictoriaHelenStone.com and www.VictoriaDahl.com.